About the author

Johan van der Berg is an Emergency Care Practitioner with a notable imagination, and a keen interest in crime and psychology. Before writing his novel, *Obsessions*, his writing was dedicated purely to academic and scientific papers. More recently his focus changed to the writing of fiction and since then, under the name Johan Parker, he has spent all his time and focus on creating this story.

OBSESSIONS

Johan Parker

OBSESSIONS

Vanguard Press

VANGUARD PAPERBACK

© Copyright 2018
Johan Parker

The right of Johan Parker to be identified as author of this work has been asserted by him in accordance with the Copyright, Designs and Patents Act 1988.

All Rights Reserved

No reproduction, copy or transmission of this publication may be made without written permission.
No paragraph of this publication may be reproduced, copied or transmitted save with the written permission of the publisher, or in accordance with the provisions of the Copyright Act 1956 (as amended).

Any person who commits any unauthorised act in relation to this publication may be liable to criminal prosecution and civil claims for damages.

A CIP catalogue record for this title is available from the British Library.

ISBN 978 1 784653 70 5

Vanguard Press is an imprint of
Pegasus Elliot MacKenzie Publishers Ltd.
www.pegasuspublishers.com

First Published in 2018

Vanguard Press
Sheraton House Castle Park
Cambridge England

Printed & Bound in Great Britain

Acknowledgements

Thank you to my friends and family for your dedicated and undoubted support. Special thank you to Segran Govender who played a big role in making my dream a reality.

I dedicate this book to my wonderful, amazing, and beautiful spouse, Charné.

Isaiah 32:17

Prologue

'I'm standing here in the cold, dark night with my eyes closed, absorbing all of the sweet senses. I feel the wind on my skin, touching me softly and dragging its fingers across my body, better than the most perfect, unimaginable lover ever could. A touch so perfect it sends impulses down my spine, calming and nurturing. I smell soft and clean, almost soapy, cologne, mixed with the smells of iron and grass. When I take a deep breath, it fills every space from the tip of my nose down to the bottom of my lungs. The taste in my mouth so natural, raw and metallic, the sort of taste you get only with vigorous exercise. Unpleasant yet so perfectly suited and wanted. I hear the wind slowly moving through the leaves outside, gently pushing each one ever so slightly out of position. I also hear dripping in perfect harmonious synchrony with the wind combined with the crickets. An orchestra conducted by nature. I open my eyes and look down at my creation: art. In my hand, the knife dripping with fresh blood; the body still seems to be warm. The blood, blackened by the glimmer of moonlight, seeps slowly from his neck, I don't think there's much left. It's almost time to cut the triangle. Oh! How it all comes together now. Do you see it? Smell it? Taste it? Do you feel it little Lily? Don't worry, I won't leave you with such a mess, I'll clean him up first. I leave you this voice recording so you can understand what went through my mind. This one was for you.'

Another one, another signature-marked body, dumped. This one is different though, this one was left for me to find, for me to admire and indulge in. How does one choose between the living and the dead? How does one choose who lives and who dies? He knows. He knows this question exists within me and that's why he left me this body to find. This one seems more like the first one. Over time the modus operandi – the M.O. – has changed. But the evidence is just so unclear. No one knows any more. I just wish that I could see how I fit into this, why am I one of the puzzle pieces? I'm just a regular girl; I'm just Lily. Pete does me these favours though, letting me onto the crime scenes even though I'm not even connected to law enforcement. He believes I'm somehow linked to the killer. Not sure how yet, but I guess he's the detective. I truly don't know what to do. They already checked the recorder for prints and unsurprisingly, none were found. The voice is muffled; it can't be recognised. He's so careful, so meticulous, never makes a mistake. Pete believes the killing was done elsewhere, the body's bled dry and not a single drop can be found where the body's staged, almost like he didn't want to spoil his thoughts on the recording with an actual picture. In a very strange way, it's artistic. He always cuts a triangle into the wrist, the left one; it's the sign. This one is a little different though, it's almost like he waited for the body to nearly bleed dry before he drew it. The triangles are usually messy, this one, however, is perfect. Only a little bit of blood seeped into the cuts leaving the triangle red and distinguishable from the rest of the skin, but not ruined by a bloody mess.

Chapter 1

June 18 1981, the Tomlinson family just grew. A girl, just what Jenifer and Brian had hoped for. Nine months went by so slowly for them; nevertheless, Lily's room is ready. The walls are coated in soft sunshine yellow with white lilies painted on the north wall, underneath the lilies in the centre of the wall, a white-painted wooden cot stands. A family of bunnies patrolling a mystical land is painted on the south wall. The east wall home only to the cupboards and door and the west wall only features a window, but it stretches from wall to wall and reaches from floor to ceiling. The window frames a picture of a large grassy backyard with a fishpond in the middle and a big oak tree towards the back. A room fit for a princess; it was perfect for this little girl.

With Brian being a banker and Jenifer a homemaker, Lily had the perfect childhood. She had a mother who entertained her during the day and a father who came home no later than four o' clock. They had breakfast together every morning and supper together every night. On Sundays Brian would start his 1974 Pontiac GTO, let it idle for two or three minutes and then load Lily on the back seat while they waited for Jenifer to lock the front door. They would go to church and after church, they would drive for an hour or two. Brian would make sure that they always arrived home early enough for Jenifer to cook Sunday lunch. A perfect picture, but Lily always dreamed of having a brother. In Lily's early years she used to say that she needed a brother; she would complain to Brian and Jenifer that she needed a brother to protect her from the monsters. Later in life the need for a brother was merely for companionship. Not that she had a shortage of friends. From when she was young, everyone noticed that she had a brilliant mind. She always did well in school, with little effort. During Lily's high school years her life started changing. Boys started noticing her. And obviously, Brian started to notice the boys. Being a nineties teenager it goes without saying that Lily was slightly rebellious. Things got worse for Brian and Jenifer, when Lily hit puberty. The beautiful princess who used to play in the backyard with Peter became the most desirable young girl in town in the span of a couple of months. Peter noticed too. Puberty turned Lily from girl to goddess. She had long, dark hair that almost touched her perfectly-rounded bottom. She had unusual eyes, a mix between striking greyish green and yellowish hazel. Her teeth were white and were framed by the most desirable, most voluptuous natural red lips. She always looked like she was wearing lipstick. This made her smile even more compelling. Also, since she was her school's top athlete, in the hundred-metre race, Lily had the most beautiful muscular legs and they were complemented by nature's gift to her, her perky, full breasts.

Lily was a sweet girl, and although rebellious, never sexually led anyone on. But with a sweet personality, a face to die for and a body to kill for, it never mattered what Lily wore, or how she acted; she was desired by boys and girls alike. She received more love letters than Brian and Jenifer received mail. Every boy in town fell in love with Lily; even young Peter. But fortunately for Brian and Jenifer, Lily was driven and did not care much for young love. Finally Lily's last term of high school was ahead of her. The once little princess now was staring her future in the face, fierce and ready to make the world perform according to her desires. She had been accepted for journalism at the best university, The University of Texas in Austin and academic year was scheduled to start mid-February. This left Lily with three months of free time; time she elected to spend in Europe. Lily approached Brian and Jenifer about the idea and asked for their permission to travel. Lily was fortunate that Jenifer had a sister, Grace, who lived in Paxos the smallest Ionian island just off the west coast of Greece. And as Grace had never met Lily, Jenifer agreed to the plan on the condition that Aunt Grace would be Lily's last stop.

Chapter 2

I'm tired, I'm thirsty and I'm moody. Since I've never been on a plane for more than two hours, I guess this is what jetlag feels like. Nevertheless, there's no point complaining when you're in Spain. The airport notification board says it's thirteen degrees Celsius outside. I don't like summer anyway so this suits me just fine. The people here in Valencia are quite friendly though, you can see they're used to having tourists. I'm booked in at Hotel Kramer, my home for the next two nights; they had a special of fifty-seven percent off per night. It's still not cheap but definitely worth the money with the discount. Still waiting for my bag to come around and in this mood I really don't have the patience to wait. Maybe I should go ask security if there was a problem and that's why I'm still—. Never mind there it comes. Oh my gosh, look at the queue of people waiting for taxis.

'Miss.' A man whispers in broken English.

'Yes?'

'You need the taxi?'

You're kidding right. Let me just reply politely. 'I do indeed, I'm booked into a hotel nearby.'

'Okay I give you a lift, my taxi is standing right there. Can I carry your bags?' he asks in a friendly voice.

'Why thank you; I'm booked in at Hotel Kramer, do you know it?'

'Of course! Very popular hotel. And a pretty girl like you stay there alone?'

Suspiciously she replies. 'Yes, why do you ask?'

'No that is not acceptable, I tell you what, my cousin she works close by, beautiful girl like you, I tell her to meet you at the front door tonight at eight, she likes tourists and will show you the city. Her name is Camila.' he enthusiastically replied.

'All right then, it sounds like a fun night lies ahead of me. Thank you.'

The ride to Hotel Kramer was nice and smooth, he's a good driver. I have doubts about tonight, but what the hell, you only live once. I'm going to take a long bath and let my jetlag fade. I feel on edge; a little bit uncomfortable but I've never been this far from home. I wonder if this is the feeling of independence. I could get used to this.

Lily puts on music, Bach. The music creates a theatrical feel to the atmosphere by gently dampening the echo from the Spanish city. Steam slowly fills up the bathroom as the hot water fills the bath; the steam gently starts to creep out of the bathroom door and creates a soft misty effect in the room. Light from outside her hotel window reflects on the mist and romances her. Lily's mind starts to wander. She visits the deeper side of her inner mind and allows the mist to fill her lungs. She closes her eyes and her heart starts to beat faster and faster. A warm feeling from within overcomes her as she wanders deeper and deeper into her thoughts. She takes off her jacket, her shirt and her pants. Left only in her semi-transparent black underwear, Lily walks into the bathroom, bends over and closes the tap. Her heart is racing and her head spinning. She reaches behind her and releases the strap of her bra, then drops it from her arms onto the floor and slowly rubs her hands over her naked breasts down to her stomach, seductively, as if there is a lover in front of her, Lily pulls down her panties and kicks them away next to her bra. Overcome by lust Lily climbs in the bath, lies down and continues to rub her breasts with one hand, while starting to rub her inner thighs with the other. For a moment Lily tries to resist the temptation, but she's in too deep, she lets go, and gently starts…

After her bath, feeling like a rejuvenated young woman, she changes the music from Bach to something more contemporary and gets dressed. Now a quick look in the mirror. 'Lily you look fine, you're beautiful, confident and you're in Spain.' *Luckily these rooms are silent; I wouldn't want to get locked up in the looney bin for talking to myself. A letter slid under the door? It's probably the rules or something. Whomever wrote this has a pretty handwriting. I'll read it later; I don't want to keep Camila waiting.*

Here I am in the lobby and it's eight o'clock. I made sure that my watch is set according to the correct European time and no one is looking for me. I should have asked that driver what his cousin looks like. Maybe he forgot to tell her, or she forgot to come. Ten more minutes and then I think I will meander off on my own. I'd prefer that to be honest. After an hour's wait at the bar and three cosmopolitans later, Lily decides that Camila is no longer worth the wait and walks out of Hotel Kramer's door and into the beautiful city.

She returned to her hotel room in the early hours of the next morning after a comedy show at Urban Café, cocktails at Sol y Luna and an unforgettable jazz show at Loco club. Intoxicated, she tottered through the door and dived onto the soft mattress, only to find the letter next to her where she had thrown it before she left. Curiosity was always one of Lily's greatest virtues and for a second she lay there thinking how nice it would be if this was another love letter. She held it in one hand for a while, admiring the sophisticated and romantic handwriting. She brought the envelope to her nose, smelling soft, clean and soapy cologne mixed with the smell of green tea. The handwriting and cologne painted a picture. In her mind with her eyes closed she saw a man, clean shaven, a handsome smile, wearing a tailor-made suit and no tie. Soon after this thought Lily fell asleep. The next morning, she awoke with a sobering fright as she was almost late for her tour bus booking. She took the letter and threw it in her bag before getting ready for her last day in Valencia.

Lily's trip through Europe was spellbinding. From Spain, she went to Monaco and from there she went to see the Rhine Falls in Switzerland, after which she visited Vatican City in Italy. From Italy, she travelled to the Netherlands where she smoked cannabis for almost two days straight in Amsterdam. Then it was Big Ben and the London Eye. The Gothenburg Botanical Garden and the Universeum in Sweden. Finland. Russia. Ukraine. Romania. Bulgaria. And from Bulgaria she went to Greece. In Greece, she spent only a day and she only went to see one thing: The Acropolis of Athens. While standing in the Acropolis, Lily remembered a letter that she still had not read. Its tea-stained paper, compelling smell and sophisticated almost ancient handwriting, made it perfect for this scene. Lily started digging in her backpack for the letter, and found it shrivelled and folded right at the bottom. She opened the letter and saw there was only writing on one side, but with no name at the bottom. As she turned it over, the back page was empty except in the middle at the bottom of the page, in the same beautiful handwriting, it was signed only "**J.**". She turned the page over and started reading.

"Dear Lily.
To you I write this letter. Not a letter of love. However not a letter of hate either. Rather I see this as a letter of admiration. You see little Lily, you are beautiful and have received more declarations of love than most cities.
But I see something more in you, something deep inside, something even more beautiful than the stars. I see the inner workings of your mind, so unique that it is worth more than gold. You see, little Lily, even if you don't see it, I do.
One day when the time is right I will reach out to you again. And when I do, please don't be concerned, I am merely an admiring friend.
P.S. I hope you enjoy your trip through Europe"

Chapter 3

Paxos, the smallest of the Ionian Islands and home to my mother's sister, Aunt Grace. I feel a little bit rattled after reading the letter from "J." yesterday. Whoever "J." is. I'm used to getting letters, but the tone that came with this one is scary. I'll just hope that it was a prank by someone at the hotel. I mean it's not difficult to discern that I would be travelling Europe if I only booked into that hotel for two days. I just hope that I wasn't followed. Even if so, I didn't recognise anyone in Greece and now in Paxos, there are so few people that it would be stupid to try and follow me here. Nevertheless, I should keep this letter hidden from Aunt Grace. She might not take it lightly with all the rumours going around of girls being kidnapped throughout Europe. If I read that letter when I got it, I would probably have thought about the same thing and been on the first plane back home.

Aunt Grace is sweet, I wish that we met earlier in my life; I can see we would've been good friends. She unpacked my clothes into the cupboard in one of the spare rooms where I will be staying for the last two weeks of my holiday. And her husband, Albert, what a gentleman; I am not allowed to do anything, not even make coffee, he does it all. Apparently they never had children, so I guess that's why they are like this with me, it's like I'm the new puppy in the house. For the next two weeks, I think I will just relax. I'm exhausted from this trip; I never really got to rest. Mom was smart telling me to come here at the end of my travels. I think after my time at Grace and Albert I will be ready for university. Next time I come to Europe I think I will visit only this city. This is more my type of town; quiet, very few people, and those that are here are friendly; it truly feels like a community. And the city itself is so pretty. Grace and Albert's house is right on the beach. The patio chairs have an unobstructed view of the clear blue ocean, from the patio down a couple of stairs is an infinity pool with the same view, and if you walk down the next set of stairs you're on the beach. It's absolutely perfect. Not to mention the house itself; five enormous rooms with en-suite bathrooms on the top floor, two of which have an ocean view with independent balconies, one of which I am happily staying in, and the other is Grace and Albert's room. On the bottom floor is one big open plan room with only a counter separating the kitchen from the dining room and lounge, and in one corner, a small downstairs bathroom is hidden behind a carved wooden door. I have never seen open space like this, everything feels so light. This is the perfect place to clear my mind and to get in the right space before attending class.

I can't wait though; university seems like so much fun. That letter made me think I might do a double major: journalism and psychology, but I'll see when I get there. The thing is I really like journalism, it's my passion and it will take me places; I'll see the world. But that letter intrigued me, made me think that I can explore the minds of others, sort of like "J." thinks he looked into mine. I still think it's a prank. Psychology just seems like an old man's job. I wonder. Maybe I should consider psychiatry, it just seems so long, first you must study to be a doctor and then specialise in psychiatry. I'm not too sure about that. I thought of criminal psychology, but that's also long. From what I understand from a conversation with Albert, according to his friends, to be a practising criminal psychologist in most countries, I will need a PhD. Then I might as well do psychiatry. I should never have read that stupid letter.

Chapter 4

Back home, fully rested and ready to take on the task of studying to be a journalist, Lily set off for university. Brian and Jenifer were proud of their daughter, but the parting was bittersweet as they knew they would only see Lily in the holidays again. Lily, on the other hand, was excited. Journalism, this is what her mind was set on. She knew that for her to be chosen for the best internship, she needed to perform to the best of her abilities and if possible, be best in class. But this was a far more difficult task than it was in school. Only the top students from the surrounding schools got chosen at The University of Texas at Austin. Therefore competition was stiff. Nonetheless, Lily didn't show an ounce of fear, she was driven and determined.

The letter from "J." travelled with her and was posted against her wall in their dormitory room. It served as a reminder of her decision and as motivation for her future studies. Julie, her roommate, was a nice girl and came from a wealthy and influential family.

'Lily, have you got all your books for this year?'

'Yes I have. My parents struggled to find one of them. Apparently, every place they visited was out of stock, but I guess if I didn't change my mind over and over about the course, I would've had it sooner.'

'You changed your mind? Are you leaving?'

Laughing Lily said, 'No, no, I was two minds about journalism and psychiatry then decided that a passion is a passion and I will always regret leaving it for a mere interest.'

'Oh I understand now, sorry blonde moment. Come to think of it that question made no sense. What made you change your mind? Please don't tell me it was your parents that told you to?'

'No my parents had no say in the matter, they also weren't too angry because I have an open bursary from the university, so the university pays either way. Do you see that letter on my wall?'

'Yes?'

'So while I was traveling through Europe, someone named "J." wrote that letter and slid it under my door at one of the hotels. I still think it's a prank, but that's beside the point. After reading the letter, it made me think. I developed an interest in how people think and why they behave the way they do. And it started with why this person decided to write me that letter. I also considered psychology—criminal, but found out from my uncle it will pretty much work out to the same amount of time to do medicine and then specialise in psychiatry. And since people always want pills for everything, I thought if I do psychiatry, I can research the human mind while making good money. But journalism is just so… *fun*. I can still research all of that and do what I love, plus this will take me places.'

'That makes sense. It's pretty creepy how that person wrote you a letter; I think it must be a man. And the way it's written, it comes across almost as if he knows you, or at least has met you.'

'You can't smell it any more, the scent has completely faded, but the letter smelled of very expensive cologne. I think, apart from the creepiness, he must be a gentleman,' Lily said, staring out the window.

Julie started giggling and said, 'You say it almost as if you fell in love with the guy.'

'In love? No way, I don't fall in love.'

'Lily what do you mean you don't fall in love? I've had a couple of boyfriends in school. Jugs Julie the boys called me.'

Lily laughed. 'Well I can see why.'

'Yes, they're not small, are they? But I like it; it makes the boys look twice. Not that I let them touch the twins.'

Still laughing Lily said, 'Twins.'

'What's so funny?'

'I love your expressions Julie.'

Julie and Lily spent the rest of that night laughing and talking about all sorts of teenage topics. They spoke about sport, movies, books, school, holidays, but mostly about boys. Lily realised that even though she kept saying she never fell in love, there was one boy that she was particularly fond of: Peter, the boy from across the street. If she ever came close to falling in love, Peter would probably be the one. During Lily's trip through Europe Peter didn't wait for life to start. He always wanted to wear a badge, "Detective Peter Jones," that's what he wanted people to call him. He wanted to wear a coat and a hat and carry a gun. He wanted to be the judge, jury, and executioner. Soon after Lily left for Europe, young Peter finished his two years' military service and joined the Police Academy in pursuit of his big dream. By the time Lily was ready to leave for university, Peter was finishing his last couple of weeks at the academy. But nothing would stop Peter from sneaking out of the academy for a couple of hours to say his goodbyes to

Lily. Lily thought of that day Pete sneaked out; he came in uniform, clean shaven, with a neat haircut, and he smelt good. He made her heart race for a couple of seconds. She had never seen Pete that nervous, but the reason was clear soon enough; as he said goodbye, Pete grabbed a kiss, a kiss she will never forget.

Crunch time. My first big exams are coming up next week. But when that is over I can go home and rest. Half a year behind me and I never thought I would be this exhausted. This course is tough, but luckily I have Julie. We have all the same classes, and all the same stress. We've become so close over the past couple of months. If only she stayed close to my parents I would be able to see her during the holidays, I guess we'll have to call each other, maybe we can arrange for a visit once or twice, I'm sure dad won't mind me driving out to her for a couple of days.

'Lily...'

'Pete!' Lily runs and jumps into Peter's strong arms, she lets go after a couple of seconds and grabs his arms around the biceps. 'Look at your arms. Wow, that's nice.' She found herself staring at Peter as if he was a movie star and started to blush.

Nervously Peter says, 'Umm, how are you? How's university?'

'It's nice, I really enjoy it there and I made—'

'I missed you...'

Lily's gorgeous smile is unleashed as she looks at Peter with glimmering eyes. Suddenly her heart starts pounding and she starts to feel warm inside. She softly replies while tucking her hair behind her ear 'I missed you too Pete.' *What is going on? Julie cursed me with all her love talk, look at me now.*

'Can I take you to dinner tonight?'

'Sure, pick me up at eight?'

'That's perfect, my shift ends at six, see you later Lily.'

Lily smiles, waves, and runs into the house. Not sure how to act or even how to dress, she searches her room for some acceptable clothes. She tries on jeans, then takes them off, then puts on sweatpants and takes them off. She pulls a dress off the hanger. Looks terrible. She throws the dress on the floor and looks in the mirror. Standing there only in her hot pants, she is quickly reminded of her night in Valencia; the night in the bath. She can't help but wonder how a similar night would be… tonight, with Peter. For a second she fantasises and wonders what it would feel like with Peter on top of her in the back of his car. She picks up the dress again, puts it on and looks in the mirror. *I think this dress will be perfect actually; it's not too long, but not too short either. It's easy to put on, and just as easy to take off… Why am I thinking of this? Sex with Pete? I've never had sex before. But what if he thinks… Never mind I'm sure he's thinking of the same thing. I just can't look too desperate, but I must be prepared. I'll leave the bra, the dress gives enough support, but these hot pants won't do. I need something a little sexier, a little bit more alluring. Somewhere in my cupboard I have some red lace underwear. They'll be perfect with the black dress; my bum won't show lines.* At nearly quarter to eight the phone rings.

Brian answers 'Tomlinson residence.' Some time passes. 'Okay thank you I will pass on the message, see you soon.' Brian puts the phone back on the hook and calls. 'Lily. My girl, Peter says that he can't make it any more, they were sent to a late call; an apparent murder.

He says that he will come by the house tonight straight from work, shall we dish up a plate for him?'

Disappointed, Lily replies. 'Yes please Daddy.'

Peter never got to Lily that night. She understood, but it still put a dent in their relationship; Peter was never the same after that night. What Peter found was most disturbing. A body, lying face down. When they turned it over it was one of Peter's cousins. They weren't particularly close as his cousin was quite abusive to his wife and child. However, it was still his cousin and in their younger years they had spent many hours playing together and still shared memories from those more innocent days. The body was shirtless and bruised over the abdomen, arms and head; almost as if while alive, he had tried to defend himself from someone. A clean cut from left to right just below the larynx was noted by forensics as the cause of death. But someone had cleaned him: there was no blood on his neck, face or chest. It seemed he had been bled dry elsewhere. The only bit of blood found was in a triangle cut into his left wrist with the apex pointing towards the hand. The forensic staff said that it had to have been done post mortem, probably before the body was moved and dumped. It was a sad day for their town; Peter's cousin was the first reported murder in decades. The murder set the tone for the rest of Lily's first year at university. Conflicted with her feelings for Peter, together with the stress of leaving her parents in a town with a murderer that could not be found, Lily felt disheartened.

Chapter 5

Peter's cousin Freddy came home late from work. As he pulled into the driveway with his blue pickup he noticed the half-cut grass in the front yard and his five-year-old son's bicycle on the walkway. He pulled in front of the big metal garage door, climbed out, and with uncontrolled rage ripped the door open which made a loud blast as it hit the top. He got back in his truck, parked it, and slammed the garage door closed again.

'Fucking people never do as I ask,' he muttered angrily as he strode across the uncut grass. He opened the door and stared Monique in the eyes. After a couple of second's pause, he said, abruptly, 'Evening.'

His foul mood was obvious to Monique, but she decided to act as if she hadn't noticed. 'Hi love. How was your day?' But she only received a threatening look as Fred walked to their room to get out of his work gear.

Storming back out of the bedroom, he screamed, 'Why the fuck are the clothes not ironed?'

'My love I was busy today, I'll do it tomorrow I promise' Monique has seen this play one to many times before and she knew what was heading her way.

'Busy? Busy with what? Or with who? Did you bring another man into my house? Answer me Monique!' Their son Donald started crying from Fred's ear-splitting shouting. 'And shut that fucking child up, he's a bloody nuisance!'

Fearful, Monique ran to Donald. 'There, there, my boy, Daddy had a bad day. You're okay. Mommy's here.' She looked at Fred and all she saw was rage.

'My love be reasonable please, I don't even have friends. I went grocery shopping today, I cleaned the whole house and the windows and started with the grass.'

'You need to learn to prioritise Monique. I've said this to you before.' Fred pulled his pistol from his hip holster, smiling as he did so, tapped it against his leg and put it back in the holster.

'Fred! The window!' He turned, as a dark figure disappeared from the large lounge window.

He ripped his gun from his holster again, ran out the door and fired three shots into the darkness.

'Run, you piece of shit coward! Come back and I'll kill you!' He walked back into the house and sat on his chair in front of the television. After about an hour's mind-numbing news Freddy got up, took the keys to his truck and yelled down the passage, 'I'm going to get some beer,' and left.

At the Liquor Store he cheerily said, 'Evening Howard.'

This face was all too familiar to the store owner. 'Evening Fred, trouble with the wife?'

'Bitches.' Freddy shook his head and looked Howard in the eyes. 'I would've left the dog if she hadn't got that kid. Teaches you some lessons. Life hey? Always use a condom when you bang 'em.'

'Come now pal you've got a pretty wife, she's good to all.'

'Bye Howard.' Freddy shook his head again and marched out.

'Cheers Fred.'

Now Freddy walks to the car, whistling an inharmonious tune and hears a noise from behind his truck.

'Psst.' But Freddy ignores the sound; he feels untouchable.

'Psst,' he hears the noise again and decides to investigate. He walks slowly around, sliding his hand along the body of the truck, looks around and finds nothing. As Freddy turns back around to get in his truck he faces the butt of a shotgun. A mighty blow sends him to the ground and a second blow to the back of the head knocks him out cold.

Freddy opens his eyes and looks around the half-lit room. He starts trying to move his arms and legs but he's bound to a standing trolley. Freddy's not a small guy and he's far from weak, but he finds it impossible to free himself. *Whoever did this really doesn't want me going anywhere. Where the hell am I? Shit what happened? I remember the noise and then nothing after that.*

'Hello!' Freddy's call goes unanswered.

'Hello-o-o-o!' He screams louder and just before he tries again he hears someone behind him, near his shoulder.

'Shh.'

'Hey who the fuck are you?'

'Shh, be still Fred.' A man replies with perfect articulation.

'Look man, I don't know who you are and I haven't seen your face. Let me go and nothing will come from this. I'll give you whatever you want.'

'I have what I want. I wanted you.' Calmly a masked figure appears from behind Freddy, walks to a table in front of him, turns around and stares at him.

'Fuck you man! Who do you think you are? Why don't you untie me and let me kick your fucking teeth in!' Freddy rages.

'No need to worry, I'll untie you soon enough, I believe in a fair fight, I'll give you an equally equipped opportunity to defend yourself. But I felt like talking to you first.' The man calmly replies.

'Untie me and we'll… chat.'

'Mr Jones you are as predictable as a Neanderthal, I know if I loosen those restraints that you will immediately try to overpower me. And we both know after that you'll probably try to kill me. You see Freddy you have a problem with aggression and that's why you're strapped to that trolley, to give me a moment to talk to you before I release you. I have absolutely no intention of killing you tied up. That would make me a coward would it not? But I must warn you Fred—' The man steps closer to Fred and puts his face millimetres from Fred's and whispers 'I have every intention of killing you here tonight.'

Fred puts his face even closer and says. 'We'll see.'

'Fearless Fred. Tell me about yourself.'

'Fuck off and untie me.'

Unexpectedly, the man punches Fred in the stomach. The blow is so much harder than what Freddy expects from this small man.

'Don't make me torture you. But make no mistake, Mr Jones, if that's the only way, then I will, and I will enjoy it. You might as well entertain me and save your strength.' The man's voice never changes; always calm, always collected 'So I ask again, tell me about yourself, Fred.'

Winded, Freddy coughs and barely squeezes out the sentence. 'I'm not an interesting man, there's nothing really to tell.'

'Hmm.' The man pulls Freddy's chin up, looks him in the eye and says. 'There's no point in telling lies.' Another punch in the stomach. 'I'm not ill informed about you. Absent father, a mother that died of aggressive cancer when you were nineteen, a child with a girl you never loved but only wanted to "bang" as you call it. Your favourite cousin Peter avoids you because of the way you are. You see Freddy, I don't just randomly pick the people I do. There's a reason I chose you and I did some research. What I am interested in, is why you are like this. Why are you always so aggressive? Why are you abusive to your wife and child? And why do you take inappropriate pictures of that beautiful girl? You know which one I'm talking about right?' Fred looks at the man and immediately goes pale. His heart bangs in his throat. 'Right? The beautiful one. Your cousin Peter's friend. But I don't need to remind you, do I Fred?'

'How do you—' Fred replies softly.

'How do I know that you snuck into their house while she was alone? How do I know that you silently climbed onto a ladder to take pictures of her while she was in the shower?' Freddy stares mutely at the man 'Where's your confidence now Fred?' Freddy remains silent as he tries to figure out who this masked man could be 'I've been watching you. You see Fred you're an animal, and I hunt animals. You're a sick sociopath and I will remove you from society, it's better that way.'

'And you? You watched me do all of this, then kidnapped me and tied me up.'

The man stands in front of Fred for a moment and calm as always says. 'You and I are not similar, Mr Jones. I am functional, I am always in control. But most importantly, I don't prey on the weak.' For the first time, the man raises his voice. 'Enough messing around: Why, Fred?' and winds him for a third time.

'I don't know!'

Once again as calm as an ocean breeze, the man looks at Fred and says, 'Tell me about your childhood.'

'When I was in Primary school, all the kids used to tease me. We got by, me and my mom, but we weren't rich. And with my dad not being around and my mom having to work till late at night, I was alone for most of my life. Every once in a while I saw Peter, but as the years went by, he came visiting less. Towards the end of my high school years I grew a bit, I started building muscle with very little effort; I guess those were my father's genes. But still no one liked me. Until one day one of the popular boys pushed me in the row. I turned around and nearly beat him to a pulp. Since that day everyone feared me, as they should have. I've never in my life felt anything like it, to just let go. I like the feeling of rage.'

'Why aren't you happy with Monique?'

Surprised that the man knows her name he replies, 'I don't know what love is.'

'That is the most honest thing I've heard anyone say in years, Fred. Don't you love your son?'

'He cries too much. I never cried.'

The man paces up and down between the table and Freddy. He stops with his back to Fred and asks, 'Why do you beat them?'

'I don't know.'

'Fred. One more lie and you're going to make me lose my temper.'

'I like it. I like it when they scream.' Freddy replies.

'And the girl? The one you take pictures of?'

'I want to fuck her. I want to tie her up, gag her and fuck her till she cries, then Pete can have her.' Freddy's sociopathic rage-filled expression returns.

The man turns around, takes off his jacket, but keeps his vest and mask on. 'There he is. The monster. The animal. The one I've been waiting for. I must say Fred,' he slowly walks toward Freddy while rubbing his hands together. 'I didn't expect this to have been mostly driven by lust. Tell me, did you envision the same for Monique?'

Fred starts laughing. 'Envision? I did it. I fucked her so hard.'

The man takes a deep breath while closing his eyes and asks. 'The bullying wasn't the part that bothered you most in school was it? It was the fact that the girls didn't want to fuck you, that's what angered you the most right?'

'Bitches.'

The man walks around Fred and whispers in his ear. 'When I untie you, relax. I'm going to walk over and stand by the table. You stand here for a second and catch your breath and stretch if you must. I want you at your best. When you're ready, take off your shirt and we'll begin. The keys to the door are in my back pocket. If you want to get out, you'll have to take them. From my dead body.' The man unties Fred and waits for him by the table as he catches his breath.

'I never thought you'd really untie me; that was a mistake.' Fred rips his shirt off and runs towards the man. He swings his arms vigorously at the man but only manages to hit the air around him. The man is unbelievably agile and accurately anticipates Fred's every move. The man starts to retaliate with powerful punches and kicks across his abdomen and arms as Fred tries to protect his face. The man relentlessly beats Fred and kicks him to the floor. Bruised and in pain Fred looks at his arms to see if one of them might be broken. To his surprise both are still intact. As he turns back onto his palms to get up, a knife falls in front of him. The sharp edge catches the light almost blinding Fred. He picks up the knife, stands up and notices the masked man remains unarmed. For a second Freddy thought that it was over, but this is his lucky break. This is his way out. He runs towards the man once more, slicing from side to side, but misses every time. Fuelled with rage, he tries to stab the man from above. But in one swift movement the masked man grabs Fred's arm, turns him around and holds him in a steely grip. Fred can no longer feel the knife in his hand. But before he has time to think, Fred feels a cold burn across his throat. He feels the blood run down his chest. He struggles for breath. He stops resisting. The man hugs Fred from behind, holding him.

'Thank you for this gift.' For the first time in Freddy Jones' life, he truly felt gratitude. The man then said 'Your family is safe, I promise.' The man took off his mask, but Fred's vision had already started to blur and all he could see was a bright, white smile. The man took Freddy by the legs and dragged him to the other side of the room and tied something to his ankles. He then took his wrists and tied them to his waist and hoisted Fred up over a funnel. Fred could not see where the blood went after that. As Fred's hands went pale, the man took a scalpel and cut a perfect triangle with the apex pointing to the hand into Fred's left wrist. Only a small amount of blood seeped into the wound, leaving the triangle red, but not bloody. After Fred's body was bled dry, the mysterious man cleaned the room and Fred's body. A large glass jar filled with blood, with "FREDDY JONES" printed on it, was sealed and placed in a walk-in fridge situated in the next room. Freddy's jar was not the first.

Chapter 6

This promotion is a unique opportunity. I couldn't do much about Freddy as an officer; as a homicide detective however, I can make a difference. Captain Deloitte from the Criminal Investigation Division is still on the fence about whether or not he should make me part of the investigation; he says it's a bad idea because of my personal involvement. I just need to convince the shrink that I'm fine and I'll be on the case. Look at this place, shrink's lair, not what you'd expect.

'ID please.'

'Sure, do all shrinks have security like this?' Peter's voice echoes through open floor foyer.

The security officer armed with his Glock 17 looks straight at Peter and hands his ID card back to him. 'First elevator on your left, fifteenth floor.'

'Thanks. Which office?' Peter asks abruptly.

The security officer smiles, 'First time hey? Fifteenth floor.'

Peter swiftly walks through the bulletproof glass doors into the clinical, white lobby. He notices that there are no waiting areas or paintings; it looks more like a psychiatric hospital to him. But in the middle of the lobby a light shines from one single glass tile. Peter ignores it and walks over to the elevator. Next to the button a silver plate indicates floor numbers and their respective departments. Floor number 15—Dr Alexander Rayne, all other floor numbers in the twenty storey building are connected to departments, except for floor number fifteen, with the sole occupant being Dr Alexander Rayne. Peter frowns for a second while waiting for the elevator and analyses the silver plate. He notices there is no building name and assumes that all departments must be individual contractors. The doors of the elevator open with a swoosh, but no alarm goes off to alert people it has arrived. Peter stands in front of the open doors and looks into a dark space; the elevator has no lights. He hesitantly steps in and as if with his first step, the elevator starts to glow. A shiny black tile floor with tinted mirrors and a roof that looks like the night sky engulfs him and swiftly delivers him to the fifteenth floor. As Peter steps out of the strange, dark elevator, the glow is gone and the doors shut behind him. His heart starts to beat and he breaks out in a sweat when he turns away from the doors and faces the corridor. A short corridor, probably only ten paces, but it's in the shape of a tunnel. The tunnel is painted with deadly scenes of war, torture and murder.

A soft voice at the end of the tunnel calls out. 'Detective Jones?'

Peter walks faster to escape the scene and replies hastily. 'That's me Ma'am.'

'All right down there?'

Peter exits and feels a small sense of relief. 'Yes thank you. Dr Rayne's assistant I presume?'

'No,' she smiles at Peter and takes his hand 'I'm his student, I'm actually on my way out. He just told me you were coming. You can wait here, he'll be right out, have a nice day detective.' She smiles at him again, kisses his hand and disappears into the shadowy elevator.

The waiting room is as big as an average dining room and has a single couch in the middle of the room, facing the door. The walls are painted charcoal and the roof sapphire black. On the wall behind the chair, more murder, torture and war stories are told, and although it makes Peter uncomfortable, it suits the entrance to the devilish tunnel. The side walls have no paintings and the door takes up almost the entire front wall; a large ebony double door with sharp, dark metal handles. Peter sits down on the black leather couch and admires the artistic and bloodcurdling theatrical scenery. The doors slowly open and a figure appears: black shoes, black tuxedo pants, snow white shirt with a black tuxedo pullover and grey tie, short, dark hair and seductive smile.

'Detective, I'm glad you made it. Step into my office.'

'Good day Doctor.' Peter gets up out of the chair and walks through the enormous doors into an office that takes up the entire floor. He starts looking around and is amazed by the remarkable room. The wall in front of him is home only to a window and on the floor, there is more art with an elegant fountain as the centrepiece. To his right is a meditation area, and two doors show the way to the bathrooms. To his left he sees Dr Rayne's desk with a couch in front of it, facing the window. On that side of the tunnel is another door, but there is no indication of what's behind it.

'I can see in your face you like my office, Detective.'

'It's big. How come you have a whole floor to yourself?'

'Well it's my building, Detective.'

Rich bastard. 'Doctor I just have one question. Why the scary entrance?'

'It's not scary Peter. It's interesting that you see it like that. It's all about perspective. Come have a seat and we'll begin.'

'The door behind me; what's in that room?'

'Inquisitive one you are. I can see why you made detective. No need to worry about what's behind that door. It's a personal room. Now, let's begin. Your captain thinks that you will be a liability if you have any emotional involvement in the case; he thinks you might seek revenge if the killer is caught. So, he sent you here, to me, and it is my job to determine whether or not his concern is valid. I've read your file and I'm familiar with your history. Can you tell me how you felt after the murder? After discovering it was someone close to you?'

'I'm fine Doc, we can skip these formalities, do a psych. evaluation and you can let me go.'

'Hmm I see. You're very suspicious of me. The entrance set the stage I would say. Let's then build a rapport today, then I would like you to return daily for the first week and once a week thereafter. So today you can ask the questions. Does that seem fair?'

'All right, but as soon as you see I'm fine, you let me go?'

Dr Rayne smiles. 'Peter once we start, you won't want to leave, but as soon as I think you're ready, I'll send the appropriate letter to your captain.'

Peter closes his eyes and listens to the trickling of the fountain, it reminds him of soft rain with the gutter dripping in a water puddle. The smell of fresh morning dew fills his nose as he takes a deep breath. 'Why would you describe the entrance as art, when all it explicitly portrays is death?'

'There is more to it than that. You might see death in all those scenes, but if we had to divide the scenes into their individual concepts you will see it my way. In the war scenes I see two things; I see how one side of the war conquers and how another side is defeated, is that not how life is? Inside ourselves we fight continuous battles, but one side always has to win, and one side has to lose. In the torture scenes I see two things once again; the people torturing the victims are desperate. There's something that the victim has that the torturer does not, and they are willing to take it by any means necessary. I also see the victim, brave beyond compare. Have you ever been in a situation where you know, you absolutely know, that you will die, Detective? In that moment, the victim shows courage and bravery, they abandon fear and start to accept their fate. No one is braver than those victims. Lastly you see scenes of murder, where I see a struggle for control and power. You see Detective, there is more in death than what you allow yourself to see.'

Chapter 7

'Doctor I've done as you asked. It's been two weeks now; six sessions. Why do you still not think I'm ready? This murderer is out there somewhere and I can help catch him.'

'I understand your frustration, Detective.'

'Then tell me, Doctor, am I ready?'

'Before I answer your question I would like to ask you one.'

'We're wasting time, please just—'

'Detective.'

Peter sighs 'What's the question?'

'Do you think that acting within the law is always the way forward?'

Peter's pupils briefly dilate and his heart starts to throb. 'I'm a detective, of course it's always the right thing to do.'

Dr Rayne rubs his chin and sits back in his chair. 'I'm pretty good at what I do and I can see when someone tells a lie. It's okay to feel that sometimes there's more to do. I've sent the letter to your captain that you are fit for the case.'

'Thank you, Doctor, It's been—'

'However, I also stated that I would still like to see you weekly. As a safety precaution. You understand that right?'

'I will do whatever you feel necessary as long as I'm on the case.'

'I have no doubt about that. Our sessions will change a slight bit from here on.'

'Okay?'

'I would like to prepare you for your case. I would like to guide you in catching him.'

'No offence Doc, but do you have investigation experience?'

Dr Rayne laughs and in a friendly but stern voice replies. 'No young man, but I've read books. Just trust me Detective, I can help you. I might not know much about investigations, but I know people. I've dealt with the worst.'

'All right then, if you say you can help, I'll take it. Where do we start?'

'For today I would like us to ease into it, go grab lunch, meet me back here in thirty minutes.'

'Don't you have other appointments?'

'One, but she'll join us. You've met Diana? My student from last week?'

'I remember her vaguely.'

'Good. See you soon Detective; don't be late.'

Peter goes for lunch across the street, he was craving sushi. While he waiting, he thinks for a moment about the murder; how perfectly it was executed. Then Lily comes to mind, sweet and beautiful Lily. He had once loved her, but no more. The love he had for her is now replaced by a feeling he cannot explain, a kind of hunger. He can't wait to walk into the office and crack the spine of the case. In his mind it already happened; the file opened with the smell of paper and plastic, pictures of a man with no blood, a whiteboard with no leads, and a hum in the office created by the voices of thirty people all making phone calls at once. If only he had a lead, a starting point, something to work from. He runs the details through his mind, but nothing. *The perfect murder*, he thinks. He is confronted with the question: how do you catch a ghost? For a second Peter wanted to back out, because it would be easier not being a part of a failed investigation. Evidence is non-existent and hope is lost with the victim's blood. He finished his meal and returned to Dr Rayne.

'Hello Detective,' a sweet and calming voice rings as Peter enters through the large ebony doors.

'Diana, what a pleasure.'

'I see the art no longer bothers you?'

'I changed the way I look at the paintings.'

Dr Rayne touches his shoulder. 'All right Detective, let's make our way over to the meditation area.'

'Meditation?'

Diana takes his hand and leads him over. 'How can you catch a monster if you can't face your own demons Detective?'

'She's right. First we need to clear your mind of all the clutter, only then can we proceed.'

Peter said, unconvincingly, 'I guess it won't hurt to try.'

Diana looks at Dr Rayne, smiles and asks. 'Only meditation?'

Alexander smirks. 'For now yes.'

Diana lays three mats down in the shape of a triangle. 'All right Detective, sit wherever you feel most comfortable, cross your legs and place your hands on your knees. Back straight and chin up.'

The trickling of the fountain is the only thing breaking the silence. Calm and relaxing. Peter looks at Dr Rayne; his eyes are closed, it doesn't even look like he's breathing. He turns his attention to Diana; her eyes are open, dark brown. She looks back at Peter with seduction that almost undresses him. 'Close your eyes,' she says 'Free your mind, focus only on your breathing, feel the air as it enters your nose, cold, and almost burning. Then feel how it exits your nose again, warm and soft. Just keep focussing on that. Count one as you inhale and two as you exhale. One, and two. One, and two.'

One, two, one, two, one, two. My head feels light, my body relaxed. Almost as if I'm weightless. I can hear Dr Rayne's breathing, and Diana's. Diana. That look she gave me. The kiss on my hand the other day. Her smile. Her beautiful lips. Peter opens his eyes briefly and looks at Diana, her back straight, her breasts out, her legs crossed. He can't help but slowly gaze between her legs, her tights appropriately revealing.

'Detective.' Diana smiles 'Eyes closed. Focus. One, and two, one, and two.'

Shit she saw me look. One and two, one, two. Peter's breathing increases as he thinks of Diana and the moment she saw him looking between her legs. *Why would she smile though? One, two, one, two, one, two. Calm down. Hear the trickling of the water, focus on the silence. Feel the air move in and out, in and out, in and out, one and two, one, two, one, two. The blood, what did he do with the blood? He cleaned it off, why? How? How! That's it! We need to...* 'Doctor! I have it.'

'What is it Detective?'

'I apologise, I have to interrupt, and I have to go down to the precinct. The blood had to be cleaned off by something. It sure as hell wasn't normal soap. It had to have been something strong. Something purposefully made I'm thinking. If I can swab the body, maybe the chemicals can be traced. Thank you. I'll see you next week. Diana, I'm sorry.'

Diana stands up. 'That's quite all right Detective. Alexander, we'll carry on with him next week; you and I will continue on our own, right?'

Dr Rayne stands up, shakes Peter's hand and turns back to Diana. 'Of course my dear.'

Chapter 8

The wipers wedge left and right to keep the windscreen clear as water droplets fall and burst onto the glass. With an idea in mind Peter hurries across town, he wants to plot the name of a chemical on the whiteboard. But an accident up the road stops him in his tracks and he is stuck in traffic. All he can do is sit in his car and listen to the pouring rain and watch how each lightning bolt splits the sky. Consumed by his idea, he decides to cut out of traffic and face the oncoming lane. With a bit of luck and a short prayer Peter escapes traffic unscathed, dodging cars left and right, flashing lights and leaning on the horn. He pulls into the precinct, jumps out of the car, forgetting to switch off the ignition. The doors of the police station crash open as he runs straight through them.

He barges into the captain's office. 'Am I on the case?'

'Yes, but Detective—' but before the captain can finish his sentence, Peter disappears as quickly as he came in. The captain puts on the chase, running after Peter like a madman, calling, 'Peter!' Since he is more athletic, Peter pulls away from the captain and he starts to flag. 'Detective!' The captain struggles to keep up and as he runs, more police officers start to follow. 'Stop him! Detective! Stop!' They're all too slow and only see the doors of the coroner's rooms close behind him.

'Doctor, I need to see the body!' pants Peter, as the doors swing open behind him.

'Detective!'

'Captain there's no time to explain, just listen, I need to see the body.' The room fills with people all talking at once.

The coroner puts his hand in the air. 'Silence!' he beckons Peter over. 'I'm sorry Detective, but that's impossible. It's been over two weeks since the murder, we checked everything that we could and found nothing. The body's been released for burial. He's no longer here.'

'Monique... we need to call her Captain; we need the body back.'

'Pete she's been trying to get a hold of you, the funeral service is in three days—'.

'Call her! We need the—'

The captain grabs Peter's arm tightly. 'Detective listen to me! The body was cremated last night, I'm sorry.' He let go of his arm.

'Detective I assure you, there was nothing to find.' The doctor adds.

'Did you scan his body with backlight?'

'Of course.'

'And found nothing?'

Tetchily the Doctor replies, 'No Detective, as my reported stated, nothing.'

'Don't you find that odd? Think about it. Blood leaves a trace under the backlight, as does bleach which is most commonly used by killers to get rid of blood.'

Irritated the captain asks, 'What's your point Detective?'

'My point, Captain, is that the doctor didn't do his job properly. He should've swabbed the skin for chemicals, because if there was no blood and no trace of household cleaners under backlight, it means something better suited was used. Something purposefully made for crime scene cleaning. But you didn't swab the skin did you? Because there was nothing to be found, right?'

Silence fills the room and the atmosphere is changed by the coroner's failure. The captain breaks the silence. 'Detective Anderson!'

'Sir?'

'Take a team of five people. Before the end of this day I want a list of all available crime-scene cleaning kits on my desk. Detective Harris!'

'Sir?'

'Go home and rest, you're coming back for the night shift. I would like for you also to take a team of five people, and when Anderson's done with his list, you find me places where you can buy those products, local, national and international, understood?'

'Yes Sir.'

'Detective Jones!'

'Yes Sir?'

'I'm going to give you a copy of the case file; you go home and work through it. Check every detail. Do you need help?'

'No Sir, but can I suggest a consultant?'

'Who?'

'Either Doctor Rayne or his apprentice Diana, also a doctor?'

'Can we trust them?'

'Yes Sir.'

'Put them on the list of consultants, but they only work on the case under your supervision, not on their own. They don't get copies of anything, understood?'

'Yes Sir.'

The captain turns to the room of people. 'You're all dismissed, let's catch this bastard. We have a lead, now get to work and don't stop until we have something. Go home if you must rest after your shift, if not, stay and work the case.'

Peter follows the captain to his office; he looks at the precinct from the captain's door, it looks like a beehive. With hundreds of worker bees focused on one specific task. If you ignore the sound of ringing telephones, it almost sounds like a hive; continuous humming albeit with the aroma of roasted coffee beans in the mix. 'Detective, here's your copy. Now Pete, listen to me.' Peter holds onto one end of the file and the captain the other 'If at any moment you are not coping with what you find in here, you tell me. I don't want you stuck in a looney bin on my account. Understood?'

'Yes sir. But no need to worry, I have a weekly appointment with Doctor Rayne.'

'I thought it was over?'

'It is, but he gave me the option to return even though I'm fit for duty.'

'Good. Let's catch this guy.'

Chapter 9

The kettle starts to whistle and it echoes through Peter's quiet house. In his winter pyjamas and gown, he shuffles from his steamy bathroom to the kitchen. His hair still wet, his skin flushed and veins dilated from the hot shower. He fills his cup with lemongrass tea. Over by the kitchen table lies the file; Freddy's case file, unopened. An old record player made of cherry and maple wood that he found in a second-hand store stands in front of the table. Slowly his fingers flick the records over. With the soft rain trickling against the window, he chooses Tchaikovsky. He takes a glass out of the cupboard together with a Pinot Noir Chardonnay blend, opens it to let it breathe and places it next to the file while sipping at his tea. Comfortable on the chair he finishes the tea, pours a glass of wine and opens the case file filled with papers, notes and reports. The list of suspects is a blank page and since he already knows every detail of the scene, he flips over and skips the scene notes; he wrote almost all of it. The notes written by the other detectives are inconclusive and add no value, they had nothing to work with; no evidence, no witnesses, no case. He opens the autopsy report:

    Autopsy report   : Freddy Jones
    Cause of death   : Exsanguination
    Gender   : Male
    Age   : 27
    Blood   : Exsanguinated, only trace of blood was in the wrist wound and bladder. Type A+, not

enough volume for blood testing (toxins, drugs or poisons).

Hair : Dark brown, cut short, no abnormalities found in hair.

Eyes : Brown, no petechial haemorrhage or other abnormalities found.

Head and Neck : A contusion 2 cm wide and 4.2 cm long to the forehead just off centre to the left above the eyebrow from blunt force trauma with a hard object. Hairline fracture of 1 cm found in the same region. A contusion 2.3 cm wide and 4 cm long to the occiput in the centre from blunt force trauma (suspected to be the same object). No further abnormalities found on the head and face. A 15 cm clean laceration found on the front of the neck below the larynx, varying in depths from 0.1 cm to 1.9 cm cut from left to right from behind by a right-handed person with sharp object. No further abnormalities found on the neck.

Chest : No abnormalities found on the chest.

Abdomen : Contusions in varying severity found over all four quadrants of the abdomen from blunt force trauma. No internal organ damage or other abnormalities found.

Pelvis : No signs of sexual abuse or forceful rectal penetration. Bladder empty from urinary incontinence, small amount of urine found in bladder with minor traces of blood as a result of direct damage from blunt force trauma. No further abnormalities found.

Back : Post mortem cutaneous dystrophy over scapulae and buttocks owed to potential transportation of body post mortem in supine position on hard surface. No further abnormalities found.

Extremities: Defensive wounds (contusions) over posterior aspect of forearms, mainly over ulnar sections, simple fracture of the left ulna, radius intact. Right radius and ulna intact. Offensive wounds (contusions, abrasions and superficial lacerations) found on the knuckles of both hands. Triangle cut into left wrist, apex pointing to the hand, two tips pointing outward left and right respectively, all sides 3 cm at a depth of 0.5 cm cut with extremely sharp object (potential use of scalpel suspected) No further abnormalities found.

After reading the autopsy report, Peter feels dejected. He finishes the bottle of wine while staring out the window, watching the rain and thinking of the case. His only lead had burned with Freddy. As he takes the last swallow, he closes the case file, packs everything neatly away and gets into bed. But it's difficult for him to fall asleep that night; he's haunted by feelings of despair and regret. If only he had spent more time with Fred, maybe he wouldn't have turned out to be the type of person he was and maybe he wouldn't have been killed. But he knows that those thoughts only created a false reality. There is no way of changing the past. He looks up towards the ceiling as a warm tear rolls down his temple, and for the first time since Freddy's death, Peter truly mourned him.

Chapter 10

The next morning Peter walks into the precinct feeling relieved and peaceful. But something has changed in the office since last night. It can only be progress. He walks across the room and looks around at everyone's desks, all empty. But inside the captain's office, the dark room with only a little bit of sunlight showing through the blinds, a shadow sits on the chair. Peter walks in and switches the captain's lights on. He is in his chair sleeping; same clothes as last night, tie on the table and the first couple of buttons on his shirt undone. Evidently the captain never went home. Peter softly walks over to the captain and gently shakes his shoulder. 'Cap. Cap, wake up.'

'Peter, my boy, forgive me.'

'No problem. Where is everyone?'

'We found the list of all the crime scene clean up kit traders. I sent everyone home that stayed the night. Just waiting for dayshift to come and we can divide the crew to investigate.'

Peter notices the captain's wedding ring is no longer on his finger; not entirely sure if he ever saw one, but the pale indentation in his ring finger speaks for itself. 'Did you stay here last night sir?'

'I was too tired to drive; thought I'd grab a catnap here.'

'All right well I'm going to head over to my desk and start reading through the list, try and figure out what time they open.'

'Okay Detective, close the door behind you.'

'Sure.'

Sitting by his desk, Peter stares at the list of companies who sell these cleaning kits. *I wonder. Would this guy be smart enough not to get caught by this? Everything he did was so meticulously planned, every bit but this one part. Hmm… taking down Fred must have been quite the task. I need to speak to Dr Rayne; I need to start figuring out how this animal operates. I'm thinking either this guy has done this before, or he really thought about this for a long while. Those are the only two options. First time killers usually make mistakes. But let me not jump the gun, either way though, whether this guy planned properly or whether he has done this before, we'll need a bit of luck. I won't put my money on this list being the factor that makes us catch this fucker.*

'Jones!'

'Anderson!' the excitement is imprinted on Peter's face.

'Is that the list?'

'Yeah, this is it. Look if this guy bought the stuff locally, then sweet, there are only three shops in our area, all within an hour's drive. The other five we'll have to ask the local authorities in these states to check it out.' Peter shows Anderson the list. 'Those kits found online are too difficult to get into the country. We're too strict. Look at the note at the bottom written there; apparently, it's law that only parties registered with the National Crimes Unit can buy this stuff. So either this guy bought the shit on the black market, or we can trace him. Whether he has a phony registration or not, we might just catch a break here.'

'Where's Cap?'

'Sleeping in his office, doesn't seem like he went home.'

'Fuck. Rumours must be true then, I guess his old gal left him. Anyway that's none of my business, what is my business is this list. What do you say Jones? Wanna hit these places with me?'

'Let's do it. Just write a note and slide it under the captain's door. I'll wait in the car.' Peter swings his coat over his shoulder and walks down to the car while detective Anderson does as he is asked.

Anderson slams the door closed. 'All right Jones, let's do this. I reckon we take the furthest one first?'

'Sweet.' It takes Peter and Detective Anderson almost fifty minutes to get to the first shop. Driving against the flow of traffic always helps. As they step out of the car they see the big building with police signs on the front door. 'Looks like the place; Fusion Cleaning,' Peter says, smiling.

Anderson enters the door first. 'Morning, morning. Can I see the manager please?' He shows his badge over the counter.

'Good morning officer—'

'Detective. Anderson and Jones.'

'My apologies Detective, I'll quickly call the manager for you.'

After some time a slender man returns. 'Detectives, good morning. I'm James and I'm in charge here. What can I do for you today?' he says in a loud, friendly voice.

Peter puts the list on the table, points to James's shop and asks. 'Can you provide a list of all people or companies that bought crime scene cleaning kits from this shop over the past six months?'

'I sure can Detective, but I must say that if you're looking for something fishy, it's unlikely that you'll find it here. We don't supply to any private companies. We only supply to you guys, nationwide. We signed the cop-shop contract some nine years ago. Since then it's been exclusive. That's why we have your badge on the front there. I'll give you the list, but all that it gives you is a name and signature of the guy that signed for it wherever we delivered to, and then also the reference number for payment by the state. You know government, strict bastards, everything has to be perfect. What's the problem if I may ask?'

Detective Anderson walks around the waiting area while Peter carries on talking to James. 'We believe that a suspect potentially got a hold of a kit somewhere and we're trying to find him.'

'Well let me tell you what you can do Detective. As I said, here we don't sell to the public, so if it was one of our kits, it had to have gone missing from one of your departments. I'll give you the list with every sale over the past year. I'll also give you our inventory list to prove nothing's missing from our stores. What you do, is you take that list and cross reference every product we sent out to the crime scenes that they cleaned. If it's ours, at least you'll know where it went missing.'

'Thanks we'll do that, we're kind of in a hurry.'

'Sure, sure, sure, let me run quickly.' The slender man disappears.

'Anderson.'

'Yeah?'

'If we don't find the loophole at one of the other shops, then we have a fuck ton of work to do. Did you hear what this guy just said?'

'Yeah.' Detective Anderson says, sighing.

Ten minutes later James reappears. 'Okay here we go Detectives. Here's your lists. You have yourselves a nice day now.'

A couple of minutes later the police car parks in front of the second destination; Ronald's Stain Removals. 'Ronald's Stain Removals?' Detective Anderson says while laughing and pointing at the odd sign.

'Hold thumbs Andy. I don't want to be the unlucky bastard cross referencing all that other shit. The name's dodgy; it has potential.' They walk in and find a man packing boxes onto shelves. 'Morning, Detectives Jones and Anderson, we're looking for the owner of this place.'

'Detectives huh? The name's Ronald, how can I help?'

'Ronald we're investigating a crime potentially involving some of your products. We'd like to ask you a couple of questions.'

The man starts to fidget with his hands, looking at the front door and then over at the counter. 'What do you mean "crime"?'

While Peter is talking to the man, both he and Anderson pick up on the change in atmosphere and Anderson slowly starts to move more to one side. 'Homicide.' Peter says.

'Homicide huh? What's that got to do with me?'

'We believe whoever committed the crime used a crime scene cleaning kit, not many places you can get hold of one of those, so we need—' but before Peter can finish the question, the man throws a box at Anderson and runs straight at Peter, making for the front door. Ronald didn't bargain on Peter being the runner he is. Peter gives chase immediately, pulling his weapon from his side mid-run and firing a warning shot in the air. The man stops, apparently thinking he got shot and starts tapping his body when suddenly he feels a shocking blow to his ribs on his right side as Peter tackles him. Like an unstoppable train, Peter collides with him at full speed, throwing the man up into the air and onto the ground. 'You're under arrest!' Peter screams, pulling the man's arms behind his back and slapping the handcuffs onto his wrists. 'We'll talk at the precinct.'

'Let me go man! I ran out of instinct, I don't like pigs!'

'You're coming with us. You have the right to remain silent. Everything you say can and will be used against you in the court of law. You have the right to an attorney, if you cannot provide one, one will be—'

'I know my rights.'

'Good. Saves me the energy.' Peter walks Ronald to the car and puts him in the back 'Thanks for the help Andy.'

'Seemed like you had him; didn't want to get in your way.' Detective Anderson replies laughing.

The man sits in the interrogation room staring at the mirror. Captain Deloitte, Detectives Anderson and Jones stand on the other side of the one-way glass in silence, looking at the man as his fingerprints are run through the system. You can see this is not his first time in that chair. He looks at the mirror almost as if he sees right through it, waiting for someone to enter the room and start talking. Almost an hour goes by while the man is left by himself. Then, the print results came. Captain Deloitte briefly skims through them and gives the file to Detective Harris.

Harris walks into the room with a box of cigarettes and two glasses of water. 'Smoke?' He lights one for himself and holds the packet out to the man.

'Don't smoke. You the good cop or the bad cop?'

'My name is Brady Harris, you've met my colleagues Peter and Andy; they're the ones that brought you in. As you probably already know by now, this is a murder investigation and you are here because we think you supplied the cleaning kit to the killer.'

"Think"; you've got no proof of that.'

'Mr Brown, or can I call you Nathan?'

'Whatever.'

'Nathan we know that Ronald was your uncle that died some three years ago. We also know he left you the business. We also know you spent some time in prison for assault in your younger years and we also found out from the FBI that you are currently being investigated for fraud and tax evasion. So, help me help you, today. We're busy looking deeper into your background as we speak, and with every passing minute, your options are diminishing.'

'Man I had nothing to do with no murder. You damn cops think you can intimidate me? Well if you have something to lock me up on, do it, or else let me go.'

'It's not really that simple for you. Because we suspect that you have some degree of involvement, we can hold you for forty-eight hours. And we will. The way I see it is that either you helped out a buddy, or you did it yourself and tried to cover your tracks.'

'No man you got it all wrong, it wasn't me.'

'So you know who did it and won't talk. That's fine, I'm charging you as an accomplice and for obstruction of justice.'

Nathan leans forward. 'Get me my lawyer.'

As Detective Harris starts to reply the door opens and he is handed a piece of paper. He sits back down and reads through it, then looks Nathan in eyes and says. 'You're gonna need one. You see, this paper has two pieces of information on it. Number one is that multiple kits have disappeared from your stores over the past couple of years since the business was put in your name. Second is that every time those numbers did not balance, you deposited a cash amount of two thousand dollars into your own account. You're officially under arrest.'

Nathan goes pale; he never thought they would find those details so quick. He held up his hands. 'All right, all right, but I need a deal.'

'What did you have in mind?'

With fear in his eyes Nathan replies. 'Look man you don't know what you're dealing with. I'll talk. But then I want to go into protective custody.'

Detective Harris briefly looks over his shoulder at the one-way glass, waits a couple of seconds and hears someone knock twice on the glass from the other side; twice for yes, three times for no, that was the rule. 'Sounds like you've got something valuable to tell us. Deal.'

'Protective custody, you agree?'

'Yes you've got a deal. What do you have for us?'

'What about the other charges?'

'Dropped if you help us, but we have no say over what the FBI decides. In the event that they find you guilty, we can re-negotiate depending on where your information leads us.'

'Okay you got a deal. So, here's the story: shortly after my uncle's death I get a phone call, the man on the line called himself Jay. He asks me for some cleaning kits under the table for his business. At first I asked for his registration papers and he then said not to worry about it. I declined and put the phone down. But he called back immediately and said he won't take no for an answer and unless I want to end up like Ronald, I should hear him out. So I listened and he offered me two grand for every kit I give him. But get this, he told me if I go to the cops, I'll disappear. There's not a lot of people who use that expression man, and those who do can usually make it happen. I don't know much about everyone in town, but the Savage family came to mind only because whenever this guy called, someone would usually pick up the kit within ten or fifteen minutes; they're close. And these guys are dangerous and they're a very influential family. You need to keep me safe, those guys are fucking mad. They'll kill me if they know I spilled.'

Fuck, the Savage family, that's going to make this investigation a little complicated. Should've known those bastards are involved in something like this. Detective Harris taps on the table with one hand. 'We'll make the necessary arrangements Mr Murphy.'

Chapter 11

'I've never heard of them,' Peter shouts across the room.

Detective Harris pours some coffee into a cup. 'Pete, these guys are probably the strangest people in town. John and Sandra Savage moved here about nineteen years ago together with their four children. Oldest name's Thomas, then there was Rachel and Bradley who are twins, and the youngest, Celeste. This family is quite something. They have more money than you can imagine and for some reason they also have quite a bit of influence. Now in our town we're lucky not to have any gangs or mafia families. Instead, we got the Savages. Every now and again some of the people in town disappear for a couple of hours and go to the Savage farm. This might seem insignificant, but there's always complaints of suspicious behaviour when these parties are held, and because of the connections they have we can never get a warrant to enter the property, the request is always declined high up. Now we've tried many avenues to get one, just so we can investigate them, but not once have we been successful. And we've received some major claims from people about this family.' He sits down by the table, and slowly sips at his coffee. 'Assault, rape, sexual abuse and stalking.'

'Why don't we use those testimonies from the people who filed the complaints as evidence and motivation for a warrant?'

'We tried that. The only problem is that the complaints are never filed by the people themselves, always by a family member. The victims just say it's part of the path or part of the journey. It's some or other religion or something that they run there.' Detective Harris blows over his cup and the steam from the hot coffee rolls over the white edge.

'So that's it?'

'Just trust me on this one. You won't get far.'

Peter leans back in his chair, chews the back of his pen and then suddenly sits forward. 'Do we have a list of the members?'

'What are you thinking?'

'We might not get to the Savages, and I know that you said the people won't split on them. But if we can get a way in, we might be able to do this undercover, right?'

Detective Harris blows the steam over his cup again and takes a sip. 'Great idea, but if we can't even get a warrant to search the property, they definitely won't commission an undercover operation. That I can promise you.'

'Come on Brady you're acting like these fuckers are untouchable.'

'It's not an act Pete.'

'You know what I mean. Somewhere we have to get a break. Someone has to care about what these guys do.' Peter looks at Brady and sees no response. He can see in Detective Harris's face that he truly has tried, unsuccessfully. 'Let's see what we can do tomorrow, I'm heading home.' He grabs his coat, whips it over his shoulder and with a wave of the hand and a nod of the head, he walks off.

Detective Harris pulls a file over his desk. The file is thin, the spine is not cracked, and at first glance it appears to be empty. On the front is written 'Savage Family' but the file seems untouched. He opens the file and pulls out the contents; six marked photos and nothing else. John Savage. Sandra Savage. Thomas Savage. Rachel Savage. Bradley Savage. Celeste Savage. He takes the six photos and stares at each one before flipping over to the next.

John. No one knows what he does or where his family comes from; everyone here seems to think he's a gem of man with his clean-shaven head and face. I don't like him. I see straight through that devilish smile and ice-blue eyes. I must say he's good looking for his age, you wouldn't say he's fifty-five years old. I wonder if he could be the killer. That face, the suit, the leather gloves, well built, seems strong. Could be him. Although, maybe it was his wife, Sandra. Yummy mummy, if you ask me. What is it with this family and age? Whatever god they pray to must be good to them if they look like that. Look at her, one year younger than her husband but she barely looks older than her daughter. I like the whole forties look though. Dress, heels, corset. She looks like a vampire princess with the black hair and blood-red lips. She could be the one. I've spoken to her once and she's quite intimidating I must say; always has the right answers.

But then there's Thomas, the little shit. Oldest of the Savage litter, my money is on him. He's a twisted twenty-eight-year-old and he looks like a mad man, crazy, messy, dark hair, blue eyes, athletic build and tattoos. If anyone needs a psych., it's him. I remember a complaint where one of the neighbour's dogs kept getting out and ran into their yard, barking. Little Thom, with a smile on his face, chased the dog with an axe. He hung the corpse over the owner's gate. No witnesses would testify, they were too scared of him.

The twins Rachel and Bradley might also be good for it. Bradley shaves his head like his father, almost looks like him too, well a twenty-five-year-old version. Dresses like John, looks like John, acts like John, same devil smile as John. And you never see him without Rachel, so if it was him, then she had to be part of it. Rachel's quiet, but always keep an eye the quiet ones, my dad used to say. Straight dark hair and blue eyes; sweet-looking girl, but I get a bad vibe from her, the way she stares at you. She pulls out your soul and tears it into little pieces with her eyes and eats the pieces with her smile.

Celeste the twenty-two-year-old youngster, and in my opinion the only one that doesn't really fit in the family. Sweet and innocent and probably one of the friendliest people I have ever met, but you can't tell.

This whole family makes me sick. They're all masters of manipulation. If they were involved in this it will be difficult to catch them. Just by looking at their mansion and cars, everything is obsessively in order, nothing but Thomas's hair is ever out of place. If one of them did it, they would be too smart to have anything lead back to them. I mean even the statement from Mr Brown says that someone working for an influential family bought those kits, but there's nothing really connecting them to the crime. Fuck. We still have no leads, only hunches.

It's seven o'clock and everyone staggers into the office, all still half asleep. Peter falls into his chair, sits back and closes his eyes for a moment. He gets up and walks over to the kitchen area. The kitchen is directly in front of his and Brady's desks. A short distance, but it seems like a marathon for the first cup. He pulls two cups out of the pale-blue metal cupboard and places them carefully next to each other. Harris takes it black with one sugar, Peter, white and bitter. Yawning while he pours the coffee he spills on the counter, but doesn't bother to clean up, leaving a single black ring on the counter top. He walks back over to the two desks in their section of the open plan office and gives Detective Harris the black coffee. 'Morning.'

'Thanks Pete, and good morning to you too sunshine,' he says, laughing.

'Fuck off. It's too early. Where's Anderson?'

'Late, you know how he rolls. So, I sat here last night thinking about the Savage family; I think we should hold a meeting. Let's get everyone working the case in and chat about them, get a feel for everyone's opinions.'

Peter takes a sip. 'You know for now it's only us three right. You, me and Anderson. Cap said he doesn't want to waste resources on something with no viable leads. The moment we bring something concrete, he'll give us whatever we need.'

While talking, Harris assembles a portable whiteboard. 'Hmm okay. Makes sense, not ideal, but it makes sense. When did you speak to the captain?'

'Last night in the parking lot. He said to continue, just submit progress reports.'

'And about the Savages?'

'He didn't even blink. He probably suspected them from the start.' Peter says while holding his cup with both hands and slowly sipping at it.

'Fellas,' Anderson says in passing them towards the kitchen.

'Andy, listen, Cap said it's us three on the murder case for now until we have some good leads,' Brady shouts towards the kitchen.

'We got anything yet?' Anderson yells back.

'Savages!' Peter screams.

'The Savage family.' Anderson whispers to himself while making his way back to his colleagues. He sits down on the desk. 'Right, let's go through this.'

Brady posts John Savage's picture in the top left corner. 'John Savage, fifty-five-year-old male, the head of the house, rich, meticulous.' He posts Sandra Savage's picture in the top right corner. 'Sandra Savage, fifty-four-year-old female, wife of John. She's smart, she's sexy and she's intimidating; trust me this lady will have men falling all over her.'

He posts the two boys – Thomas and Bradley – beneath John's picture; Thomas in the middle and Bradley in the bottom left corner. 'The two boys in the family. Thomas, the oldest one, in the middle, is twenty-eight, and Bradley, at the bottom, is twenty-five. Thomas is a psychopath. Remember the story about the Turner family's dog that got killed with the axe? Thomas. Bradley, on the other hand, seems to imitate daddy, he dresses and acts like John.'

He posts the two girls' photos on the right below Sandra's picture. 'In the middle we have Rachel, Bradley's twin sister. She's quiet, but fuck she scares me, she's got murder in her eyes for sure. At the bottom we Celeste; the youngest of the family, twenty-two-year-old sweetheart, but I wouldn't trust her, she's still a Savage.'

Anderson looks at the board.

'Harris you've worked this family before, what's your take?'

'I don't know man. Honestly I wouldn't be surprised if it was any of them. At first I thought of Thomas, but I don't know, that dog case screams impulsiveness. But then again it was a dog, not a murder.'

Peter walks over to the whiteboard and taps John's face.

'He looks like the type of guy that could pull something like this off, but if they have that much money, why not just pay someone?'

'See now that's the problem.' Brady says while looking at the board from a different angle. 'All of them truly have the potential to have done this, but as you say Pete, they could've paid someone to do it.'

Peter laughs. 'In that case why not add three more suspects, Andy Anderson, Brady Harris and Peter Jones.' He says as a joke. 'You guys know we really got fucked here right? We got the short straw. We've got nothing. No leads. No real suspects.'

Brady looks ruefully at Andy and slaps Peter's shoulder. 'Everyone in this city is now a suspect.' And then silence fills the air.

Chapter 12

The wheels of the black Lincoln limousine hum on the tar. The headlights catch the edges of the trees as they drive through the forest on the private road towards the Savage farm. The road is dark. Smoke from the Cuban cigar mixes with the forest air and leaves a forest cabin and smoky fireplace smell in the car. The air coming through the half-open window and open sunroof is cool. Stars fill the night sky, but barely visible through the sunroof. The straight road starts to wind. Left, then right; left again, right again. The car slows down as it approaches the large metal gates, but before it comes to a complete stop, the gates open. The window rolls down completely. On both sides of the driveway there are large open gardens with small hedges separating the road from the evergreen grass. The driveway ends at a fountain, with a statue of a knight sitting on a rearing horse, sword in the air and water spraying over him from ten sides, all streams colliding in one single spot above the tip of the sword. The water creates a magical dome over the victorious scene. On both sides of the fountain are parking areas; about thirty cars can comfortably be parked there. But tonight, there are only seven. The limousine stops and the driver walks around and opens the door. A slender grey man gets out and walks around the fountain towards the great glass front doors. A man dressed in a black tuxedo with a bowtie and white gloves open the doors for him, nods and points the way through the reception area towards the back door on the other side of the enormous house. He walks past ancient paintings on each wall. On the left, a large lounge with a fireplace and no television or radio. In the middle of the room a red Persian rug sits neatly underneath a square wooden table. On the right is a large dining room, with an eighteen-seater table and from there, a door leads to the kitchen. The man walks further, stairs on both sides, both leading up to a single balcony with a single door opposite. Beyond the door are the bedrooms, but no one has ever been up there and the number of rooms is unknown. He walks underneath the balcony through an arch. On his left and right are two closed doors. He walks further down the passage and once again past two doors, one on each side. On his left is an art gallery and on his right an indoor pool. Then, finally, the back door. He exits the house and for a brief moment stands on the large patio facing the stairs down towards the back lawns. He looks around and admires the property. Then he walks down the steps and follows the path, passing wide lawns on each side leading towards a pond. On his far right he can see stables. On his far left there is a hall with burning lights and two more men in tuxedos, standing, one on each side of the door. The man follows the path towards the hall and as he approaches the door, John Savage comes out.

'Mayor Briarheart, so glad you could make it. Welcome.'

Smiling and happy to see John, Mayor Richard Briarheart pulls him closer and gives him a hug.

'Evening John, my apologies for changing my mind at the last moment. I initially had too much work to make it tonight, but fortunately Susan, my assistant, took care of it for me.'

'Not a problem Richard, as you can see we have fewer people here tonight than we did last month. There's a play at City Hall. An unmissable performance they say.'

The mayor puts his finger in the air pointing towards the sky.

'Ah yes of course, Romeo and Juliet. Now I remember, my wife is there tonight. Nevertheless, those who really need to be here will be here.'

'Go have a seat. I'll join you shortly.'

The mayor walks into the hall. The large U-shaped table takes up most of the room. In the middle there's a bed, a chair, a table and a water drum. He takes a quick look around to see where he wants to sit and sees that, apart from himself, only seven of the fifteen inner circle members made it tonight; this excludes the Savage family. Tonight's important: they will initiate a new member into the group. Initiation is always done on an evening like this by the inner circle members. They are the elite of the group. The elders, so to speak. To become an inner circle member is near impossible; you can't apply, you're chosen, and over the past six years' no one new has been chosen. The mayor looks around to see who made it; at the head of the U-shaped table sits the Savage family, everyone but John—he's still outside, probably fetching the new member. On the right, there are always the men: Rob Patterson, attorney. Jacob Taylor, pilot. William Smith, financial advisor. On the left, there are always the women: Kathy Larson, principal. Evelyn Brown, book store owner. Scarlett White, physical therapist. Emily Bride, pharmacist.

The mayor walks to his seat. 'Good evening ladies and gentlemen.'

Like a symphony orchestra in a single hum, the room replies, 'Good evening Mayor.'

John enters the room with a beautiful young girl trailing behind him. He claps his hands, creating a solid deep thump because of his leather gloves.

'Good evening everybody. I'm glad that you could all make it tonight. Unfortunately, because of the play at City Hall, we're missing a couple of our inner circle members. Nevertheless, we have more than fifty percent attendance and therefore the initiation of this young lady will continue. It's always better to have a full house. But considering the circumstances, this is not bad. As usual we start with a lovely dinner.' He turns to the young girl. 'My dear go have a seat next to the ladies over there.' He turns back to the inner circle members. 'Now, you are all familiar with initiation procedure, but for the sake of our guest, I will repeat it. We will first have dinner. The name of the new member is not important and she will be addressed only as "the initiate". For the first month, she will be called that, and only after a month of being part of us, will we let her have her name back. It is important to remember that even when out in public, she has no name for the first month. After dinner we will then initiate her into the group.' Once again John turns to the young lady. 'How it works my dear is that you get a choice of three initiation rituals: pain, fear, or humiliation. You will not be told beforehand what each of these rituals entails. Only after you have chosen a category will we explain the differences between the three. Also, when you have made your decision, you cannot change it. But, if you are uncomfortable with the procedure, you are more than welcome to leave. However, remember, a person only gets one opportunity to enter the group. If you leave here tonight without completing initiation, you can never return.' John turns back to the room and opens his arms. 'Now that the formalities have been dealt with, the evening can, begin!' The room cheers and applauds. 'There is champagne on the table; over by the bar we have the finest scotch, brandy, and cognac.' He turns to the ladies, clasps his hands together, squeezing them tight. 'I know you ladies prefer wine.' He winks at the young girl. 'All you have to do is ask, our ladies are respected, and therefore they are served. If you need anything, call over one of the butlers and they will bring whatever your heart desires.'

What am I doing here? I yearn for something but I'm not sure any more if this is it. I'll have to trust my friends, I mean they seem fine. They all went through this. Argh if only I could calm down! I can't even drink something without shaking. Chad said to choose the pain initiation. He'll be kicked out if they know he gave me advice about the choice. I don't like pain though, getting hurt, tortured. I wonder if they're going to torture me. They all seem so happy and friendly though. The only thing here that really scares me is the bed. I don't like it. I know what people make you do during rituals on beds. If they make me sleep with someone I'm out. I'm still a virgin, and I'm not planning on giving that to anyone tonight. She puts her pale, shaking hand in the air.

'May I please have another glass of wine?' One of the butlers walks over and fills her glass with the same wine as the previous time, Merlot.

At least the dinner was nice. It was probably the best seafood dish I've ever had, I definitely need to introduce myself to the house chef. Can't they just get on with it? The suspense is ruining me, I'm all sweaty. No! Please don't tell me the lady next to me can smell me! Shit, is that why no one speaks to me? Oh my word, this isn't happening, I'm going to cry! Slowly and inconspicuously the girl turns her head left, moving her arm outward to smell if she smells like sweat. Nothing, nothing but a sweet, clean smell. She turns to the right, moves her arm and takes a breath. Nothing, clean, no stench. *Thank goodness. I can see the pits of my shirt are a little wet though, never mind, I'll hide it. I'm glad I decided to wear this. They said to wear something formal, but I don't like dresses. Suit pants, boots and neat white button shirt. I would've felt so uncomfortable in a dress right now.*

John Savage stands up and clinks his fork against his glass. 'Ladies and gentlemen I hope that you all had a wonderful meal. Although the festivities are enjoyable, we are here with a purpose tonight.' He points his open hand, palm facing the roof, at the young girl. 'My dear would you please walk around the table and stand in the middle of the gap here.' While she makes her way to the centre of the room, John continues. 'We are here tonight to welcome a new member into the group.' With no one saying a word, they all look at the girl and clap. 'Sweetheart, we are all very pleased to have you here and we are extremely excited to see what the future holds for you here with us. Now, tell us, what is your choice of initiation? Pain, fear, or humiliation?'

She stands holding her hands in front of her, trying her best not to shake, trying her best not to stutter. After a moment's pause she softly replies, 'Pain.'

'Sorry my dear I didn't quite catch that, can I confirm, did you say pain?'

'Yes sir.' Louder this time. 'Pain. I choose pain for my initiation.' Said with the utmost confidence.

'Hmm.' John pushes his chair back and makes his way round to her. 'Pain. Interesting choice. May I ask why you chose pain out of those three options?'

Oh no! Please don't tell me he knows. 'To be honest, fear is worse than pain to me. And I don't like to be humiliated, none of the three choices seem ideal, but pain seems like the more acceptable one to me.'

John puts his arm around her shoulder. 'Ladies and gentlemen, the girl chooses pain! Now I'm sure you're wondering what these three options require?' He lets her go, walks over to the table he sat at, turns around, faces her, leaning against it. 'Let's start with fear. If you had chosen fear, then you would have had to choose two of the inner circle members, one man and one woman. Each of them would then be allowed to torture you in a manner of their choosing, without inflicting pain, to the verge of death. They would make you feel like you were going to die. You would go through that fear twice, once with each of the members you chose. If you chose humiliation, you would have had to perform sexual acts. Once again you would have to choose two of our inner circle members, one man and one woman. You would then have to perform oral sex on the same-sex member, and have intercourse with the opposite-sex member on the bed placed here in front of the other inner circle members.' A feeling of relief overcomes the girl. 'But you chose pain, so as you can probably see the trend, you have to choose one man, and one woman from the members sitting here. We will start with the lady and end with the man. They will each be given a whip. They will then lash you four times each, across your exposed behind. You will stand over by the table with your back facing the members. You will have to pull up your shirt, to shoulder height and pull down your pants, as well as your lingerie, down to your knees. You will then lean on the table; I will tie your hands to the table and your ankles to the table paws. I assure you that apart from the restraints, no one will touch you, no one will sexually abuse or rape you. You will only be lashed. If at any point you feel you've had enough, scream stop, and it will be over, but remember our discussion earlier, if you stop the initiation ritual before it is finished, you will not be accepted into the group. Do you have any questions?'

Shocked she looks at John. 'You said to choose between the three. And I chose pain. What do most of the people choose?'

'Most of them choose humiliation.'

'That's rape is it not?'

John smiles. 'No, my dear, it's only rape if consent is not given, and agreeing to the ritual is giving consent.'

'Can I make a request?'

'It depends.'

'I chose pain, and only pain. If I have to pull my shirt up to my shoulders and my pants and panties to my knees, that would expose all of my private bits. That's still humiliation.'

He looks at the inner circle members, his eyes alighting on each of them. 'You're right. What is your suggestion?'

'I don't mind pulling my shirt up to my shoulders as long as my bra can stay on. Exposing my bum I don't like, because if I bend over, everyone will see more than just my cheeks. So I will pull my pants down to below my buns, but my panties must stay, I have a thong on, so the other bits will still be hidden. I don't want to be tied down; I promise I will stand for the lashes. And lastly, I don't want anyone standing in front of me while my shirt is up, even if my bra is still on.'

He thinks for a second and turns towards the female members. 'I can see where she comes from, so I would like you ladies to tell me if her request is unreasonable.'

Scarlett stands up. 'No John, it's not. It's within her right not to be exposed, if she agrees not to move while being lashed, I see no problem in it. She still has self-respect and dignity. Let the girl cover her private areas.'

'Gentlemen, because she is a girl, you have no say in the matter, Ladies is there anyone that objects to what Scarlett has just said?' He looks at the four women. But no one makes a sound. 'Good. My dear your request has been granted, you will only expose your bottom and back and you will be allowed to be free standing.' John walks around to his seat and sits down. 'Now, who do you choose?'

'Miss White and Mr Taylor.'

'Scarlett, Jacob. Do you accept her choice?' Both nod yes. 'Good. Scarlett when you are ready, the whip is on the table.'

The girl stands by the table, and with tears in her eyes and shaking hands, she pulls her shirt up above her breasts. She looks down and her eyes fill with tears, blurring her vision until the tears drop. She struggles with the button of her pants. She battles to undo it as her hands are shaking too much. Finally, she gets it right. She pulls the zipper halfway down. With her thumbs in at the sides, holding her shirt with her teeth, she wiggles her bum and pulls her pants down to just below the cheeks. A white lace thong is revealed, sitting neatly between the buns. Standing upright she holds her shirt with her hands almost as if she's praying. The first lash cracks like thunder on her left buttock cheek. But she makes no sound, not even a squeak. A tear rolls down as the second lash tears the skin as well as her thong. Again on the left cheek. The third lash creeps up her spine on her lower back, she can feel the blood run down, giving her goose bumps. Scarlett pulls back the whip for the final lash, it lands mostly on the right cheek, but the edge of the whip sneaks in between the two. This being the most painful of the four, she can no longer keep quiet, she cries out loud, tears streaming and shoulders shaking. Jacob walks over. She knows that it's all in the technique and it doesn't matter whether it's a man or woman lashing her if done right. Jacob looks at her for a second and he is reminded of years ago when he was lashed. He looks at her back, blood running down her spine. The first lash only left a purple stripe, but looking at her cheeks, he knows that those hurt the most. He pulls the whip back. One, two, three, four. The four lashes all fall within the space of three seconds. Not a single one on her back, all four over her butt cheeks. All four of them bleeding. Crying and in severe pain, she drops her shirt and painfully pulls her pants back up over her swollen behind. The blood from her back stains her white shirt, and the blood on her bum seeps through her pants, leaving them wet.

Chapter 13

I'm so tired. Why can't I just get a break in the case? I've been working on this thing for months now and nothing. Without any evidence on the body, no one will issue warrants for anything. I guess that makes sense from their perspective. We've tried everything, but no one will talk; no one will help. It's as if this killer just never existed. Peter sits in the back of the cab, with his body hunched over his legs. His knees graze against the seat in front of him as they go over bumps. Leaning back, he almost sits on his kidneys. He stares out the window while his head rests heavily on his left hand, and with his right he plays with his pen. *I don't know how to avenge Freddy if I don't catch this guy. I feel like a failure. I should've stuck to routine; I should've just kept going to Dr Rayne. It just felt like I was too clouded, it felt like there was nothing more to gain from him. Asking me stupid questions. The whole damn point about returning to him was for him to help me catch the killer; today I'll confront him. Today.* The cab comes to a halt and Peter makes his way through the lobby, into the elevator and up to the fifteenth floor. The doors open and Peter walks through the painted entrance, but he's been there so many times that he no longer notices the brutal paintings. He pushes hard against the black doors and they open with a crack. He finds Dr Rayne in the middle of the room, waiting. But as he enters the room his attention is drawn to his left when the doors that are always closed, slowly creep closed, and lock. Dr Rayne is in front of him, one hand in the pocket, silent.

'Doctor. We need to talk.' Judging by the way Dr Rayne stands, it seems almost as if he's been waiting for him. 'You were expecting me?'

'The lobby called. Did I forget to schedule an appointment for you Detective?'

'No Doctor, I came of my own accord.'

'I usually work on an appointment basis only. But I guess you're here now, so we can continue if you want.'

'Is there someone else here Doctor?' Peter says as he turns towards the closed door.

'Yes.'

'Do you want me to wait outside until you're done with your other patient?'

'No. But let's sit over by the meditation area, we can meditate for a couple of minutes and then begin.'

'Doctor I'm not here for a session.'

'Why are you here then Detective?'

'It's about the case. You said in one of my earliest sessions that you would help me catch this guy. That's why I'm here. I would like help with the case.'

'Come Detective, let's first meditate and then we can talk about it.'

Peter pulls his backpack over his shoulder. 'Doctor I don't have time for this, I brought you a copy of the case file so you can look at it and help me with this. We've waited so long already and wasted enough time. My captain was even instructed to pull back all resources from this case. I'm the only one left working on this and all that I have left is you. So please, help me. You promised.'

Dr Rayne waves away the file. 'Detective I think you might have misunderstood when I said I would help you. Maybe I should've put it differently. I don't want to look at the case file. What I meant when I said that is that I would prepare you to *think* like him, which would give you a much clearer perspective on your case. I'm not a detective; I probably won't be able to make the connections that you can.'

'We have a serial killer here in New Orleans and you have absolutely no interest in looking at the file to help me catch him?'

'Technically, Detective, he's not a serial killer, he only committed one murder. He only killed your cousin. Fred.'

Frustrated with himself and Dr Rayne, Peter snaps, 'I'm not stupid Doctor, I understand that. But if you would just look at the damn file you will understand why I say he is.'

'Peter.' For the first time Peter hears Dr Rayne refer to him by his first name. 'I know you're angry, but I'm not the one that you're going to blame.'

He realises what he did and calms down. 'I'm sorry. Doctor please, all I'm asking for is your help. If you don't have the time, can Diana look at it?'

'I think of the two of us, Diana's probably the busier one right now. Let's sit. Let's meditate. Then we can talk about the case.' Peter puts his bag down, both of them take their shoes off and sit down. 'Now close your eyes, back straight and rest your palms on your knees. Feel the tension in your body. Feel how heavy your body feels on the floor. Bring your attention to your breath.' Peter's body feels heavy, and his mind cluttered. 'Think about your breathing. Mentally note as you breathe in that you're breathing in. And as you breathe out mentally note that you're breathing out. Breathing in. Breathing out.' Silence fills the air like a cloud and softly the silence is broken by the trickling of the fountain like soft rain. Peter starts to drift. 'Now feel how the tension falls away from your head and it becomes light. Feel how the muscles relax, your cheeks, your jaw, your tongue, the muscles in your face and scalp, all relaxed. Feel how the tension moves down into your neck, feel how you breathe all of that tension out.' Peter starts to inhale through his nose and exhale through his mouth. 'Feel how the tension on your shoulders moves down your arms and into your hands. Relax and calm. Feel the tension move from your hands and into your legs where they touch. Your arms and shoulders are light, like they're floating.' Peter's body starts to tingle. 'Now the abdomen, feel whatever discomfort there is. Then when you're ready to do so, let it dissolve.' Peter notices the full feeling in his abdomen. But as he relaxes his abdominal muscles, it disappears. 'Feel your pelvis and the tension in your legs, feel how all of this tension moves down and into the floor. You're light. You're weightless. Feel how the air starts to fill the space between the floor and your body, feel how light you are, as light as air. Then bring your attention back to your breathing. Feel how the air enters your body, and exits your body. Feel the air fill your lungs making you lighter. Feel the air exit your lungs.' Time becomes irrelevant. All that matters is the here and now and Peter indulges in the weightless feeling. For what feels like hours, they sit in silence, hearing only the trickle of the fountain. 'And as the practice finishes, wiggle your fingers and toes and bring your attention back to the room. Then, when you're ready to do so, slowly open your eyes.'

Refreshed and relaxed, Peter glows. 'Thank you Doctor. I actually needed that.'

'Before we tackle the case, I have only one question: why did you stop coming here?'

'I don't know Doc. It felt like there was nothing more to gain here for me. We started talking quite a bit about me, and never about the case. I think also now that I thought about it, I also felt somewhat distracted by Diana.'

Peter's answer surprises Dr Rayne. 'Diana?'

'Come now Doctor you can't truly say to me that you're not distracted by her.'

'Oh. I see. You're physically attracted to her. Lust.'

'Aren't you?'

'Maybe there was a time where I felt lust for her. But I see her in different way than how you see her.'

'You see her more like a daughter?'

Dr Rayne laughs. 'Detective I'm thirty-three years old and Diana is twenty-five. There's hardly the appropriate age gap to produce those feelings. No I don't see her as a daughter. What I see in Diana is difficult to explain. It's her mind that attracts me. I like the way she thinks, and I see some of that in you too. Anyway. Why don't you ask Diana to dinner?'

'Wouldn't that be unprofessional?'

Confused Dr Rayne answers. 'No. She's my intern, which does not make Diana any part of yours and my relationship. I'm your psychiatrist, not Diana. If you want to take her out, you're more than welcome.'

'I might just do that.' Peter happily replies. 'The case.'

'Yes of course. I don't really care much for reading the file. Why don't you rather tell me where you're stuck and we'll see if I can provide some insight.'

'Do you remember the body?'

'Yes I do. He had a fatal laceration below the larynx, cutting the carotid arteries as well as the trachea. He also had defensive wounds over his arms. Two wounds to the head. He had no blood and then he also had the triangle cut into the wrist.'

'You have a good memory Doctor.'

'I'm blessed.'

'The big thing is that there was no evidence. None whatsoever. We then caught a man, Nathan, who sold crime scene cleaning kits to the killer and he said that it was never the same person picking it up and that this man said he worked for an influential family. He also said that if Nathan would not help him and if he went to the police, he would end up dead.'

'So where's Nathan now?'

'Protective custody.'

Dr Rayne rubs his head while thinking. 'Did you get everything you could from Nathan?'

'We think so.'

'Do you know where they took him for protective custody?'

'No that's above my paygrade.'

'I see. Okay so Nathan was a dead end too.'

Peter starts flipping through the file. 'Not entirely, he also said that when this man called, someone would pick these kits up within fifteen minutes of the call. Which means that unless it was meticulous planning whoever bought these kits, has to be in town.'

'Or know someone in town.'

Peter nods his head. 'Or that yes. We then thought that it must be one of the Savage family members or someone in their cult, but no one will say if they're part of the cult or not.'

Dr Rayne frowns at Peter and sits forward. 'That's a bold claim to make. Apart from your interpretation of that statement, do you have any other information or evidence leading you to think it might be one of the Savage family members?'

'No but who else here in town fits that description Doctor?'

'Lots of people, Detective. Although I can see why they sprung to mind first, they're not the only influential family in town. Wouldn't you agree?'

'I guess so, but who else seems like they might do something like this? It's just them and that fucking cult. Based on a few complaints, we know a couple of names that we suspect might be in the cult, but they don't talk, they just deny being involved with that family.'

'Wouldn't you?'

Confused, Peter asks. 'Wouldn't I what?'

'Deny being part of the Savage family's group.'

'Cult.' Peter corrects Dr Rayne.

'Group.' Dr Rayne corrects Peter. 'They're not religious. Therefore they're not a cult.'

'How do you know they're not religious?'

Dr Rayne smiles. 'Everyone knows that they're not religious, Detective.'

Suspiciously Peter stares at Dr Rayne. 'Okay then, group. So who else Doc?'

'Detective any family with lots of money has influence in this town.'

'Do you have influence Doctor?'

'Am I a suspect, Detective?' Dr Rayne confidently replies.

'Well I don't know what or who you hide behind those doors.' Peter closes the file, his hands start to shake lightly as he imagines Dr Rayne as the killer. 'For all I know you could be killing people in there.'

Laughing Dr Rayne replies. 'My dear Peter, when the time is right I will show you what I hide behind those doors; today, however, is not that day.' But Peter remains silent. 'Detective I know you're wondering if I killed your cousin, and I also know that even if I deny that fact, I have as little evidence to prove my innocence as you have to prove my guilt. If you still want my help, we can continue. If not, you can leave. I won't take offense.'

Peter thinks for a moment. 'We can continue, but Doctor if it was you, I promise you I will find the evidence against you.'

'I would expect nothing less.'

'Could it be someone in the group?'

'Of course. But then again the killer can be anyone. If you're thinking of a cult connection, we've established that it can't be sacrificial, because they're not religious. So unless you can think of a possible motive, I can't see why the Savage family or their group members should receive special investigation above me, or your neighbour, your friends, colleagues, or even you. Remember you have no motive, no evidence, and therefore you really have no suspects.'

'Thanks for pointing that out.' Peter sarcastically replies.

'There's no need for sarcasm Detective, you asked me for help remember.'

'So what are you saying Doctor? Should I just give up? Should I just let Freddy's killer run free? Because all you did today was help me understand that according to the evidence I'm looking for someone with no motive to kill him and possibly someone that has killed for the first time despite the practiced, almost surgical, precision.'

'A psychopath.'

'What?'

'You're looking for a psychopath, Detective. I understand why you think that he's a serial killer, I understand it as much as anyone. But in court nothing you have will mean anything. You need to start looking for someone with signs of psychopathy.'

'Okay?'

Dr Rayne looks at Peter and in a disappointed tone says. 'But that's your problem. Psychopaths are the most difficult to catch in your field. They're meticulous. They're always two steps ahead. For now I would say you'll have to wait. Maybe you're lucky and he does something similar. Actually that's what you can do for now, look for cases with similar findings.'

'We already did that.'

'See why I said I might not be of much assistance for the investigation itself?'

Peter puts the file back in his bag. 'You proposed to help. So tell me Doc, how can you help?'

Dr Rayne stares deep into Peter's eyes. 'I can change your mind to think like him.'

Chapter 14

1 December 1999. The day before Peter's birthday and Lily's in town after completing her first year at varsity. She promised Peter that they would go out for his birthday and celebrate and chose the day before his birthday just so that she wouldn't be late, because she knows that he will be busy tomorrow. Lily's in her room and getting ready for their dinner date, however she learned a lesson from her previous experience with Peter. She's not expecting much. In fact she only sees this dinner as spending some time with an old friend. There's a small restaurant in the French Quarter near the Saenger Theatre and the food there is divine. It's Lily's favourite place and whenever she has the opportunity to go somewhere, Nature's Piece of Heaven is the place. Peter is in for a treat. Lily planned the whole night already and she can't wait to meet him.

Having lived in this beautiful town, Lily believes that so many local people forget to appreciate it fully. Everything is seen on such a regular basis that they forget to see the beauty. Tonight, Lily will show Peter the beauty again; he needs it. Peter's been so despondent lately, he hardly ever smiles. She arranged with him to meet her at the door of the Saenger Theatre at seven. The sun set just after five and it is now five to seven. Lily stands just outside the theatre, the sky clear and filled with stars. A crisp breeze fills the air; a smell so clean. In the background Lily can hear a muffled performance from inside the theatre, but it is smothered by the sounds coming from around the corner: jazz. A local musician plays his saxophone and enchants Lily. She closes her eyes and envisions every note. She can feel the emotion that he blows into his instrument, almost as if she connects with him. It's beautiful. Caught in this moment she doesn't realise Peter is approaching her. He looks at Lily with her skinny jeans and her plum coat, neatly topped off with a black beanie, and as always Peter can't help but admire her pure beauty.

'Hello there, stranger,' he says, while sneaking up behind her.

'Oh my gosh! You gave me such a fright!' And she playfully punches him on his shoulder. 'You almost gave me a heart attack.' She pulls him closer and gives him a firm and extended hug. 'I know it's early, but happy birthday! I hope tomorrow will be the best birthday you ever had.'

'Thanks Lily, but I think tonight will be my best birthday.' He winks at her. 'So now we're here but I can hear there's already something going on inside the theatre, which leads me to believe we're not watching a play, right?'

'Look at you going all detective on me here.' Lily giggles. 'But no we're not. I have a different plan in mind for tonight.'

'Oh yes?'

'I realised lately that you're not yourself, so I thought that tonight, I will show you this city like you've never seen it before.'

'Sounds promising.'

'I love the French Quarter.' Lily says, her eyes roaming over the buildings. 'It's like when they built this place, every person that had a part in it put a bit of themselves in it. Don't you think?'

'Hmm yes it's amazing. I never thought of it that way, but I like the look of the buildings. The city seems to have its own personality.'

He excites Lily. 'I know right. Anyway, have you ever been to Nature's Piece of Heaven?'

'No I don't think so.'

Lily laughs. 'If you have to think then it's a no, Pete. Trust me, you would've remembered if you went there. I think it serves the best food available on the planet.'

Peter raises his eyebrows, puts out his arm for Lily to hook in and points the way. 'On the planet you say. Well then, my Lady, I think we should go have a look. Or would you rather spend the night out here?'

Lily rolls her eyes back. 'My lady eh? Well then, Sir, our table awaits.' At the table Lily makes Peter laugh for the first time in months. Her charm overwhelms him and almost cuts the negativity from his mind. She's a free spirit and can only see the best in every situation, something Peter has lost. She orders her meal; stuffed and braised veal heart.

Peter frowns and orders a medium rare sirloin steak. 'You're going to eat heart?'

Lily licks her lips with closed eyes. 'I know it sounds odd, but you must have a bite. There is nothing that tastes like it. It's stuffed with bits of bacon, onion, mushrooms and peppadews. Just the thought of it makes me drool.'

'You're going to eat a baby cow's heart. How on earth does that make you drool?' Peter asks, disgustedly.

Lily laughs. 'Well if you're going to say it like that, obviously you might think of it as strange. But it's the sweetest, most tender meat you can eat. You'll see.'

'I'm not sure I want to taste.'

'The tough detective Peter Jones that hunts murderers scared to try a bit of veal?'

Peter rubs his chin, purses his lips and squints his eyes, looking like a quizzical monkey. 'Hmm okay I'm convinced. By the way, how's university going?'

'Amazing! I have a great roommate and the course is great fun. I'm glad I decided to go. But I mean it's only the first year now so there's still quite a bit to go. The more important question is how you got detective status so quickly?'

Peter shrugs with pride. 'I met the criteria to apply and I showed great potential, always working harder than I should. Captain felt that it would be a new change. The first couple of weeks I was considered detective, but I didn't really feel like part of the team you know. I'm the youngest ever detective of the unit, so it comes with a bit of judgement. And on top of it all, some of the department felt that it was a charity decision because of the whole Freddy story.'

'That's terrible.' Lily says, shaking her head.

'They're quiet now. Trust me. Those guys quickly realised I mean business. Sometimes they still tease me, but it's all a joke now.'

'I'm happy that you're doing well. Youngest ever detective of the New Orleans Criminal Investigation Division. That's quite an accomplishment Pete! I'm proud of you.'

With a shy smile and a nod of the head, Peter replies. 'Thanks Lil. I try.' The waiter comes with their meals, beautifully prepared. 'Okay so here goes, give me a bite of your baby cow's heart.' Lily laughs, cuts off the apex of the heart and slices a thin slice and adds some of the filling to her fork. Peter puts it in his mouth and slowly chews. 'Hm. Mmm.' He swallows the bite. 'Not bad actually. In fact I like the taste, it's just getting over the fact that it's a heart.'

'I told you it's good,' Lily says with excitement.

After dinner Lily suggests to Peter that they visit Jackson square, she says that it is an important part of their city's history and that Peter has been neglecting it. Peter wants to take a cab; however, Lily feels that that is where the problem lies. Everyone always drives everywhere and in doing so misses their own city's beauty. Tourists never drive; they always walk. Lily won this argument with little effort. As they walk down the streets of New Orleans they are surrounded by the beauty of the old buildings in the French Quarter. Smells of food fuse with the crisp smell of the breeze. The clear sky paints a striking picture above them with different shades of black and blue, the white stars, and the silver moon. As soon as the sound of one musician fades out, the sound of another fades in. While walking they hear the sound of people, laughter, trumpets, violins, saxophones, guitars, and drums. Never a moment of silence. For a moment Peter sees the great city through the eyes of Lily, and it leaves a feeling of euphoria. The city serenades both of them by painting beautiful pictures, and singing songs of love and happiness.

But before they could make it Jackson Square, they come across an art gallery called Pure Imagination. They enter and find a clean and well laid out gallery. In the middle of the room on the floor is a square plastic sheet, and on the sheet they see a man painting. The gallery is silent and all that can be heard is the stroke from the man's brush. The walls are filled with paintings, methodically arranged. The paintings are all filled with colour and range from scenes from nature, to portraits of naked women, to abstract art. All of them are signed by Michael Lafayette, the owner of the gallery. Except one. This painting is the centre piece of the wall directly opposite the entrance. The wall is a floating wall; you can walk around it. Hidden behind the wall on the left is an office door, and on the right a bathroom door. The rest of this wall is home to all of Michael's abstract art. The paintings are arranged in a perfect square, all the same size. In the middle of the square is the painting that is not signed by him. The painting is square and large, it must have only just fit through the door. It features only four colours; white, black, yellow, and red.

Lily and Peter walk around the room admiring every painting. After circling around the room and standing by the door again Peter turns to the painting on the back wall again: it shows a dark, shadowy figure looking at the sun which is in front of him, with blood dripping from his hands. Peter can't help but see the similarities between the paintings at Dr Alexander Rayne's office and this painting.

'Excuse me sir.' Peter approaches the artist. 'I don't mean to bother you.'

A small and lean man with shoulder-length dark hair appears from behind the canvas. Peter and Lily are greeted with a pearly smile and green eyes, in one hand a brush, and in the other a palette. 'Good evening guys,' he replies cheerfully. 'How can I help?'

Peter sighs. 'This is a silly question I know, but did you do all of this?' Peter gestures around the room.

'I did indeed. Sorry I'm quite rude; my name is Michael. Michael Lafayette and this is my studio.'

'Pleased to meet you Michael, I'm Peter and this is Lily.' Lily waves with a smile. 'The painting on the back wall there, was that also you?'

Michael turns and looks at the painting, gazes at it for a moment and turns back to Peter and Lily. 'I would like to claim responsibility for that, but unfortunately not. That painting was a gift and is also the only one here on display by another artist. Why do you ask, Peter?'

Peter steps closer. 'I'm just wondering. I thought I could get some better insight.'

'What do you mean by that?'

'A friend of mine is a psychiatrist. His name is Alexander Rayne and in his office he has some very similar art to what you have there. I didn't fully understand it at first and I have a better idea about the scenes now, but I thought that if it was you I could ask why it was painted or where the inspiration came from.'

Michael smiles. 'Sorry, wish I could help.'

'No problem, I saw the red on your palette now, it's the same colour and I thought that maybe I just missed your signature somewhere on it.'

Michael looks at his palette with surprise. 'You are very observant, Peter.' He is impressed.

Peter laughs and Lily giggles. 'I'm a detective.'

'Aha now it makes sense. No I sign my work. You are right about the colour though. The painting was a gift from an anonymous person. A truck just stopped here one day and said it had a delivery for me. I at first thought it was supplies and told them I ordered nothing. The driver then just said no it wasn't an order placed by me, this is just the delivery point. So I got the painting and a letter and an unmarked jar with sticky almost dried dark red paint in it.'

'Okay I see, that makes sense. What did the letter say?'

'Now there's something that might mean something to you. It gave me the instruction to just add a bit of thinners to the jar, which would reverse the coagulation and make the paint usable, and then the artist just said that he painted the painting with colours of snow, sunlight, darkness, and blood. He's very artistic.'

'He didn't give a name?'

'No sorry, the back of the letter was simply signed with the letter J.' Suddenly Lily's heart starts to pound, a feeling of nausea fills her stomach and she becomes light-headed. It's the same person who wrote to her when she was in Europe.

Chapter 15

'Good morning.'

'Lily, if I'm not mistaken?'

'You remember me?'

'Of course. You and your boyfriend Peter were here last night. Peter seemed to take quite an interest in the picture on the back wall there.'

Surprised that Michael remembers them, Lily replies, 'Oh no, he's not my boyfriend. You're good with names.'

Michael laughs. 'On the contrary. No, I just remember you because not many people introduce themselves to me. People tend to walk through and pass a compliment or two, and then leave.' Lily mills around the room for a while, and then makes her way in silence over to the picture of the shadow with blood dripping from his hands. Without Lily noticing, Michael has put down his painting equipment and is now standing behind her, he whispers. 'Beautiful isn't it?'

'Intriguing.' She replies without blinking. 'What do you think he tried to imply here?'

'Oh that's almost impossible to say. I can tell you from my perspective that some of the paintings I paint have purely a figurative meaning, all symbolism. But then there are some that portray reality as I see it. Without knowing the person, it's just a picture. A very artistic and graphic picture, but the meaning of it eludes me.'

Lily walks closer to the wall, never looking at Michael. 'But if you had to guess?'

Michael folds his paint-stained arms and joins Lily in front of the wall. 'There are two perspectives we can look from. If we had to look at this from a purely symbolic perspective, I think that the artist here may feel that he has made a terrible decision. The decision would somehow have harmed another, not necessarily physically, but in some or other way, hence the blood on his hands. I also think he would feel as if no one knew about this deed or that no one sees him for who and what he truly is. Maybe he even feels as if no one wants to see him, that's why he would paint himself as a shadow. I think that he would definitely seek help or guidance. People tend to look towards the heavens only when they need help. The sun is the source of all life on our planet, maybe he looks towards it to get his life strength back. This whole painting from a symbolic point of view in my opinion seems to be a cry for help. It seems like he has a lot of regret.'

'And the other perspective?'

'He killed someone. He killed someone and he's not afraid to proclaim it to the world. The blood is literal and the shadow probably because he feels darkness inside of him. The sun would just be him boasting, he could kill in the light of day, and he feels powerful and confident enough that no one could touch him.' Michael takes a deep breath and gives a long sigh as he exhales. 'He probably walks among us.'

Lily and Michael stands in front of the painting, each of them lost in their own thoughts, then Lily asks. 'Which one do you think is most likely the inspiration?'

'I'd rather not think about it. The one option is quite grim, and the other quite evil.' For the first time Michael turns to Lily. 'But this is the essence of art. It makes us dwell in our own minds. Which one do you think it is?' He walks back to his canvas. 'For all we know, it might just be a picture inspired by another picture.'

'I doubt that.' Lily replies. She walks over to Michael. Standing beside him she says. 'I received a letter once.' Silence fills the air. 'From someone calling himself "J".'

'And what did he say?'

'Nothing really important, but he gave me the letter while I was in Europe.'

Shocked Michael replies, 'You met him?'

'Oh no, he slid the letter under my hotel room door. It scares me to think that he may have followed me there.'

'He could've given you the letter here, couldn't he?'

Lily frowns. 'What do you mean?'

'I mean I think it may have been coincidence that you were both there. Otherwise he would've given you the letter here. It's quite something to travel to Europe only to deliver a letter don't you think?'

Lily starts to feel anxious. 'What if he's not from here, but followed me back?'

'When did you get the letter?'

'End of last year. When did you get the painting?'

'I think around three years ago. So he's most likely from here. Maybe he's someone from around here who just likes doing things for other people?' He scratches his head with the back of the brush. 'Did he say something negative in the letter?'

'No, he said it was a letter of admiration.'

'Has he made contact again?'

'No. Well not that I know of.'

Michael strokes his brush against the canvas. 'It's weird though.'

'What if he's a killer?'

Michael stops, and turns his head towards Lily, looking at her with his green eyes. 'Should we report this?' He bites his lip nervously. 'I'm quite worried now.'

'No let's first see if he contacts either of us again. If he does, then I'll tell Pete and he can find he guy.'

'Of course! Peter's a detective, I almost forgot.'

Lily licks her lips, her breathing changes. She wants to say something, but doesn't know how. Michael turns and gives her his full attention and she looks him straight into the eye. 'Michael, would you like to go for coffee some time?'

Flattered he replies. 'That sounds wonderful. Whenever you feel like it, just come to the studio and we'll do it.' He winks at her. 'Maybe I can even paint a portrait of you.'

Chapter 16

It's nearly six, and in an hour's time Peter's birthday dinner will start. Last night he had a great time with Lily and although he would love for her to be there, he can't be distracted, not tonight. Apart from the usual people, Peter also invited his colleagues, Alexander and Diana, and the Savage family. There's a bigger play here, a deeper plan. Tonight his birthday is merely an excuse to get certain people to talk to him, an excuse to let the key players come to him. The moment he invited the Savage family, they offered to host the party, because he's such an upstanding citizen they said, someone New Orleans can be proud of. He has previously apologised to the family, admitting to his mistake in making them some of his prime suspects. He's convinced that they don't suspect his strategy. They were smart though, the party is held at the historic Gallier Hall across from Lafayette Square, so he still can't access their house. John replied with a letter explaining that this birthday dinner will be a tribute to an excellent detective and added that excellence needs to be celebrated. He also said in the letter that he will invite some of the most important people in town to celebrate Peter's birthday with him. Peter has no doubt that John Savage has ulterior motives. Peter stares out of his kitchen window, waiting for the car to pick him up. *I wonder who will be there tonight, it's almost seven now, the car should be here soon. The sky is beautiful. The moon hidden by thick clouds, so dark. I like how the lightning in the background lights the clouds up every so often, outlining them, showing the true face of the storm that's bound to pass through our town.* Thunder rattles Peter's windows, and the first couple of drops can be heard on the roof. What a sound; so powerful, so full of authority. Peter can't help but think how powerful God is in creating such an occurrence. The wind howls as it quickly starts to encompass the house, surrounding every corner, every window, and every door. In the matter of a heartbeat, one drop becomes two, two becomes ten, and then suddenly, a mass of water plunges down onto the earth below as the clouds open up. Rain hits the ground so hard that it creates almost a foot of mist just above the ground. In the distance Peter can see light breaking through the thick rain, right on time. A slender shadow briefly obscures the light as it runs hastily to the front door, the bell rings and Peter is faced by the driver under a large clear umbrella. They run to the car. And with feet wet and the cuffs of his pants soaked Peter leaps in as the slender man opens the car door. Not even fifteen minutes pass when the car stops at the Gallier Hall. Rain is softer here, but lightning continues to dance behind the clouds, letting its thunder thump. As Peter enters the hall he is welcomed by clapping and cheering and a jazz band in the background. There seems to be almost a hundred and fifty people there. Most of the faces unknown.

'And a warm welcome, Ladies and Gentlemen, to our guest of honour. Detective Peter Jones!' John's voice echoes from the large speakers. The driver leads Peter through the great hall over to the front, and onto the stage. John's strong arm wraps around Peter's shoulder. 'Tonight is a tribute to a truly historic moment, it's the birthday of the youngest ever homicide detective in New Orleans. This man, ladies and gentlemen, is a reputable soldier, he left for the military at the age of seventeen, and made quite a name for himself. He then joined the police force and almost immediately applied for detective and what a magnificent...' John's voice fades into the background and becomes muffled to Peter; he blocks John out entirely as his eyes move over the arranged tables and he starts to scan the room. *One, two, three, four, five, six, seven, eight, nine, ten, eleven, twelve, thirteen, fourteen, fifteen, sixteen, seventeen, eighteen, nineteen, twenty tables. One, two, three, four, five, six, seven, eight around that table. One, two, three, four, five, six, seven, eight around that one. One, two, three, four, five, six, seven, eight, that one's also full, all of them are full. That must be around hundred and sixty people. That's quite a lot. I can't imagine all of them are involved with the Savage family, but who knows. Doctors, seems like nurses, I recognise some of those firemen, some of my school teachers. Alexander, Diana, the Savages, Mayor Briarheart. Scarlett White? Now that one is a surprise, didn't expect to see my physical therapist here. Rob Patterson one of the criminal attorneys, no surprise there. That face over there, so familiar, hold on, is that, what's his name again? Come on Pete think, think, think, think! Michael! The artist from last night. I wonder who invited him. Is that Lily, next to him? Fuck. I didn't want her here tonight. Cap must've told John about her, and it seems she brought painter boy with her. The last thing I need is a distraction, unless of course it's the sexy Diana over there. Focus Pete, focus. There are the boys! I must remember to tell them about the plan, I don't think Cap's going to like it very much, Brady and Anderson on the other hand, they're going to love it. Seems like John's speech is almost over, smile and wave, smile and wave.*

Peter brings his attention back to John for the final word. '...but I mean who can predict the future. As I promised, the speech was short and sweet, I hope. Now dinner will be served, we will kick off with some prawn starters, and I must say, compliments to the chef! I had a taste; I couldn't resist. That will be followed by some lovely lamb shank, and finished off with the chef's signature dessert, which is a surprise to us all. Let us feast!' John leads Peter to his table with his colleagues, it seems to be the general arrangement, everyone with similar occupations sitting at respective tables. Here we have Peter, Anderson, Brady, and the Captain, each with a date, except Peter. After the main course and while they are awaiting this signature dessert, the Captain makes his way across the room to speak with the Mayor. This gives Peter a golden opportunity.

'Boys. Listen here quickly.'

'Pete when you start like that it sounds like bad news.' Anderson says.

'I'm not going to lie, it's not necessarily good news, but I still think you'll like it. Are you guys up for an unsanctioned undercover op.?'

Harris puts his head in his hands. 'What the fuck Pete?'

'I apologised to the Savage family so that they would accept my invitation to my birthday, I had no idea that they would take over arranging it. They think it's over, it's not, this is a play.'

'Okay? What's your plan?'

'Look at the opportunity we have here. John said that he was going to invite every important person in town.' Peter looks around the room and turns back to his partners. 'What I've realised, is that all the key players in their little club will probably be in this hall tonight. Think about it.'

Brady and Andy look at each other with smirks on their faces. Brady shrugs. 'Why not. But you know if Cap finds out, we're fucked, right?'

'He won't. The way I see it, either the person that did it, is in here, or the person behind it is. Someone in this room knows something. By the time Captain finds out what we're busy with, we'll have some viable suspects.'

Andy looks at them and speaks softly, almost whispering. 'I have a bit more experience than the two of you. Let me give you some tips. Don't ask questions you would ask in an interrogation, it's a dead giveaway; all you have to do tonight is analyse the people's characters. We don't talk about this for the rest of the night, we continue to party and have fun. Tomorrow we'll meet at Pete's house and discuss what we found here tonight, so remember the names that you think fits the killer's profile. And for crying out loud, don't get drunk, you'll miss details.'

'We don't have much to go on.'

'No, we don't, but think, work it out: who here fits the profile of a serial killer? When that person stands out, write down his name. And focus on the guys, remember Freddy was a big boy, for a lady to take him down would be a tall order.' Anderson says pedantically.

I need to get this out of the way. Peter walks over to Lily's table. 'Hey Lils. I thought I wouldn't be seeing you tonight.'

'Peter.' Lily gets up and hugs Peter tight. 'I wasn't but then Michael invited me; he had a plus one invitation without the plus one.' Lily laughs.

Michael sticks his hand out and greets Peter with a firm grip. 'Good evening, Detective. It's a pleasure to see you again. Last night when I saw you I didn't realise that tonight was arranged for you, if I did I would definitely have asked what you wanted for your birthday.' He says as a joke.

Peter smiles. 'And I would say a house on the moon. Sorry Michael I don't mean to sound like a sceptic, but I didn't expect to see you here.'

Michael looks up at the magnificent roof of the Gallier Hall and glances out the door. 'No I understand, it's actually quite simple. John invites me to these things, especially when they are held here. He feels it's his obligation to my parents. Unfortunately my parents passed away and I inherited everything they had, including their legacy. Did you see the square opposite the hall when you entered tonight?'

'Not tonight but I've seen it before.'

'It's called Lafayette Square. I was adopted by the Lafayette family when I was born and they said that my great, great, great grandfather or something was a war hero and that was a tribute to him. He's not really my biological grandfather, but my parents always made me feel like I was a blood relative of all of them, they were great people. In any case because of that, our family name is seen in the same regard and has some influence in this town.'

'You don't seem like the political type?'

Michael smiles and lifts up his hands. 'I'm not.' And laughs. 'With some of the money I inherited, I opened the gallery. Art is my passion and all of the people here that knew my parents know that I won't get involved with the same things they did. I don't want to run the town, I just want to live here, so they don't bother me. But for the sake of the family name I come to these events.'

Peter sticks his hand out as if saying goodbye. 'Well from my side, I'm glad you came. I'll chat to you guys later again, let me be polite and go talk to some of the guests.'

Lily turns to Michael as Peter walks off. 'Who would've known. You intrigue me Michael Lafayette.'

'My dad used to say I must live out my dream and never do things I don't like.'

'Sounds like he was a wise man.'

'He was. I'd like to introduce you to someone, as I believe that you study journalism. He's name is Francis Linwood. He was one of my father's oldest friends and he is the chief of the New Orleans Weekly. Maybe you can get involved with the paper.'

Lily smiles gracefully. 'I'm only finished with my first year you know.'

'I'm sure he can fit you in somewhere.' Michael replies confidently.

Peter stops behind John at the Savage family table. But because of his previous suspicions, the welcome isn't as warm as he would've liked. 'Evening Savage family.' But he only gets a couple of waves. 'I just wanted to thank you all for the party, I'm having a great time.

John gets up. 'It's only a pleasure. This is my family, Sandra my wife, my two sons Thomas and Bradley, and my daughters Rachel and Celeste.' Peter takes each one's hand as they are named. 'After dessert you and I must have a drink together, I'll introduce you to some of my friends.'

Peter mingles for a while, meeting and greeting. Some of the faces are well known, but some he's never seen before. The three detectives masterfully investigate the crowd, like wolves dressed in sheepskin. They move from table to table and person to person, chatting at the bar, flirting with the ladies and connecting with the chaps. The three tables behind the Savage family curiously keep to themselves, discussing business perhaps. Surely, they must be the Savage's closest connections? But there's no way in, it's as if the detectives don't even exist in that moment.

Finally dessert is served, and what an elegant dish it is. A cocktail glass with caramel cheese cake at the bottom, topped with cream beaten by the chef himself, drizzled with a dark almost black sauce. On top a single strawberry rests peacefully. It's evident why this is his signature dish; every bite melts in your mouth hyper-stimulating every taste bud. As John promised, he leads Peter around the room, introducing him to some of the town's most noble and influential characters. After a long night filled with dancing, drinking and good music, the driver takes Peter to the car.

On the way home Peter is intrigued by the driver. The slender man – Ryan Hunt – seems to have some dark secrets, avoiding questions about his occupation and his past. He comes across as militant and serious.

Chapter 17

Peter places the white pin board in the centre of his living room; he moves the couches against the wall and places the table in one of the corners. He places three chairs a couple of feet from the board, indentations are visible on the carpet from where the couches used to stand. Andy came with some steaks and Brady with the whiskey. While they're busy chatting, Peter cuts pieces of papers, only large enough to write a name on, and places them on one of the three chairs. Out of one of his kitchen drawers he takes a small container filled with coloured map pins, and puts them with the papers. After some time of searching he finds three permanent markers, one for him, one for Brady, and one for Andy. He writes down the names of the Savage family, John, Sandra, Thomas, Bradley, Rachel, and Celeste. He pins the names on the right-hand corner of the board in an almost circular formation, and at the bottom of the board he pins only the letter X. 'All right guys, obviously we said that it must have been a man that did this, however I've thought of something.' Peter points at the family names while he speaks. 'These people are seriously connected, I mean John and his wife last night talked to the Mayor like he's family. That got me thinking, what if a woman is behind all of this? Think about it, Freddy was a scumbag in the eyes of women. And any of these women could have used their influence or money, and got someone to kill Fred.'

Andy nods. 'Makes sense, I focused on the men last night though.'

Peter replies, 'That's all right, I never had the opportunity to share that last night, so I only focused on the ladies.'

Brady writes something on a paper, takes a pin and walks over to the board. He pins Mayor Richard Briarheart's name above the family. 'I spoke to this guy briefly last night; surely he must know what's going on. As you said Pete, John and Sandra are definitely friends with this guy.'

Anderson walks over and pins Rob Patterson and William Smith's names to the left of the family. 'Every criminal family needs a criminal attorney and financial advisor; these two sat right behind John.'

'I have four female names: I like Kathy, but same story, she sat close to them and mingled almost entirely the whole night with Sandra. I also have Emily Bride, Scarlett White and Evelyn Brown that seem close to the Savages.' Peter pins principal Kathy Larson name below the family, and on the right, he adds Emily the pharmacist, Scarlett the physical therapist and Evelyn the librarian.

Brady pins Jacob Taylor's name below William Smith's name on the left of the family. 'I had a beer with Jacob last night, and he seems to fly the family around in one of his choppers quite often. He also owns a charter flight company, which comes in handy if you need to transport some things under the radar.'

The three detectives sit on the chairs sipping at their whiskey and looking at what they've created so far. Peter points at the board and says, 'You know guys, that looks an awful lot like an inner circle and outer circle of a cult. I know Alex said that they're not religious, but even for a crime family, that makes sense don't you think?'

Brady looks at Peter, frowning. 'Who the fuck is Alex?'

'Dr Alexander Rayne,' he says in a monotonic voice, dragging out Alexander's surname.

'You think he's involved?'

'I don't. I do think he has something to hide, but I don't think he's connected here.'

Brady sighs almost like he has something to say, then pauses, and says, 'Don't you guys think it's odd that Evelyn Brown has the same surname as Nathan Brown?'

Both Andy and Peter look gobsmacked. 'The little fucker, he played us. We need to get him out of protective custody, we'll check later if he's connected to her, but if he is, he's coming back here.' Peter writes his name on a paper and pins it on the left of the board. He takes string and two pins and connects Nathan and Evelyn's names. 'You know he's also connected to the killer.' He takes more string and connects Nathan's name to the X at the bottom of the board.

'Now we're making progress.' Andy says. He writes down the name of Gilbert Wilburn, pins it more to the left and lower on the board than Nathan's. 'This guy is a philosophy lecturer at The University of New Orleans, him and Kathy are good mates.' He takes string and connects Gilbert Wilburn to principal Kathy Larson's name. 'If you're right Pete, she could've gotten him to do it, I bet you she's fucking him anyway. He's also a very unpredictable person. Strong. Assertive.' Anderson takes string and connects Gilbert with the X.

Peter writes Ryan Hunt's name on a piece of paper. He pins it halfway between the circle and the X, then connects Ryan to the middle of the family's circle and to the X with string. 'I don't trust him, he's supposedly their driver. He's strict, he's slender but strong, and precise. He's also a bit shady. Fuck I can't believe that we already have three connections somehow to the killer, directly related to this group.'

Anderson stops Peter. 'Suspects, that's all they are so far Pete. Don't get ahead of yourself.' Next to Ryan's name he pins Benjamin Black and connects him to Jacob Taylor. 'A while ago this fucker was investigated, now while he's way too connected to do something like this himself, he's always under the spotlight. But he's a thug, he owns the Royal Aces casino and the Penthouse strip joint in town. He could easily have someone do the deed for him. And I'm pretty sure your cousin would've gone to one, if not both of those places. But I can't connect him to the X yet, not yet at least.'

Brady smiles and walks over to the board. Below Benjamin Black's name, he pins the names of Edward Valentine and Oscar Reid. Peter looks at Brady and asks, 'Edward Valentine? As in the chef Edward Valentine?'

Brady replies. 'I caught him and Oscar talking last night. So Oscar owns PCL import-export. And he imports stuff for Edward that is difficult to get, but then I overheard them speak about Ben. At the time, I didn't know who Ben was, however, both of these guys owe him favours. I'm pretty sure Ben is Benjamin Black. Also, Oscar sometimes uses Jacob's charter company.' He connects Edward Valentine to Benjamin Black and to the X. He also connects Oscar Reid's name to Benjamin Black, Jacob Taylor, and to the X at the bottom of the board.

Peter runs his hands through his hair. 'I'm all out of names. Are you guys done?'

Andy just nods yes and sips his whiskey, but Brady writes two more names and Anderson says, 'Fuck Brady, don't you just want to put the whole party on there?'

Brady smirks with satisfaction. 'Just two more.' He pins to the left of Ryan Hunt the name Shane Clemente and below him to the left, directly under Gilbert Wilburn, he pins the name Victor Quinn. 'I spoke to Victor, who owns Mystic Tours, about starting a business, and he said to me that if I ever want to start a business and need a good financial advisor, I must let him know and he'll set me up with none other than: William Smith.' He connects Victor's name to both William and the X. 'And Shane Clemente is a general surgeon, who has a connection to Emily Bride, the pharmacist, *and* to Evelyn Brown. Emily supplies all of his medication, and Evelyn supplies him with medical textbooks.' He connects Shane's name with Emily Bride, Evelyn Brown, and finally the X. 'Now I'm done,' he says, sounding satisfied.

They all sit in a row, in silence, staring at the board. Peter breaks the silence. 'So apart from the Savage family who make up the inner circle, we have eight outer circle members. That's sixteen people.'

Andy interrupts him, 'Your math sucks Peter, there are fourteen inner and outer circle members.'

'Okay. Fourteen members, and apart from them we have eight more suspects, but one of the last eight is probably the triggerman.'

Andy interrupts him again, 'Fuck Pete.' And he laughs. 'Remember Benjamin Black wouldn't do it himself. So either Nathan, Gilbert, Shane, Victor, Ryan, Edward, or Oscar would be the triggerman.' Counting on his fingers as he says it. 'So seven.'

Peter frowns and closes his eyes, 'It's the whiskey.' He takes another sip. 'So now what?'

Anderson's voice becomes grim. 'Now we have to search these names on our system and build profiles, this we can only do at the office. The key is not to get caught, so be careful.'

Chapter 18

Peter and his colleagues have been working hard over the past three months under the radar, but with little success. At least the captain is unaware of their endeavours. The board with their connections has gone cold due to a lack of evidence. The case has been closed since no real progress was made. It's now spring and the city is swarming with tourists. The air smells of flowers and shrubbery. The city is so colourful, painted with light green leaves and flowers of all colours. Perfection. There's noise everywhere, a constant buzz. Except in the mornings; the mornings are quiet. Next to the river, if you listen carefully you can hear the birds sing, trees rustling and the river flowing.

A knock at the door. 'Police! Open up!' the police officer shouts.

A man walks to the door and looks through the peephole, he sees the back view of a police officer who is looking at the quiet street. He opens the door. 'Morning Officer, how can I help?' the man says.

'Sorry to bother you so early Sir, we received a call for a break-in in this street; would you mind if I check your property and your house?'

The man peeks past the police officer. 'I don't see your cruiser.'

'No Sir, my partner is patrolling the block to see if there is any disturbance. I'm going from door to door just to ensure that all is in order. Would you mind if I take a look? Or do you feel that everything is okay here?'

'Not a problem, Officer, you can take a look around.'

'All right I'm going to circle the yard and when I'm done I'll ring the bell to check the house. Keep the doors locked until I return please.' The officer walks off. A couple of minutes later the doorbell rings again. 'Sir, are you still in here?'

'Yes. Yes, I am. Everything clear?'

'From the outside yes, let me just quickly check the house and then I can move on to your neighbours. Please be vigilant, it's difficult to say if it was a prank call. Better to be safe than sorry.' The officer walks into the house and checks behind every couch, the kitchen, the dining room and then moves upstairs. 'Do you stay alone Sir?'

The man follows the officer closely, feeling uneasy with the potential of a break-in. 'Yes Officer, I am alone. Well, for now. My wife is in New York for the next couple of days. She'll be back on Wednesday.'

'All right well I hope that you have a quiet Sunday, and please, if you see or hear anything, call 911 immediately.' The officer checks all the rooms and walks into the master bedroom last. 'Everything seems clear.'

'Thank goodness. Thanks for your trouble, Officer.' The man turns around and walks out of the bedroom. But before he reaches the door he's bashed behind the head with a heavy object and he falls to the floor. His vision slowly turns to darkness.

Chapter 19

Peter's phone rings; there's no answer. The phone rings again, still no answer. On the third ring, Peter's muffled voice says, 'Peter Jones, hello.'

'Pete, it's the captain here. Are you up?'

'What time is it?'

'It's half past twelve.'

'Sorry Cap I was asleep. What's happening?'

'Get dressed, we have another homicide. A woman called 911; she got home just before twelve and found her husband on the bedroom floor. It sounds bad.'

'Where must I meet you?'

'I spoke to Harris and Anderson, meet me at the precinct, we'll all go from there.'

'Okay give me twenty minutes.' Peter says.

Fifteen minutes later Peter stops at the precinct. The three detectives get in the cruiser with Captain Deloitte and make their way to the crime scene. Even in this busy city, the police lights flare into the air; a dome of blue lights visible for miles. Yellow tape cordons the house, closing the road entirely. This is good, it keeps curious eyes off the scene. Media people crowd the barrier like vultures, each of them hoping to get the scoop. If not for the police officers monitoring them, it's highly probable that one – if not all of them – would take the opportunity to sneak in. Even with the cruiser lights and the occasional blaring siren, it proves difficult for the captain to navigate through the crowd. He parks the cruiser inside the barrier, and before they even speak a word, they know this will be a messy scene, it's evident because everyone is here. Spotlights from the fire truck light up the house like the sun lights the moon. Everything seems to move quickly but almost in slow motion. The forensic guys in their white suits move silently, with neutral faces. A black van with its rear doors opened faces the cruiser. The victim's wife is inside it. It must be the wife. She's slouched over, her head in her hands with some person, probably a counsellor, speaking with her. It looks like she's crying. What a terrible thing it must have been for her to find her husband in whatever state he's in. A man hurries over to the cruiser; he opens the driver's door. 'Captain, we need to hurry.'

The three detectives climb out with the captain. 'What do we have Officer?' the captain asks.

'One male victim, face down. Coroner reckons he must have died some time on Sunday, an accurate time can only be given upon a full examination. His wife returned from New York tonight and found him like that.'

The detectives are led to the room where a man lies on the carpet; the smell is awful. It smells like fermented rice and acid and iron, pungent. His pale body lies prone on the carpet. His head turned slightly left, it almost looks like he's crying. A small amount of vomit is spattered on the floor, mixed in the lake of blood. His arms are underneath him, a failed attempt to brace for the fall. 'Fuck. The smell is revolting,' Brady says.

Peter walks around the body and checks the room. 'Doesn't seem like anything was taken.'

Brady and Andy quickly scan the upstairs area of the house and return to the body. 'Definitely nothing was taken. Whoever was here, they were here for him. I didn't know people could bleed this much.'

The captain looks at one of the forensics guys. 'So what's your take on this?'

'We're waiting for the blood spatter analyst, but so far it seems the cause of death is from a cut to his throat. The only other wound I could see without turning the body over is the hematoma on the back of his head. He was hit hard. But the blood man wants him as we found him. We can't see either of his arms; he's lying on them as you can see. So far I don't have much for you, but we've only been here for a short while.'

'How long before the analyst gets here?' snaps the captain.

'He's just getting his equipment from the car, won't be long now.'

'Have you guys found any prints?'

'No. Nothing. There's also no sign of forced entry. The only prints in the house belong to him. Which was odd to start with, but his wife said that apparently he cleaned the house on Saturday. We've still got a couple of areas to dust though, maybe something will come up. I wouldn't bet on it though. The path from the door all the way here revealed nothing. He let his killer in.'

The blood spatter analyst walks into the room in silence; he greets no one. He walks around the body and takes lots of pictures. Then lies down on the floor; takes more pictures. He kneels, and he gets up and takes more. After about ten minutes of flashing he says, 'You can turn him now. We'll take more pictures and then the body must be removed. I'll need the room then for my analysis to be accurate. Detectives, have you done everything you wanted in here?'

'I took pictures of everything,' The man in the white suit answers.

'In that case we just want to see the rest of the body and we'll be out of your hair,' replies the captain.

'Okay let's turn him.' The detectives put on gloves and help the analyst turn the body. The cut on the neck is clean, the blade was sharp.

'He or she was right handed, not the tallest person either,' the blood spatter analyst observes. 'What's that on his wrist?' He looks closer. 'A triangle? That's interesting. I need to capture that.'

Peter goes pale and walks out, the captain and two other detectives follow him. 'Do you still think we should've closed Freddy's case?' Peter bitingly remarks to the captain.

The captain mutters, 'Shit. We'll have to open it again. I'm going to speak to his wife. You guys wait in the car. We'll talk about this shortly.'

'I can't help but wonder. This was sudden, and it's only a couple of weeks after we stopped investigating our suspects. Do you think he knows?'

'Boys, we don't even know who he is yet,' Anderson remarks.

'We'll have to work quickly, and we'll have to show the suspects to cap.'

'We might have a break here,' muses Peter. 'The previous scene was clean and the body was dumped. At this one he left the body in situ, and it is a messy scene. Fucking blood everywhere; vomit. Something's not right here.'

Anderson rubs his chin, 'I agree with Peter. Something's up here, out of place. The previous MO was perfect and well executed—'

Brady interrupts, 'I get what you're saying, but think about it for a second. Looking at only the cut, it was still done meticulously. But as you say, the body wasn't cleaned and it wasn't dumped either. But that cut was absolutely edgeless. The killer here hit this guy behind the head, as was done with Freddy; maybe Freddy didn't go down as quickly and took the opportunity to fight back. This guy has no defensive wounds and a clean cut, which makes it look like he was bashed behind the head, went down, and then was killed. Maybe that was the plan for Fred?'

'The blood? The body? The scene? The MO has changed.'

'Has it?' Brady says smirking, 'What is the one key factor missing here?'

'There's nothing missing, everything is here apart from the weapon.'

'There is something missing. Nathan's missing.' Brady points at his temple. 'Nathan supplied the cleaning kit. If the killer moved the body from this scene, he would have definitely transferred some of the evidence, wouldn't you agree? That's risky if you think about the previous murder and he doesn't do risky— he plans. So this gives us one more clue about Freddy too. Wherever Fred was killed – and the same as with this guy – the killer knew he had time, he knew he wouldn't be interrupted because this guy's wife only found him three days later. The difference here is he couldn't clean up after himself, so he chose to leave the body at the scene, rather than risk getting caught some other way.'

'You know what that means right? Nathan can't be a suspect anymore.'

Brady muses, 'Well we can't say that just yet, I got some inside info that his protective custody is very lax, he has freedom to do whatever he wants, he was just given a new home and new identity. But he's close, they didn't take him far away because there was no real lead. He's not more than an hour's drive from here.'

Peter replies, 'We need to speak with whoever offered this deal, we need to bring him back and revoke his protective custody. But he can't know that he's a suspect.'

'But if it was him, he'll know about the second killing,' Brady points out.

'We'll have to ensure that he thinks someone else is on the case then,' Anderson says. 'He's our only connection to this fucker. He's coming back, I'll pull some strings.'

Chapter 20

'Harris! Jones! Anderson! In my office!' Captain Deloitte barks. The three detectives file into his office. 'Close the door behind you.' Brady closes the door. 'So I got a phone call this morning, from an FBI agent. Now imagine my surprise when a name that you fuckers searched for on our system was red flagged on their system. Benjamin Black. Initially I didn't think much of it, but then she faxed me a list of names that were searched for on that very same day. That is why you are here. First, I got some interesting names.' He pulls the fax up and starts reading the names, staccato: 'I have Benjamin Black, I have Gilbert Wilburn, I have Oscar Reid, Shane Clemente, Victor Quinn, Edward Valentine, Nathan Brown? Why are you searching for *Nathan*? Oh, wait I know! It's because you called the people in charge and ordered them to revoke his protective custody—'

Brady interrupts, 'Cap we can—'

'But it gets better!' the captain snarls. 'The mayor! The *mayor*? Scarlett White, Evelyn Brown, Rob Patterson, William Smith, Emily Bride, Jacob Taylor, principal Kathy Larson? What the fuck are you guys doing? And there's still more. The one thing I told you *not* to do, you do! Do you know who the next names are? Of course, you do, the whole Savage family!' Captain Deloitte throws the fax on his desk in rage, but it flutters down softly which angers him more. 'What are you busy with? First you blame these people for murder, then you apologise in public and then you investigate them again! What do you think will happen when this gets out?'

'I know it looks bad. But let us explain. All the names on that list are suspects. The apology was fake,' Peter holds his hands up. 'But with good reason, we needed an in. We needed to speak to the Savage family to try and figure out who was involved with Fred, but then they hosted the party for my birthday and it gave us the perfect opportunity to scope out the people who are involved with them. We believe that someone on that list might be responsible for Fred's murder, and now this one too. And that someone on that list might also be the trigger man. We brought Nathan back purely because he's Evelyn Brown's cousin, and we believe that she's involved with the Savage group. He's also the only direct connection we have to the murderer. I know it looks bad Cap, but please, just trust us.'

The captain sits in his chair staring at the three detectives for a while and then calmly replies, 'Don't ever do anything behind my back again. I looked like an idiot when this FBI agent spoke with me over the phone and I had no answers. Next time, come to me.'

'Will do Sir,' Anderson replies.

'You might have a problem; Kelly Young is her name, the FBI agent. She's on her way here and will be in the office tomorrow morning. It seems she's taking over the case. Now as a courtesy I'll ask her to keep the three of you on the case, but I can't promise anything. Don't do this to me again.'

The next day at seven o'clock, a luscious Asian FBI agent walks into the office. She turns heads with her beautiful straight black hair and dark brown eyes. You can see she's fit, but tiny. Already she has every man's attention, without saying a word. She walks into the captain's office and closes the door behind her. She sticks out her hand to greet him. 'Good morning Captain. I'm special agent Kelly Young from the FBI.'

The captain quickly gets up and takes her hand. 'Agent Young, it's a pleasure to meet you.'

'The pleasure is mine. Captain I have a long day ahead of me so I'll get right to it.' She takes a file out of her bag and hands it to the captain. 'This is a file that we've compiled over the past year or so. It contains details about Benjamin Black.' They sit down. 'Obviously some of the details are redacted—sensitive information, I hope you understand. There was a search on your system for Mr. Black and it is a concern to us. Mr. Black is involved in numerous criminal activities, but we have encountered difficulty linking him to some of those activities, however we have informants that confirm those involvements. Over the past two months Benjamin seemed to disappear. We know that he was in your town for an event hosted at the Gallier Hall in December last year and we placed an undercover operative at the party to monitor his activities. Obviously I cannot disclose who our undercover operative is. My question is what is he involved with here.'

'Involvement is a strong word; suspicion would be better suited. Three of our detectives investigated a murder last year but because of a lack of evidence and therefore suspects, the case was dropped. But recently another murder was committed with a similar MO. The three detectives had a list of suspects, based purely on character and these suspects' involvement with a certain group. The group was investigated due to a connection made by Nathan Brown, one of the names on the list that you sent to me. The rest of the names on that list are all the old suspects. Because of the latest murder, we did a search on the system for all those suspects.'

Curious, Agent Young asks, 'Why were they only searched for after the second murder?'

'Because that list was compiled without my knowledge.'

'I see.'

'Where does this place us, Agent?'

'I will be in town for a couple of months. I am going to conduct my investigation on the FBI case from here. I will also assist with the murder investigation because of Mr. Black's suspicious involvement and if it can be confirmed, then we will take over the case. For now I would like to meet with the three detectives if possible to discuss it with them. Would you mind if we use your office?'

The captain nods graciously, gets up and walks to the door. 'Not a problem Agent, I'll send them in.' He calls, 'Jones, Harris and Anderson, in my office please. Special agent Kelly Young wants a word. Bring both case files.'

The three go into the office with files and notes in hand. The mind map, however, remains at Peter's house. Agent Young gets up and moves to the other side of the captain's desk, sticks her hand out to greet each of them and sits down. 'Good morning Detectives. I'm sorry to be here so early but we have a lot to discuss.' She holds her hand out, asking for the case files. 'Can I see those?'

'Here you go Agent Young.' Brady replies, almost in love.

'Thank you. I noticed your search for some names on the system; it raised a red flag at our department because of one particular name: Benjamin Black. I've explained the relevance of this to your captain. For now I hope you understand that I cannot share details with you. However due to mutual interest in one of these names, I will try to assist you in your murder investigation. If we determine that these crimes are not linked to those I am already investigating, then I will step back and you will remain the sole investigation unit on the case. But, if the cases do seem to have a connection, I am going to have to take over the case and unfortunately it will not be investigated from here, but from our headquarters. I hope you understand that the other case is much more than just a murder case. Any objections or queries?'

All three say in unison, 'No.'

'All right quickly run me through these two cases. I will then take them with me to the hotel tonight and work through them thoroughly.'

Peter replies. 'Before we go on, Agent.'

'Call me Kelly.'

Peter nods, 'Kelly before we continue, I would just like to inform you that at my house we have created a mind map with connections to the murder. We also have notes. When you are ready we can meet at my house, the four of us, and we can show you how far we've progressed so far in terms of suspects.'

'Okay.'

Brady starts to talk, 'As you can see from the pictures in the files, the murders are very similarly executed. However, in the first one, the body was staged and dumped elsewhere, and in the second one the body was left at the scene of crime. In neither of the cases did we find any evidence to which we could link a suspect; no DNA, no prints, and no murder weapon. The murder weapon was clearly a very sharp object. The cuts on both victims are clean and precise. The ME determined that, for both victims, the murder was committed by a right-handed person, most likely a man. He also found – using some mathematical voodoo that they have – that the perps would be roughly the same height, if not precisely the same height. We were fortunate to catch a man named Nathan Brown.' Kelly studies the crime scene photos with immense concentration while Brady talks. 'Nathan was the man who sold the crime scene cleaning kits to the suspect. However, he told us that different people always picked it up. After we found and questioned him, he was sent into protective custody. We now have reason to suspect that he might be more involved than we previously thought. Back to the point: the first murder was clean and the second was not, we think that the reason for the difference is the absence of Mr Brown. If the killer is truly as skilled as he appears, then he wouldn't have moved the second body, because in doing so, he would have transferred some of the evidence. Unfortunately, that is all we have at this stage.'

Anderson quickly sits forward. 'We also believe that this might be linked to a particular group. And they're blocking us. We are unable to get warrants for pretty much anything.'

'Quite frankly, Detective, you don't have much to go on. Meaning you don't have much to motivate for a warrant. That can change though. Our connections supersede any law enforcement in your town; not even your DA can stop us.' Detective Anderson gives a pleased smile with her response. 'When I saw the list that you guys searched from, I looked into the names very briefly. And now, looking at these pictures, I want you to consider something. A while ago we took down a very dangerous organisation. And in that case I saw something similar to this. The organisation was run by a masterful, incomparable puppet master of the highest order. And he committed some of the murders himself, for amusement. I want you to consider that your killer might not be working for the group, but that the group might be working for your killer. If there is a connection, and I do say *if*, then we have a difficult task ahead of us.'

'Are you saying our cases may be linked?'

'I'm saying that even though the organisation in question has been taken down, Benjamin Black is one of the very last members of that organisation that still prowls the streets. He was a lower order member and we've been tracking him to flush out higher order members. So yes, Detective, his involvement here might not be a coincidence. This means that the Savage family might be part of something much, much greater than you could imagine, and your killer too; who knows?'

Chapter 21

A stranger intercepts Lily while she makes her way through the crowds to her next class. He gives her an envelope and all he says is, 'Have a nice day Lily.' She wonders if it is secret admirer… She enters the class and sits at the back. As she opens the envelope she smells soft, clean and soapy cologne mixed with the smell of green tea. Her heart starts to bang in her chest. The smell is familiar. She pulls the letter out slowly, it's the same tea-stained paper. The letter, when opened, reveals the same artistic and sophisticated handwriting. Again the bottom, signed only 'J.'

"Dear Lily,
I hope this letter finds you well and that you will not be scared off by it. I have made some calls to several of my friends, and the result of that will be that soon you will receive a phone call from Mr Francis Linwood. He will give you the opportunity to write a blog in the New Orleans Weekly.
I also found out through the grapevine that you met another one of the people I admire. Michael Lafayette. He's very talented isn't he?
I promise you once again that my intentions towards you are pure. I'm looking forward to reading your blog.
P.S. I hope you do well at university."

Her cell phone rings. 'Hello.'
'Hi, is this Lily speaking?'
'Yes it is?'
'Lily this is Francis Linwood from the New Orleans Weekly. We met at your friend Peter's birthday party in December last year.'

Chapter 22

Agent Young sits in her hotel room in silence. The balcony door is open, as well as all the windows. The curtains are tied back so that the wind doesn't damage them. She opens the two case files on the bed. Sitting in her T-shirt and pyjama pants, she works through the files, sipping on white wine and nibbling some sushi. The breeze is nice. It's cool and fresh. Music from street is all she needs; she likes New Orleans. It's got character. She reads, and reads and reads. A gust of wind blows into the hotel room, chills her slightly. *A gown would be nice. Let me check in the cupboard. Perfect! Not my colour, but it'll do. Mother always told me not to wear white gowns, they get dirty too quickly.* Kelly walks out onto the balcony. *This city is amazing. I love it here, maybe one day I'll take a different job and move here, do something not involved with crime.* Wind blows through her hair. The sky is dark, the moon big and the stars bright. Apart from the solitary musician, the streets are quiet, it's late. *This case, I wonder... I wonder if it's linked. I haven't seen this MO before, but he's risky and bold. He's not afraid at all. This killer thinks he can't be caught, he taunts them. I can't imagine that this is his first time, it's just too well executed. Even the second one, it's messy, but it's well done. Perfectly planned. If he's connected to Benjamin, then he's definitely not some hired hand. The detectives don't realise the seriousness of the situation, but how can they? When the time is right I'll share what I can with them, but it's too soon. For all I know it may just be a coincidence, Benjamin being here. But if I don't act quickly then the organisation will start to operate again and then everyone's screwed.* She looks up at the stars feeling a bit helpless. It's difficult for Kelly doing all of this on her own; the Bureau feels that this is all over and that Benjamin should be arrested; there's no need to keep him on the streets when the organisation has been dismembered to the point it has. *The two murders were just so random, the victims have no connection to anything or anyone of interest. I can't see how they're connected, if they're connected. I'll have to have a look at this mind map at Detective Jones's house, maybe it'll provide some clarity.* Kelly walks inside and closes the balcony doors behind her. She's exhausted. She feels the soft carpet beneath her feet as she walks. It reminds her of her childhood where she used to walk on the soft, short grass in the garden. She closes the case files and places them neatly on the counter top and gets into bed. But insomnia gets her; her mind won't shut down. Usually it's a good idea to watch a boring television show, when there's no interest, but the mind is distracted, it tends to shut down. That's the plan. But all there is to watch at half-past-two in the morning is cheap pornography, and that won't do. Porn doesn't sit well with Kelly, she feels it is a tasteless misuse of one's body for money, no more than prostitution with a prettier bow tied around it. In Kelly's younger years, a woman confided in her, telling her about the abuse she had suffered in the industry. Sure, in the movies with bigger budgets the girl has more authority about how the scene should proceed, she's also the star of the show, but in these cheaper movies, the girls get abused and almost raped. Well, that's what the girl said that she spoke to in any case. Apparently some of them enjoy it, but to others it's just another means to an end. These thoughts of pornography distract her briefly enough for her to fall asleep. The curtains remain open and a glimmer of light shines through the hotel room. In her dream Kelly runs along a dark road, woods on either side. A deep breath follows her, a shadow of... something. The earth starts to shake beneath her and she can see lights up ahead, a house perhaps, but she can't get there; the faster she runs, the slower she moves. Her chin is drawn up to the moon, and it is almost impossible to look back down, she physically can't look down! Her heart beats and the breath comes closer. Every now and then she can see the light shaking in her stride but then her head is drawn back up to the moon. Her legs start to slow; she can feel the breath now. She starts telling herself it must be a dream, it must be a dream, it must be a dream. In the dream her eyes are closed now, squeezing the lids tight. It must be a dream, it must be a dream, it must be a dream she repeats over and over. She can feel her legs regain strength, her neck relaxes and she can see the light. It must be a dream. Her stride becomes longer, she gains speed. The breath is now losing pace, trailing behind her more and more. It must be a dream; it must be a dream. The light is now bigger and brighter. The breath has faded; she can barely hear it now as the woods start to clear on either side of her. Before the bright light is an open field and the light is mounted on top of a high roof, a hotel—no, a church. With a sudden shock, Kelly awakens from her nightmare in a sweat, she gets up and closes the curtains.

Chapter 23

The entrance to Dr Alexander Rayne's office never becomes less theatrical. It also never becomes more welcoming. What is more welcoming though, is the fact that today Dr Rayne is not alone, Diana is here too. 'Detective. I must say that in all my time as a psychiatrist, I've never met anyone as erratic as you. You ask for my help and disappear for months, twice in a row now.' Dr Rayne says as he sticks his hand out to Peter.

'At least this time I made an appointment,' Peter jokes.

Dr Rayne chuckles. 'At least.'

'Hello, Diana,' Peter offers his hand to Diana.

'Oh nonsense, Detective,' Diana says, pushing his hand away as she comes in for a kiss. Her lips are soft and warm; they smell of berries. 'I think that's better.'

Peter starts to blush and stammers, 'I'll never say no to a kiss from such a beautiful girl, I need more friends like you.' He takes a chance and winks at her.

'Have a seat, Detective,' Dr Rayne says as Diana disappears into the always-closed room.

'Diana won't be joining us?' He asks, pointing at the mysterious door.

'We'll join her in a moment.' Dr Rayne sits back in his chair, he doesn't say a word. Peter and the doctor look at each other for a long while before the detective becomes tense. 'Detective why did you come today?'

'I want to take you up on the offer that you made in our last discussion.'

'You want me to change your perspective.'

'Yes.'

'Why now? Months have passed and I never saw hide nor hair of you.'

'There was another murder.'

'It seems that soon I will have to start committing murders, to see you, of course.' Dr Rayne smiles.

'Do you?'

'Do *you*, Detective?'

'I'm a detective.'

'And I'm a doctor; is that a no?'

'Of course it's a no.'

Dr Rayne sits forward, his index fingers placed neatly together over his lips. 'And that's your first error.' He licks his lips, almost touching the fingers. 'You still approach this killer as someone who morally argues like you. I can guarantee you, Detective, that this killer doesn't care about what job he has, or how much money he makes, or how much respect he generates. None of that matters. Tell me: how do you see this killer? Describe to me how you think he behaves, approaches life, those sorts of things.'

'I think he either has a double life, or a single life. He either lives as this innocent character in a story that exists only in his mind and then whenever he feels the need, the second part or ulterior part begins where he is a ruthless killer. Or he is an obvious psycho that lives only for the hunt. I think that he is drunk on power, he also needs to prove something to the world. He needs to have control.'

Dr Rayne nods without a sound. 'What you describe there is a blatant killer and I think almost nine times out of ten you would be correct with that, but sooner or later the people you describe get caught. I think that the killer you are dealing with is nothing like that; you completely misunderstand him.' Peter frowns questioningly.

'Let me explain. I am pretty convinced that Freddy wasn't his first kill, it was just too well done, and his second kill I'll bet was pretty much the same, right?'

'Pretty much.'

'This man – whoever he is – doesn't live a double life and he certainly doesn't live a single life as you theorised. If he did he would've been caught by now. Instead I reckon that he doesn't want to *take* control, but rather, he believes he already *has* control. If that makes any sense. Something in his life that happened or continues to happen makes him feel like he will never get caught; never, no matter how risky the kill. That kind of killer is what you're dealing with. Think about Freddy for a second. That murder was executed with near-surgical precision. No blood, no evidence, nothing was found, right?'

'Yes.'

'Then why would he have given you the body in the way he did, why would he mark the wrist, if he's never done it before? The answer to that is simple, it was a shrine of some sorts, dedicated to one group or even one person. He wanted that body to be found, and seen, by at least one specific individual. And that is why I think he lives a normal life, with murder as an extension, like a third arm, it comes naturally to him. He doesn't feel abnormal, but he surely feels superior. You need to learn what it feels like to have such control, because only then can your mind shift in the way that his mind has shifted, where right and wrong run parallel to each other. When that shift has happened, you can freely jump between the two. Detective, you are very mature for your age, and you have a good background, but your mind is young and few things are set in stone.'

Peter seems confused. 'I don't fully understand your point, Doctor.'

'What I'm saying is that this man's mind had to have been changed at a young age, and that's what we'll do to you.'

'It makes sense.'

'But you'll have to trust me.'

'I do trust you.'

Dr Rayne gets up and leads Peter to the closed door where Diana went in. 'Detective, if we go through those doors, then you're not a police officer any more, do you understand?'

'Okay?' Hesitant.

'You said you trust me, now do so.' Dr Rayne pushes the door open.

'What the fuck?' Peter says as he enters the room. He finds a girl, blonde, and bare inside the room. She's tied down over an adjustable wooden table. It's at the perfect height for her to stand with her legs spread open, each foot tied firmly to a paw of the table. She's bent over and lying with her chest and stomach on the table. Her hands are tied together, the rope runs tightly over the table and off on the other side. She's blindfolded and gagged. Every now and then she mumbles something in a nervous tone. Behind her Diana stands, watching Peter as he examines the girl's naked body. He's obviously conflicted by the need to set her free, and natural lust. 'What the fuck is this?'

'Don't worry, no one will ever know what happens here today, we don't use names in here.' Diana says.

'I'll know! And what do you mean, "what happens here today"?'

Dr Rayne takes Peter's shoulder. 'I need you to listen carefully. I need you to take control. I want you to imagine that you captured this girl, and you're alone in the woods. There's no one for miles around.' Dr Rayne turns down the lights.

Peter's confused and upset. 'Yes, so?'

'He wants you to act on your instincts,' Diana says. 'Whatever they may be.'

Sarcastically, Peter replies, 'What if I want to kill her?'

'Then so be it,' says the doctor from behind him. After hearing that, the girl starts to panic, she struggles and pulls on the ropes, but with no success. She cries and says something through the gag, but it's impossible to make out. 'Silence!' Dr Rayne says sternly, but the girl continues to cry. 'She was prepared here for you,' he says to Peter. 'So stop thinking about it, and do it.'

Diana and Dr Rayne stand behind Peter as he moves closer to the crying girl. He looks at her, spread-eagled and tied to a table, she can't see him, and she'll probably never recognise him. He looks at her with animalistic lust starting to surge through him. 'Shh,' he says; he rubs his hand over her back. She cries louder. 'Shh,' he says again, but she tries to pull away from his hand. He slaps her on her butt cheek, then walks around her, circling like a wolf circles crippled prey, stopping directly behind her. He starts to touch her while undressing himself. 'We have to be naked together,' he says urgently, to the young blonde girl. Without warning he enters her. She gives a cry, partially relief; at least he's not killing her. He thrusts hard. After some time everyone in the room realises that he's almost done. He tenses.

'Don't,' Diana says. She walks closer as Peter tries to contain himself. Diana pulls him out of the young blonde girl. 'I want to taste her on you,' she kneels and starts sucking on Peter. In a single gushing moment he releases all tension into the back of Diana's throat. He can feel her tongue move as she swallows.

When there is nothing left to swallow, Diana gets up and kisses Peter on his lips.

'Get dressed,' Dr Rayne says, and when Peter was dressed, he was sent home. The girl was released, and made a hundred thousand dollars richer. As Peter never knew that the girl was paid for her performance, he will never be the same.

Chapter 24

It's early in the morning, but the exact time is unclear. Outside Peter's window, a couple of birds dance in the air, chirruping and chirping. The morning is crisp, but not cold. The wind is absent today and it leaves a sort of obdurate silence without the howling around the house. No rain can be heard either, only the birds, chirping, chirping, chirping.

Peter can't sleep, the past few days have been difficult for him. Raping a girl of, God only knows *how* old, takes its toll on a man. It's a strange and conflicting feeling for him. On the one hand, he feels the emotion of a normal human being: he feels guilty, he wants to confess, he wants to get this terrible sin off of his chest. On the other hand, he knows that it will never be linked to him. It is impossible for that bare and blindfolded blonde beauty to link him in any way to what happened to her. This knowledge results in a feeling of boundless power; it devours him. When Peter thinks back to that event, he is aroused all over again in a way he has not experienced before. When he thinks of Diana's reaction to his vile act, the lust consumes him. Whenever he tries to sleep, he gets visions of this helpless woman, but he never has a nightmare; always just a dream, he's awoken by a feeling of power, not repentance. Nevertheless, sleep eludes him.

Peter gets up; he heard a noise against the front door, probably the paper, which puts it around four o'clock, the paperboy's never late. He walks down the stairs in complete darkness; he doesn't need the light. Approaching the door, he can't help but wonder, what if the detectives from the serious crime unit have come, maybe it got out, maybe Dr Rayne or Diana betrayed him? He shrugs the thought off and opens the door. It was the paper; he brings it inside. The kitchen light is on, the paper is on the counter, and the smell of roasted coffee beans is in the air.

Peter pages through the paper, he never reads it from front to back, always just the articles that interest him. The last page is very interesting to him: a blog, with a familiar name as the author, Lily Tomlinson.

"A mystery man.
In the darkness of the shadows, a gentleman lurks. One that never shows his face. A man so polite in the letters that he writes. I cannot help but wonder why this mystery man – wherever he may be – never comes to greet me in person. His handwriting is first class and beautiful. The tea-stained paper not only takes time to make, but shows a dedication to perfection. His smell, the strong, clean and soapiness of it will make any woman quiver. If this man really is how he portrays himself to be, then he is the sort of man that women spend their entire lives hoping for. Gentle and caring. But the shadows own him, and they dare not share. Oh, mystery man, this is my plea: that one day, we will meet."

Poetic and direct. Peter closes the paper, he is impressed by Lily's artistic feel. He walks upstairs to get ready for the meeting he has with his colleagues, Andy,

Brady, and now also Kelly. The shower head in his bathroom sprays fine water, it gives the sensation of warm rain, rather than a small waterfall, very pleasant.

A while later, the doorbell rings.

'This is the police, open up and put your hands above your head!'

Kelly elbows Brady in his side, she's not impressed with his joke. 'People can hear you.'

He chuckles, 'Nah, the neighbours know by now. Sir! If you don't open this door right this instant, we will use force to enter your house and we'll also use force to take your coffee.'

The door cracks open. 'Please Sir, not the *coffee*, anything but the coffee,' Peter jokes.

Andy stands on the grass smoking his pipe and waits a while after Brady and Kelly enter the house. 'Morning Pete.'

'Morning colleague! Cup of coffee?'

'Sounds nice. Black, no sugar please.'

'Watching your figure now I see? No more sugar.' Peter comments.

'We need to start somewhere.' Andy replies gloomily, as his coffee is served.

'Kelly,' Peter smiles at her. 'The way it usually works here is that if it's an early morning we either eat breakfast before we work, or we go somewhere afterwards. Since you're new to our... manhunt club, you get to decide.' Peter wonders if Kelly would cry and scream if she was bound to a table, naked, like the blonde.

'I think we should quickly go through whatever you guys have here, then go out somewhere for breakfast and coffee. We can always continue to talk there. What do you guys think?' She looks at Harris and Anderson.

'Sounds good.'

'Let me see this board that you guys created.' Peter never puts it away, he only puts it face down against the wall, in case someone comes for a visit. He puts it on display for her. 'Wow those are lots of suspects. Explain the connections to me?'

'I spoke last time,' Peter says.

Brady steps up to the board. 'Okay so by now you've figured out that there is a certain family that we suspect might be behind this. In our town, they run some sort of group; initially we thought it to be a cult, but we were corrected by the fact that they are a non-religious group.' Kelly listens attentively. 'The names that you see in the inner circle, the Savage family, they seem to be the head of this group and John Savage seems to be the head of the house.' Kelly nods as if she knows this. 'The names around them are the names of the people we suspect to be the inner circle members of the group. You see, they have quite the fan base and when they host events – invitation-only events – almost a quarter of the town ends up going, that's why we suspected a cult. The six family members plus the eight inner circle members, that we know of, are our main suspects.'

'How did you determine who those eight members are?'

'At Peter's party, we took notice of who interacted with the Savage family and who sits closest to them.'

'Okay that makes sense.'

'We understand that in all probability those people won't get their hands dirty themselves. Now, we heard what you said, but for now, to explain this board, let's continue with that assumption. The other names towards the bottom, those are our trigger man suspects, and as you can see each of them is connected somehow to either the Savage family, or to the other members.'

'Okay explain these connections to me,' Kelly says.

'Nathan Brown is the man who supplied the crime scene cleaning kits, he is also Evelyn Brown's cousin and Evelyn owns a bookstore, but the only problem with Nathan is that with the second murder he couldn't have been there, as he's in protective custody. Evelyn is also connected to Gilbert Wilburn, the philosophy lecturer, because he gets his books from her. Gilbert is also connected to Kathy Larson, the principal of a school for the gifted, where only the smartest kids go. Apparently he gives philosophy speeches every now and then at the school. Shane Clemente is a surgeon, and he is connected to Emily Bride, the pharmacist where he sends his patients for prescriptions. He's also connected to Scarlett White as he sends his patients to her for physical therapy after surgeries. Victor Quinn owns Mystic Tours and William Smith is his financial advisor. Next is Ryan Hunt, but we know very little about him. He seems to have been in some or other military wing, but we can't find him on the system. Ryan is the only one directly related to the Savage family and he is a butler or something, sometimes he's the driver too. Now we get to the one you are interested in, Benjamin Black. Benjamin is connected to Rob Patterson; Rob being his criminal attorney. Now we thought that since he's always under the spotlight, chances are that he won't have the opportunity to do this himself. Therefore he is connected to Edward Valentine and Oscar Reid. Edward is a chef that is known to cook for Benjamin whenever he is in town, but Edward is connected to no one else on the board. Oscar Reid is not just connected to Benjamin

Black, but also to Jacob Taylor. Oscar owns PCL imports and sometimes uses Jacob's charter company to transport goods.'

'That was quite a mouthful, it's easier to remember when you look at the mind map you created,' Kelly says, but there is admiration in her tone.

Andy asks. 'What are your thoughts Miss Young?'

'How do you know it's "miss"?'

'No wedding ring, and no change in skin colour either.'

'You're observant. Okay my thoughts. I think you certainly have some viable candidates here, I know you don't have much on them, but it's definitely a good start. Some people that stand out for me are Ryan Hunt, Nathan Brown and the two linked to Benjamin Black. You're right when you say Benjamin is under the spotlight, the FBI is always watching him, so I don't think he would've pulled the trigger, but as you say, he could've arranged for it to be done. I don't know too much about the other three.' Kelly points at the names of Victor, Shane and Gilbert. 'But I'm sure they're on this board for a good reason. Just remember what I said because it's important.' She looks at the three detectives. 'It is still very possible that the person behind the murders could have done it him- or herself.'

'Must be a man.'

Kelly frowns. 'Why do you say that?'

'Freddy was strong and he had defensive wounds; he was also a very good fighter. Trust me Kelly, any woman would have a hard time fighting Freddy off, ask his wife.' Peter looks sad as he speaks. 'And if you look at the women who are suspects, you'll see that none of them have the physique which would indicate that they are strong enough to take him, not even armed. Freddy would've shattered them.'

Kelly nods. 'I'll trust your judgement Peter. So, to correct myself, just don't let the Savage family men and inner circle men fall too far into the back of your mind.' A brief silence passes. 'Do you guys have more notes or comments?'

Andy speaks up. 'Just one more, Miss Young. I made some phone calls but I can't seem to arrange something.'

'What do you want to arrange?'

'We want to have Nathan Brown released from protective custody.'

'I'll make some phone calls later, and I can guarantee you that he'll be back in town tomorrow.'

'Thank you, Ma'am,' Andy says respectfully.

'Actually, Peter can I use your phone quickly?'

'Sure, it's on the kitchen counter.'

Kelly dials a number and the phone rings. 'Hi, good morning this is Special Agent Kelly Young from the FBI.' A pause. 'Yes I'm calling about a man who was placed in protective custody, a Mr Nathan Brown.' A short silence. 'I would like to request that Nathan be released from his protective custody, I will arrange the necessary documentation, but it needs to be done, he is critical to a murder case that we're investigating at the moment.' Another silence, this one longer. Kelly starts to frown and her tone changes. 'Okay understood, thank for your time.' She places the phone back where she found it and turns to Anderson. 'Are you sure that you were unsuccessful?'

'Yes Ma'am, why?'

'Another request was filed for his release about six weeks ago, and it was approved two days after the request was filed. Nathan's no longer in protective custody, he's in New Orleans, he's here, and he has been for almost six weeks.'

'That means he *was* in town at the time of the murder.' Peter says angrily.

Chapter 25

On the way to Dr Rayne's office Peter wonders what he might expect this time. The bullet is through the church now, there's no turning back; he's raped a girl and it's done, he can't take that back. Might as well commit now. As he approaches the building his heart starts to bang in his chest, it brings back the memory of the crying girl, it's not so sexy to him when he might be forced to do it again. Not that he was forced, he could've arrested the two of them there and then. But it's too late for that train of thought. By now the security guards know him, they don't even check him anymore, they just let him walk in.

'Hello, Detective,' Diana coolly says.

'Finding you in the lobby is new to me.'

'I'm a couple of minutes behind schedule, but that's okay.' A long, awkward silence persists as they wait for the elevator. As the doors open, Diana breaks the silence. 'You know you shouldn't feel guilty.'

'But I do.'

'Didn't you enjoy it?'

'In the moment maybe, but now I'm not so sure if it was a good idea.'

'You had to experience control, Detective, and there was no better way of giving you that experience.' Diana turns to him, 'What about the ending?'

He faces her. 'The ending was a surprise.'

'Did you like it?'

'I loved it,' Peter says, thinking it might happen again.

'You see.'

'See what?'

'All I had to do was remind you of the pleasure.' She grabs Peter between his legs, feeling an erect penis. 'And look, or rather, feel, you've already forgotten about the guilt.' She passionately kisses Peter. 'Hello, Detective. You never greeted me.'

Peter is stunned by Diana's sexuality, nervously he says, 'Hello, Diana.' She lets go as the doors open. 'What are we doing today?'

'Something different, something that will provoke less guilt.'

'Detective,' the doctor says smoothly, 'always a pleasure to see you.'

'Morning Doctor.'

'Have a seat.' Dr Rayne points Peter over to the desk. Once again Diana disappears into the closed room. 'You seem nervous, Detective.'

'I am a little bit nervous. Last time we had this meeting, I raped someone.'

'Do I sense some regret? Are you drawn to repentance? You do know that would require a confession, Detective?'

'It would ruin my career.'

'It would.' Dr Rayne sits forward, opens his drawer and takes out two tumblers and a bottle of whiskey; he starts to pour. 'There's no need to feel guilty. I explained that I will change your way of thinking, and that is what we're busy with. I need you to rid your mind of this guilty feeling. It's okay.'

'I raped someone. What was the purpose of that?'

'To teach you what it feels like to be in control at the cost of someone else's terror. Don't you think that's what your killer experiences?'

'He doesn't *rape* people,' Peter snarls aggressively.

'It was either rape or murder, Detective, only those two acts can give you that experience. And I would prefer you don't kill someone in my office.' He hands Peter one of the tumblers.

Peter sips the whiskey; it has a wonderful oak aroma. 'This is smooth. What's the plan for today?'

'Last time we made you take control, and today you will use that control.'

'What does that mean?'

'It means, Detective that you must use that control that you obtained and apply it to your own mind. You must take control of your own thoughts in order to accomplish today's exercise. Today is all about taking innocence.'

Peter frowns. 'Didn't I take innocence last week?'

Dr Rayne shakes his head, 'No you did not, you might have lost your own innocence, but you didn't take someone else's.' Dr Rayne gets up and walks over to the door. 'Come, finish your drink and when you are ready, come find us.'

After some time, Peter gets up and walks to the room. He takes a deep breath, and goes in. This time he sees a cage on the table, and inside the cage is a small puppy. 'What's with the dog?'

Diana walks to Peter. 'We want you to take innocence.' She hands Peter a knife. The blade is almost four inches long, and extremely sharp. 'We want you to stab the puppy to death.'

Peter refuses to take the knife, 'I won't do it.'

'Why not?' Dr Rayne asks, 'Because it's an animal? A dog? A puppy? Maybe because it's innocent?'

'This is animal abuse, Doctor; I won't do it.'

'And I agree with you. It *is* animal abuse.'

'Then why the fuck would you have me do this?'

'Because all killers start with animals, Detective.' Dr Rayne says in a voice tinged with impatience.

'Fuck this I'm done. I won't do this.' He steps back but Diana leaps toward the cage, opens it and takes the puppy out. 'Diana, what are you doing?'

'You need to do this!'

'You're crazy. I refuse.' Diana takes the knife and sticks it into the puppy's abdomen. It starts to whimper and then to yelp unstoppably. She puts it on the ground, and blood gushes from beneath it. 'What the *fuck*, Diana?' He can't believe his eyes.

'Will you let it suffer?' She throws Peter the knife, eyes taunting and challenging him.

'You're sick!' He runs to the puppy, hoping to save it, but Dr Rayne locks the door. 'Open it! Open it or I'll kill you,' he shouts. Out of control now.

'You're more than welcome to try, but the easy way out will be to kill the dog and put it out of its misery,' Dr Rayne drawls nonchalantly

'Why are you doing this?' But only silence answers Peter. He looks at the whining dog and a tear runs down his cheek. 'I'm sorry,' he whispers. He puts the knife to the terrified puppy's throat, and in one swift motion separates its body from its head. Blood spurts out of the open neck, covering Peter with blood, but the whining has stopped. 'Why did you make me do this?'

'So that you could kill something innocent,' Dr Rayne answers, taking Peter's shoulder. 'Detective, it's okay, remember people kill cattle and sheep and pigs and rabbits every day, to eat them. This was just another animal, like humans are just animals to your killer.'

'I don't like this anymore,' Peter says in a calm and soft voice.

'I want to ask you Detective, do you feel worse about raping the girl, or killing the dog?'

'What sort of question is that?'

'One that comes with an answer.'

'The dog.'

'And that's normal.' He leads Peter outside. 'I know this was difficult, and I don't want you killing any animals, so I'll never let you do it again. But you had to know what it feels like to kill something innocent. Think about the emotion you experienced, your killer doesn't have that. If I had to give the killer that dog to kill, in all probability, he would've done it without thinking about it. That gives you a clue about what type of person he is. I'll tell you a secret. The dog didn't whine because of pain, it whined because of *fear*. I gave it a nerve block before you got here. I can promise you it felt nothing. The point was not for the dog to feel pain, the point was for you to feel that emotion, so that you can know what the killer lacks.'

'It felt nothing?'

'Nothing.'

'Why didn't you tell me this beforehand?'

'Because it wouldn't have provoked the same emotion.' He looks deeply into Peter's eyes. 'The girl you raped…'

'Yes?'

'I paid her. I paid her and told her that someone would rape her.'

'And she agreed?'

'Everyone has their price,' Dr Rayne shrugs. He sits down in his chair. 'I didn't want you to become a criminal, detective; I merely wanted you to think like one.'

Chapter 26

Kelly walks into the office, early as usual. It seems she never starts a day late. As usual Brady and Peter are at their desks, having an early morning coffee. Andy is still not at the office; he never comes in early. His view is that if he needs to be there at eight, then he'll be there at eight.

'Good morning guys,' Kelly says with four coffees from a nearby coffee shop in her hands.

Brady gets up hastily. 'Morning Kelly, how did you sleep?'

Peter quickly squeezes his greeting in with a wave. 'Morning!'

'I slept well thanks and you?'

Peter has noticed Brady's behaviour change whenever Kelly walks in. 'Good thank you, the coffee looks amazing, I presume they're for us?' He winks at her.

'No, they're for the fairies behind your ears,' she replies jokingly. She hands Brady a cup and places the other three in front of Peter. 'There's one for you too.' She says to Peter while removing a cup for herself. 'Where's Detective Anderson?'

'He never comes in early.'

'This coffee is divine, where did you buy it?' asks Brady

'There's a small coffee shop about two blocks from here, I found it yesterday.' She smiles. 'So are you guys ready for tonight?'

Shocked Brady replies. 'Tonight?' He turns to Peter as if Peter could supply the missing information.

Peter also looks fairly confused. 'Don't look at me, I have no idea.'

'Oh crap! This one is on me, I forgot to tell you about it. Please tell me you're not busy tonight?'

In synchrony the two detectives answer, 'Nothing planned.'

Relieved Kelly replies. 'Good, we have a stakeout tonight.'

'That sounds like fun, where?'

'The Savage family is hosting another event at their house, and we're going to sneak in and have a peek at what they're doing and who's going.'

'How on earth did you get that authorised?' Brady asks.

'I know the right people. One of our undercover agents received some information about it, apparently it's a small gathering, so not everyone in town will be there, but our undercover operative will. He will set up cameras through the house in strategic places and we will sit in a van listening and watching. Unfortunately, as you guys know, that place is a fortress, there's no way to get in there without getting caught.'

'So when you said we're going to sneak in, you meant cameras will be snuck in and we'll watch it all on a screen like a couple of nerds?' Peter replies.

'That is exactly what I meant.' She looks around. 'Where is Anderson? Surely he should've been here by now?'

The captain walks by just as she asked the question and responds, 'Oh no, he's in hospital, he won't be coming in for the next couple of days.'

'I guess it's just the three of us then. I would suggest that you go home early and get some rest, and don't forget snacks. I'll meet you here tonight and we can all leave in the van from here.'

'What time do you want to leave?'

'I think if we leave here at eight it should be fine.'

Kelly, Brady and Peter all leave the office early in preparation for their big night. Finally, Peter and Brady have the opportunity to peek behind the curtains at the Savage house to see exactly what's going on. The day passes quickly and the weather doesn't seem to play ball. It's much easier to stay hidden when it's rainy, but there's usually some interference with the camera signals. Hopefully tonight will be different, it's crucial that they don't have equipment problems. Somewhere after seven Peter arrives, the first of the three, he's almost an hour early. Peter sits in his car waiting for the others. He watches the precinct from outside as the last couple of things are said during shift handover. It would be possible for Peter to sit inside the precinct and wait, but he's quite suspicious of the group, one never knows who they have on their payroll. The rain is cold and hard, and the wind makes it fall at an angle. Some officers came unprepared, and hand over the vehicles in the rain with their jackets pulled over their heads. The officers move in the same manner that ants do when it rains, single file and almost perfectly coordinated. A sudden and continuous knock on the passenger window frightens Peter; it's a man with no umbrella, it's Brady. He unlocks the door. 'You're going to wet my seats.'

'Fuck this rain,' Brady says jumping in, shivering. 'I'll clean the seats for you don't worry. Why are you sitting here in the car? No umbrella?'

'I just don't know who these people have on their payroll.' Peter searches the car vigorously for something.

'I can't find my watch, and this stupid car clock doesn't keep time, what time is it?'

Brady inspects his right wrist. 'Twenty to eight.' Peter has been sitting there for almost half an hour, without noticing.

'Your watch is on the wrong hand.'

'I don't care.' Bright, high lights pull up behind them, blinding Peter in the mirror. Brady turns around and looks out the back window. 'Must be Kelly.' He climbs out of Peter's car, slamming the door in the run to the van behind.

'Fucker almost slammed the door right through to the other side,' Peter mumbles as he, too, runs to the van.

Both of them are sitting in the back of the van and Kelly is behind the wheel. 'Hello boys.'

'Shit! What a night! Hi. How's this weather?' The two detectives are astonished by the equipment in the back of the van. 'Luckily Anderson couldn't come, there's only three seats back here.' In front of each seat is a set of four screens, each probably programmable to a different camera. Also each seat has a headset with a switch on the desk where it is connected, to change which channel's audio to pick up.

'Did you guys bring snacks?'

Peter and Brady look at each other with the same emotionless expression. Peter looks down and whispers, 'Fuck.'

'Me too bud, I also forgot. That would be a negative, Special Agent Young. That would be a negative.'

'You can never leave that to a man.' She holds out a bag filled with something. 'I've learned over the years.' She places the bag on the floor, it's filled with snacks and drinks. The motor of the van is soft and can't be heard over the rain while they drive. Kelly takes all the back roads, and it looks like she's scoped the place well. They pull off a gravel road and are now travelling on a muddy back road and they are just in range for the cameras, somewhere in the bushes. Neither Peter nor Brady know where they are. The van is black and with the rain and the thick forest, the van is invisible. 'This is the perfect spot.'

'How did you come across this place?'

'Satellites,' Kelly says, concentrating. She pulls some switches and presses buttons, and in what seems like a second, the windows are darkened and a low-wattage black light is turned on at the back. From the outside, the van is completely blackened by the night, but on the inside every marking that is in white, now glows. Only two televisions go on. 'Sorry guys, this weather interferes. I've spoken to our contact, and he says that only two cameras seem to have signal. He will place one inside the room where they sit, and the other one at the entrance so we can see if someone leaves.'

'I guess that's better than nothing.' One of the cameras at the door, is angled up from waist height. The faces of the guests can be made out clearly; the other camera is in a corner, and unfortunately when the people are seated around a "U" shaped table, half of them can be seen, and only the backs of the other people are visible. Peter places the headset on his head. 'Kelly.' He pulls the one earpiece off. 'How do I switch on the audio feed?'

'It is on.' She fiddles with a couple of knobs and switches. 'Now?'

'Nothing.'

'You've got to be kidding me.' She fiddles and fiddles, but with no success. 'It's the weather. Whenever something happens, write down every detail about that moment, and afterwards I will ask our operative if he can remember the conversation. I'm sorry guys, everything seems to fail tonight.'

'Not everything.' Peter says. 'Look who just arrived.' Peter, Brady and Kelly look at closely at the screens. Every person that they have on their board is there, all but one, and then Kelly and Brady see the person, right in the corner over by the bar: Nathan. 'At least we now have confirmation that he's connected here.'

'Initially I doubted you guys, but I must say, job well done.'

Brady replies, 'Look there are a couple of people here tonight that we don't have as suspects, and one or two that I don't recognise from the party, but this confirms our suspicion about the members of the group.'

'I agree,' Peter nods. They sit in the van for just over an hour, and the screens reveal nothing significant, people are eating and talking. At one stage John was talking to the group, but that's nothing new, nothing suspicious. But then someone's arm seems to point aggressively in Nathan's direction; it's Benjamin, and he seems very upset. 'Here we go,' Peter says. Benjamin and Nathan get up out of their chairs. Clearly, they're screaming at each other, their body language speaks for itself, aggressive and choppy movements. The two approach each other, but before a fistfight breaks out, Ryan Hunt pulls a gun out, and they both stop. For a moment they stand there, listening to whatever Ryan has to say, then return to their seats. 'Now *that* I wish I heard,' Peter says softly.

'I'll find out what the conversation was there.' Kelly's phone vibrates. She looks down, a message. 'Guys we have to go.'

'What? Why?'

'I just received a text message from our man inside, the argument was about us. Benjamin said that they know the FBI is spying on them and he also suspects that we might be watching them now. He blamed Nathan, he said Nathan is the reason why we're watching.' She switches off the equipment and starts the van. The windows lighten and she switches the lights on. 'Ahh!' She screams as a figure appears. Kelly struggles to get her gun out of the holster. The two detectives' guns are already drawn, but the man just stands there.

'Kelly, just leave, just drive, he's not armed, they're trying to intimidate us,' Brady says. Kelly pulls of shakily and the man keeps eye contact, soaking wet in the rain, as Kelly drives off. 'Okay we're clear, is everyone okay?' Brady asks.

Peter responds. 'All good from my side.'

'Kelly?' But she only cries. 'Kelly are you all right?'

She gets a word out, while nodding, 'Yes.' She drives uncomfortably fast in the rain, racing back to the precinct. 'What if they follow us?'

'They won't.' Brady puts his hand on her shoulder. The trip back to the precinct feels much faster than the trip out was. 'Are you okay?'

'They scare me tonight. I can deal with them knowing, but that man, just standing there with no warning, he could've killed us.'

'But he didn't, we're all okay. Do you want me to come to the hotel with you tonight? I'll sleep on the couch.'

'No it's okay.'

'I really don't mind.'

'Are you sure?'

'I'm sure, I promise.' Brady responds.

'I wonder what he meant when he said Nathan is the reason we're watching.' All of them go home, a little shocked. Peter to his house, and Brady with Kelly to the hotel.

Chapter 27

A couple of days later, Lily visits for the weekend. She has a meeting scheduled with Francis Linwood, it's nothing serious, but she wants feedback on her blog. *I'm quite excited to hear what Francis has to say about my blog. I've never written anything like this. I'm not sure what to write about next though, maybe I should continue with the mystery man somehow, or maybe I should do something entirely new. I'm not sure yet. I'll wait for the feedback and see if people liked the mystery man. One thing is for sure, I'd like to write a bit more next time, the first one felt so short. It also felt a bit more poetic than I hoped for, I mean I'm not writing poems here for crying out loud. I just got caught off guard. I wonder if Michael's had a similar experience; this mystery man pulling strings for him. I'll ask him when I see him, I want to visit anyway, he's such a nice guy. If only I was a bit older; he's eight years older than me. Well. No. I don't know. If nothing happens at least I've made a nice friend. He's just so open-minded, friendly and relaxed; so charismatic. And I mean all artists are sexy, but Michael... Michael is right up there with the sexiest people I've ever seen. I just want to drag my fingers through his long black hair, I never thought I'd like a man whose hair touches his shoulders, it's very sexy. His eyes, that is what melts me, striking green, amazing.* Lily continues to think of Michael for a while, then of his art. Michael's art is amazing and extravagant, he is a very talented artist. It seems from his gallery that he can paint in any style or genre; every category and every painting is flawless. Whether simple or intricate, he never misses a stroke, never makes a mistake. Each painting is absolutely perfect. Lily's plan is to see Francis first, then visit Michael and after Michael, go to her parents.

'Lily! A pleasure as always to have this young beauty in my presence. Sit, sit, sit.' Francis pulls out a chair for her in his office.

'Hello Sir,' She replies politely and sits down.

'Sir? Thank you for your affability Lily, but you can call me Francis.' He sits down next to her. 'So, tell me, what's on your mind?'

'I just want to find out if you're happy with my blog. Did I make any mistakes? Did people like it? Do I have to change anything?' she asks nervously.

Francis chuckles. 'You are far too nervous my dear. We've only received positive reviews for your blog, and in fact we have received some requests for it to stay, not that it was going anywhere.'

'Thank goodness.'

He gets up and pours two cups of black coffee. 'Milk and sugar?'

'None thank you.'

Francis brings her cup, the coffee smells divine. 'So tell me, this mystery man, is he a character of fiction, or is he real? Oh, and if he's real, have you met him?' He asks her excitedly.

'Oh no... he's real, but I haven't met him. I only receive a letter from him every now and then. Can I ask you advice about my writing?'

'Of course! What can I help with?'

'Do you think I should continue with the mystery man or do something different?'

'Hmm... it's difficult to say. Let me think for a moment.' He rubs his chin and sips at his coffee and after a couple of seconds, says, 'Aha! I have an idea. Tell me if you like it or not. What if you spoke a little about him every time, in other words write something new about him, tell the world how you would imagine him or how you picture him to be, then write to him. As in respond to his letters? Talk to him in your blog, and let everyone read, they won't necessarily understand that you are *replying* to him, but they'll know you're talking to him. What do you think?'

'I think it's brilliant. Now I see why you're in charge here,' she jokes, feeling light and relieved.

'We have jokes, I see,' he jokes back.

'Then do you want me to write it once a week?'

'If you want to, if not, then it doesn't matter. If you write once a week for some time and then skip one or two weeks, it's okay, it will keep the readers on their toes.' He talks almost as if his only goal is to keep Lily happy.

'I'll try and write regularly, but if I end up writing more erratically, please excuse me. With university I might forget every now and then.'

'And of course, it will also be dependent on the number of letters you get.'

'Also true yes.'

'Well, I think this is going to work out perfectly, you seem very talented. And it's good that we have some young blood on our team now.'

'Thank you for the compliment.' Lily finishes her coffee with Francis, impressed with their discussion. Now there's one person she really wants to see and tell about the meeting. She hurries over to Pure Imagination Art Gallery to see Michael. She wants to surprise him.

Soon after she left the New Orleans Weekly's offices, she arrives at Michael, but she doesn't see him painting. The doors of the gallery are open though, so she walks in and notices a new painting hanging on the back of the wall. She walks closer to investigate. This is the second painting in the gallery that does not have Michael's name on it. The colours are also the same as that of the other one. It must be the same artist—it must be J. This is an interesting picture; a hooded, shadowy figure stands at the entrance to a forest, with the moon big and bright, and red. The two paintings complement each other beautifully, with a strange similarity, yet a great contrast.

'Michael!' Lily yells happily, as she sees Michael emerge from his office. 'I see you have a new painting here.'

'What a nice surprise.' Michael says in a soft and happy tone. 'It's pretty hey?'

'Very pretty. From J?'

'Yes.'

'I received a letter from him.'

'It seems like he contacts us at very similar times.' Michael replies, sounding puzzled.

'It does seem that way; so, I have a story for you.'

'What is it?'

'You know that he gave me a letter saying that I will get an opportunity to write in the paper?'

'I remember the letter vaguely.'

'He pulled some strings and somehow in some way he got me the opportunity to blog for the New Orleans Weekly.'

Michael pulls two chairs closer and puts them in front of the new painting. 'Oh yes! I remember reading it, it was about the mysterious man?'

'Yes, so Francis and I—you know, Francis from the paper? Well, we just had a chat about how to write this blog. The idea came up that I would respond to his letters in the paper, as in talk to him directly, what do you think?'

Michael lifts his eyebrows, looking keen. 'That sounds interesting. I think it's a great idea. Maybe ask him about these paintings.' He jokes and points to the paintings with his head. 'If I look at these paintings in depth, I sometimes wonder if the man who did them is lonely.'

'Why do you think he's lonely?'

'These paintings are perfect, but why just give them to me? Why write you those letters? People who are lonely do things like this, don't you think?' He stands up and examines the new painting. 'And look at the way he paints the person; in both paintings, the face is hidden and the man is alone… alone to face the world. It's sad. Either he's lonely or for some reason he feels like he is, in other words, maybe he feels superior to everyone around him, above them in a sense.'

'That's creepy.'

'In its very own way, it's beautiful.'

'Last time he gave you a painting, he also gave you a poem, what's this one's poem?'

'Nothing written, but the delivery man said that he had a message and then said that in the light of the moon, all becomes clear.' Michael looks at Lily. 'Or something like that.'

Lily sits up. 'Sometimes when I think of him, I wonder why us; why would he communicate with us? But then other times I think that it's exciting, and it is! How many people have mutual stalkers, nice stalkers?'

'I don't think he's a stalker. Do you think we've met him?'

'Do you?'

'Why else would he choose us?'

Lily gets excited; she likes thinking about things like this. 'Let's just pretend for a moment, out of everyone, who do you think it could be?'

'I bet it's some ordinary-looking guy, right in the open. And it must be someone that both of us could've met, without our own paths crossing. A pilot?'

'I've never met a pilot.'

'Hmm.' Michael thinks for a while. 'What about a waiter?'

'You think a waiter could do this?'

'I think anyone could do this if given the right drive.'

Chapter 28

A couple of days later, Nathan returns to his shop, angry with the Savage group. *I hate those people. I'm convinced that they must be involved here, who else would kill people like that, and that fucking Benjamin, what a piece of work. I'm sure he's the one, and he thinks I threw them under the bus, they threw me under the bus!* 'Piece of shit,' he whispers to himself. *I should've said no when Evelyn wanted me to join them.*

Nathan walks around the shop, and switches lights on as he goes. The police have messed his whole place up, nothing is where he left it, some of his products are missing too, and dust has gathered on the remaining products. He fetches a broom from behind the counter and starts sweeping the floor. He hears a rattle from the storage room. 'Fucking rats!' he screams in irritation. Between the police and the rats, he's bound to lose more money than what he already has by not being at the shop for the past couple of months. He walks swiftly with the broom in his hand to the back, murder in his eyes. He unlocks the door and it creaks open, but the light won't switch on. The irritation is piling up inside him; now he must walk back to find a torch. The light is dim, but it'll do for now. The torch light shines yellow on the boxes as he moves it around the room, searching for the rats. He moves the light fast from left to right, up and down, hoping to spot the rats; something catches his eye, something glossy, but it disappears when he shines the light on the same spot for a second time.

'Hey!' he calls out, but no response. More noise.

'Hey, who's there?' Nathan calls out again. A small, heavy box is thrown in his direction, knocking the torch out of his hand. The torch shatters on the floor, and he's left with only a glimmer of light from the small opening in the door. 'Hey! Show yourself!'

Without warning, the door shuts with a bang. Nathan is left in darkness. He starts to feel uneasy.

'Come on man, this isn't funny,' he says nervously. The boxes move behind him. Nathan reacts instantly; he swings the broom around and hits a box. Now he's looking for an escape.

'Psst.' Someone whispers behind him. Nathan turns around, shaking. 'Psst.' Behind him again.

'Please man, this isn't funny!' Someone runs behind him slicing his back with a sharp object. 'Fuuuck!' Nathan screams in pain; he can feel the warmth on his skin as the wound starts to bleed. He hears laughing in the distance and starts to cry. 'Please, what do you want?' he screams. But there's no answer. A hard object knocks him on the back of his head, he crashes to the floor, but he's still conscious. He screams as the axe drives through his left arm, amputating it a couple of inches above the wrist. The screaming doesn't stop, but he pulls his arm to his abdomen, blood running out as if a tap was opened. Nathan turns on his back, hoping that he can defend himself in some way, but a hack at his chest stops the screaming. Nathan can't breathe and he quickly grabs at his chest with his right hand. The killer hacks at his chest again but partially amputates his right arm below the elbow and fractures his arm above it. Now there are only short bursts of bubbling cries from Nathan. For a moment he thinks it has stopped, but after a brief pause, the killer starts to grunt and hacks repeatedly at Nathan. The axe drives into his collar bone, his chest, his abdomen, repeatedly. With a final blow, the axe stops with a crack in Nathan's skull, splitting his face and head in two, Nathan's pale body spasms briefly and relaxes as the man pulls the dripping axe from his head. A bright headlamp switches on; the killer is covered in a plastic suit found in one of the cleaning kits from the shop, he shines the light on Nathan's bloodied and mutilated body and looks around, he sees the severed left hand and wrist. The man pulls a scalpel from his pocket and cuts a triangle into the wrist, with the apex pointing to the hand, and places it neatly next to the arm where it is severed, and leaves the axe next to Nathan's body. Calm and composed the man takes off the plastic suit and places it in a bucket with some acid also found in the shop, and the suit disintegrates almost immediately. The man walks to the front desk and with a bloodied glove dials 911, and disappears.

'Detective Jones hello.' Peter sits on the couch paging through an old album, the only one he owns, as the call comes through.

'Peter, it's the captain here. Listen you need to make your way to Nathan's shop, a 911 call was made from there, and the officer on scene is quite upset, he found Nathan.'

'I'm on my way, Sir.'

'Good I've already spoke to Harris and Anderson, they're meeting you there.'

'Copy that, Sir.' Peter stops paging when he gets to a picture of him and Lily in her room, she was still in school then. Peter smiles, but as he closes the album he notices something, and quickly opens the album again, and there it is, her necklace, a triangle pendant. Quickly he calls the captain back. 'Sir.'

'Peter.'

'I might have found a connection. Well I hope so.' He says, excited.

Curious, the captain replies, 'What did you find?'

'I think I might have found a person connected with the killer; Lily Tomlinson.'

'Your friend Lily?'

'Yes, Sir.'

'How on earth are they connected?'

'I'm not sure yet sir, but I found a picture of her wearing a necklace with a triangle pendant.'

'Peter I'm sure there are many things with triangles on them, not everyone who owns a triangle can be a suspect now.'

Peter gets frustrated. 'Sir, I understand that, but Freddy always had a thing for Lily, he created videos of her and flirted with her. Please, I know it's a long shot, but we don't have much else.'

With doubt in his voice the captain replies. 'All right I'll give you this one, but Detective, if you're wrong and this goes pear-shaped, it's your head, understood?'

'I understand sir, I'm going to take her to the crime scene.' Peter ends the conversation and calls Lily. 'Hey Lily.'

'My dear friend, Peter! I was just thinking about you.'

'That's always nice to hear,' he says distractedly. 'Lily I want to ask you a question.'

'Okay I'm all ears.'

Peter doesn't know how to approach the subject. 'Lily, do you remember that triangle necklace you had?'

'Of course, I still have it why?'

'Do you remember where you got it?'

'Not really, I remember finding it in my locker at school, with a letter, the person apologised for opening my locker but he wanted to give me the gift anonymously. The letter said that it was one of a kind.' Lily's voice changes. 'Why do you ask?'

'This is going to sound strange but I want you to trust me, I think that you might somehow be connected to the murders… now I might be wrong, but I want to make sure.'

'Okay. Am I a suspect?' Lily sounds nervous.

'Not at all. However, would you mind coming to the crime scene with me? I'll say you're part of media.'

'Um… okay.'

'Great I'll pick you up in ten minutes, and thank you.' Peter puts down the phone and gets dressed. On the way to the crime scene Peter picks Lily up, and they race to the crime scene, blue lights flashing Lily's nervous, but Peter might have just found a good lead.

'Hold up Ma'am,' one of the officers says to Lily as she tries to pass under the barrier tape.

Peter pushes him back. 'She's with me, Officer.' He arrogantly flashes his badge.

'Pete what's Lily doing here?' Brady asks, emerging from the crowd.

'I'll explain later, but I think she's connected in some way; take us to him.'

'Are you sure you want her to see him?'

Peter turns to Lily. 'If you don't want to see the body, or if you think you've seen more than you can manage, tell me, all right?'

'I think I'll be okay,' Lily says as Brady leads her and Peter to Nathan's corpse. 'Oh my word.' Lily turns pale when she smells the strong metallic smell of blood and the sickening odour of faeces. There's blood everywhere, and some of his organs can be seen poking out from his abdomen, he has been eviscerated. His face is in two and only a small portion of his brain can be seen as it has retracted into the skull.

'Peter?' Kelly asks.

'I'll explain later.' He takes Lily's hand. 'I know it's difficult, but Lily please tell me if you recognise anything about this man or this shop.' Lily is covering her mouth with her hand, evidently, she's nauseous. But she shakes her head, no. 'Lily have you ever heard of a man called Nathan Brown?' But again she shakes her head. 'Each of these people have been marked with a triangle, like your necklace. If you think of anything, please let me know.'

Lily replies softly and turns away. 'I will. Whoever did this is a monster.'

Peter calls an officer over with a gesture. 'Officer please take this lady to my car. And get her something to drink.' Peter turns to his colleagues. 'This is a long shot I know, but a couple of years ago Lily received a necklace with a triangle pendant from an unknown person. I don't know how the last two murders tie in with her, but I know there might have been a connection with Freddy. So bear with me. I'm going to involve her until we can prove that there is no connection between her, and any of the victims.'

Kelly steps forward. 'You'll have to be careful, seeing things like this can change a person.'

'In my defence, I didn't expect it to be so brutal.'

'Neither did we. He still cut the triangle, even with the hand being cut off.'

In a monotone, Anderson says, 'At least we can exclude Evelyn Brown for now.'

Kelly looks at Brady, then Peter. 'I think we should meet at your place in two hours. Then we can talk about it properly.'

Chapter 29

As usual, Anderson arrives first at Peter's house, but stays outside puffing away at his pipe. Harris, being of military inclination, arrives second, always on time. 'Police! Come out with your hands up!' Brady jokes as he enters the house, but to his surprise, Kelly beat them both to it. She has already helped Peter set up the whiteboard and four chairs with a table; at least this time they have a table. 'You guys are way too eager,' Brady says in a friendly tone.

Kelly rolls her eyes at Brady. 'Actually, we're packing up, you're too late.' She smiles and walks over to give him a hug. 'Peter just went to squeeze a kidney, he'll be right out.'

'Squeeze a kidney?'

'Went to the bathroom.'

'Ooooh,' Brady chuckles.

'So far, the only thing that we've done is we took Evelyn and Nathan's names out and just placed them at the bottom, so as you can see Gilbert Wilburn is now only connected to Kathy Larson.'

Andy walks in. 'Evening Miss Young.'

'Hi, Andy,' she says as she waves.

Peter returns from the bathroom. 'Hello boys.'

Almost at the same time, the two detectives reply, 'Hey.'

'Get your drinks and come sit, I have some information for you guys,' says Kelly.

Brady pours two whiskeys, one for him and one for Anderson, and a glass of wine for Peter. 'Kelly, what are you having?'

'I'm okay thank you, I have iced tea, I'll have a drink when we've finished here.' She walks over to the board and waits for the three detectives to sit down. 'Pete I think we should leave everything like this, then we don't have to set up every time we come over.'

'I thought about it, but if I have visitors then I have to pack up again.'

'You get visitors?' Andy asks, incredulously.

'Well. Okay. I guess we can leave it there.'

Kelly points at the board. 'As you guys can see here, Nathan and Evelyn's names are now stuck at the bottom. I removed Nathan for obvious reasons and I removed Evelyn for now, because I doubt that she would have her own cousin killed. However, this does not mean that the group isn't still behind it. I have spoken to our informant inside the group and he said that the conversation that night between Benjamin and Nathan was very heated, as we could see. Apparently Benjamin was furious with Nathan, stating that Nathan threw the group under the bus, and Nathan retaliated and then there was screaming. Our informant said that Nathan and Benjamin never got along in any case. That also confirms the fact that the organisation still exists and that the Savage group plays a role here.'

'So the FBI is taking over?'

'At first our director wanted to, however I spoke with him and told him about us getting caught. In a nutshell, he will give out the word that the FBI is no longer involved with the investigation, but will leave me on the case. His hope is that with your help, we can flush out some more members. The FBI will still track Benjamin, but I have been moved to this case with you. So no, the FBI is not taking over, we will continue here and see what we can find with this group and how they are connected.'

'Thank goodness.'

'The only puzzle piece here that I can't figure out yet, is how Lily Tomlinson fits in. Peter would you mind enlightening us please?'

'Give me a moment.' Peter disappears into his bedroom, and emerges with the album. He pages to the picture of him and Lily, takes it out and places it on the table. 'For now, it's just a suspicion, but I would like us to entertain this for a while. In this photo, Lily wears a necklace with a triangle pendant. Lily says that this is one of a kind and was given to her in school by some anonymous character. It was a gift to her, and nowhere can another one like this be found. I don't know how the subsequent murders connect to her yet, but Freddy was connected for sure. It came out that Fred made videos of Lily while she was in the shower and so on. It's a long shot, I know that, but if it comes out that she's not connected, I'll gladly drop it. For now I think we should involve her, maybe she picks something up or makes a connection that we wouldn't have.'

'I agree with Pete.' Says Brady and Andy agrees with a nod of the head.

'All right, we'll pursue it.' Kelly replies. 'This leaves us with seven suspects and their respective connections. We have Victor Quinn, Gilbert Wilburn, Shane Clemente, Ryan Hunt, Edward Valentine, and Oscar Reid. The last two connected to Benjamin Black. But before we look any deeper into Benjamin, I think we should start with Shane. All these triangles are cut with something sharp, potentially a scalpel, and I'm not saying that it is, or that no one else could get hold of a scalpel, but I think it would be a good place to start. What do you guys think?'

'We have to start somewhere, and that's a logical place to start,' Anderson says.

'I agree,' says Brady.

Peter rubs his chin, 'Makes sense to me.' He takes a sip. 'I really thought it would be Nathan.'

'Me too. But I must say people never come off easy when they betray organisations such as this one,' Kelly replies. 'It was absolutely brutal.'

'It's interesting how this man adapts his MO,' Brady muses.

'I wasn't with you guys for the first one, and I think if these kits were available we probably would still not have any blood. But if you look at the murders from the first one to the last, it seems that each one becomes increasingly vicious. Hopefully we catch him before there's another murder, but I think the killer is starting to enjoy the act of killing; he's exploring.'

'Is that normal?'

'The FBI has seen a couple of cases like this in the past, luckily the killers got caught. But when they were interrogated, it came out that the longer they were out there, the more risky the murders became. Apparently, they enjoy the thrill of the chase.'

'In other words, they taunt us.'

'Exactly,' Kelly replies. 'Fortunately it also gives rise to another trend. With each kill, they became more and more sloppy as the murders progressed in brutality. And eventually, because they thought they would not get caught, their egos grew, and they took less care in cleaning up after themselves.'

'This one still had no evidence, the man left nothing behind, either,' Peter points out.

'The techs on scene said that the one bucket had dissolved plastic in there; no evidence, but the man potentially used one of the plastic suits found in the cleaning kits. The axe was also clean, they suspect he used gloves,' Brady replies.

Anderson sits forward. 'The part that bothers me the most is how these victims are chosen. They are in no way connected to each other.'

'And if they are connected to Lily... how?'

Kelly answers, 'We have to also look at the facts of the last one, remember, if it's connected to the organisation, then Nathan was potentially an example. So we have to look closer at the previous two victims, we know how the first victim is connected, or rather was connected to Lily, but not the second one yet. This is going to sound horrible, but we'll probably have to wait for a next murder to be able to make this connection.'

'Well it's not like we have anything else to go on,' Peter mutters, despondently.

'For now, our focus should be placed not on connecting our current suspects with the murders, but excluding them one by one, and if we can't exclude one, then that suspect becomes a higher priority than the rest.'

'I just thought of something,' says Anderson. 'There was quite a large space of time between murder one and two, and a shorter period between two and three, so I think Kelly is right. Nathan was collateral damage, an example. That being said, I think we might also have a window of opportunity here. Unless the killer decides to act faster, we have some time before we can expect the next murder; we should bank on it.'

'Andy's right, we have to move quickly,' Kelly nods. 'I think we should split the task. Andy and Peter, will you investigate Shane Clemente? Find out anything you can about him and his whereabouts during the three murders. Brady and I will investigate Emily Bride and Scarlett White. When all of us have our information, then we'll have another meeting and discuss our findings. Everyone okay with that?'

Andy and Peter high five. 'Is it a race?' Peter jokes.

'If it is, then make peace with the fact that you're going to lose,' says Brady, winking at Kelly. Her cheeks start to feel warm as they become flushed, and she blushes. 'A drink?'

Kelly's cheeks remain red. 'Any other questions or comments?'

'No, Ma'am.'

'Then yes, a drink. Peter would you mind if I have a glass of your wine?'

'Of course not!'

'I'll get it for you,' Brady smiles at her. 'Glasses boys.' Andy and Peter hand their glasses to Brady and he balances the four glasses as he carries them to the kitchen counter. Brady fills the glasses while Kelly, Peter and Andy sit talking.

Chapter 30

"A letter to a mystery man.
If only I could meet you, even if just for coffee. Your letters always make me smile. You seem like the perfect gentleman. There is so much that I would like to discuss with you, so much I would like to tell you. Recently I was witness to something terrible, something that few people see and I wish I could ask you for advice. I'm not entirely sure how to manage the circumstances I have been placed in. Of course, I gave consent to be part of the matter, but I am now involved, or rather I see people at their very worst, and it makes me sad. If only I could speak to them as you do to me. Your tone alone could cheer them up. Apart from this, I am well, and very excited for my future. I would like to thank you properly this time for the opportunity you gave me. And thank you for always watching over me.
Your friend, Lily."

The last page of the New Orleans Weekly is home to Lily's blog. Many people in New Orleans read it, and all of them enjoy it. Today's blog is the first time Lily directly speaks to this mystery man. A man walks on a sidewalk, slow and in thought, it's been a couple of weeks since Lily has written in the paper, but after Peter took her to the murder scene, she felt inclined to do so. The man walks by a newsstand, but doesn't buy a paper; he simply asks the attendant if there is another blog in the paper about a mystery man. The attendant turns the paper over and there it is, Lily's blog. He quickly skims through the blog as the attendant holds the paper, but he waves him off and greets him in a friendly voice, without buying one. Two days go by, and Lily is still at home, she does well enough at university that she got exemption for her exams. She wakes up in her bed, nice, and warm. She looks on her clock and it flashes at 04.37 a.m. Her father told her to put batteries in it, in case there is a power outage, but as with most young adults, she didn't listen. She finds her watch, it's 09.13 a.m. A quick calculation gives her the answer that the power came back on at 04.36 a.m. She's pretty sure that her parents wouldn't even have noticed that the power was out last night. The clock without the battery is the only clue. Lily walks downstairs to make some breakfast, the smell of her father's coffee machine still lingers, but both Mom and Dad are out. The breeze in the kitchen is crisp, she feels chilly. She switches on the kettle and places a pan on the gas stove with a little butter and turns the heat on low. While the water boils and the butter melts, she runs upstairs to fetch a jersey. The floor is cold, she'll need her slippers too. She yanks the cupboard door open and pulls the top jersey, a pink one, out. A letter falls on the floor. The handwriting is all too familiar, and the smell distinct. It always smells like soft, clean and soapy cologne mixed with the smell of green tea. But this time there's something different, the seal has been broken. Her heart sits in her throat and she almost feels nauseous at the thought of him being in her room. She forgets about the butter in the pan.

"Dear Lily.
I hope you find this letter well. Please don't be alarmed, I am going to place this letter in your room while you sleep, there is no other way I can give it to you without giving some clue of who I am. But still I promise that I mean you no harm.
Thank you for your letter, I appreciate you communicating with me and I do hope that you can somehow emerge from this situation you are in. If ever you need my help, you need only ask and I will do everything in my power to assist you; my power is great, and my circle of connections vast.
Enjoy your off time from university, hope to hear from you again soon.
P.S. I opened the letter while in your kitchen, to add a little bit; please speak with your father and address your current state of home security. It makes me uncomfortable that it was this easy to gain entry to your home, your safety is of the utmost importance. Also when you write again, please will you suggest where I can leave my next letter."

And at the back of the letter, it is, as always, signed only, "*J.*"

Chapter 31

Brady and Kelly get into the car, they're on their way to an undercover FBI office in New Orleans, a safe house that was set up a couple of years ago. It hasn't been used much, but is sufficient for the task at hand. The night before, Kelly spoke to Lucius Vance in order to get a warrant to investigate Emily Bride and Scarlett White, the condition was to do so discretely and the same condition applied to the warrant issued for the investigation of Shane Clemente. The half-rusted garage door of the condemned house shrieks as it opens, the light inside yellow, and flickering. The floor is darkened by brown dust, evidently this place has been unoccupied for some time. The smell of old newspapers, or papers in general, lingers in the air. When Kelly unlocks the door, it becomes clear to detective Brady Harris why no homeless people sleep here at night. Locks click one by one, moving out of the steel frame and into the heavy steel reinforced door.

'The doors are reinforced, as you can see; and the windows bulletproof.'

'No wonder no one has tried to get in here.'

'We leave it in a terrible state and with the condemned building signs all over so that no one would even try. This place is an impenetrable bunker. It's bomb proof,' Kelly adds.

Brady smiles, 'Bomb proof you say?' But as they enter the house, the thick, two-foot concrete walls bury his joke. 'Okay. Bomb proof, but why though?'

'The equipment in here might seem old, but it's all directly connected to our FBI server which means if anyone comes in here, they would have access; well, assuming they can break through the other security measures, they would have access to our FBI mainframe.'

'Other security measures?' Brady asks while they walk from room to room, all empty.

'Did you see the camera?'

'What camera?'

'Precisely. The camera hidden in one of the door bolts, facial recognition; also, when you touch the handle it scans your fingerprint. If it's unrecognised, the speaker systems first start to creak to imitate the imminent collapse of the building, and if you stay, teargas canisters in the roof and ventilation system will chase you off.'

They enter the master bedroom, empty, except for an old bed. Kelly walks over to the fireplace and sticks her hand up the chimney and tugs at something. Nothing. She tugs again, this time with success. The foot end of the broken and stained bed lifts three feet into the air, revealing a small trapdoor leading to the hidden basement. 'The FBI has lots of money,' she says, jokingly.

'That's pretty obvious, and impressive,' Brady looks amazed. They climb down the ladder; the tunnel is narrow, and cold. As they get to the bottom, Kelly touches a switch and a bright white light illuminates a small room with three computer screens and two chairs in front of a single desk. When the screens are switched on, one shows the FBI security screen, the other stays black and the last one is split into eight equal parts that show the views of the hidden cameras around the house. Brady stares at the screens. 'Who would've known.'

'Remarkable, isn't it?'

'Very.'

Kelly types in the name of Scarlett White and searches the FBI system. The two look at the screen, waiting for results. White's name does not come up on the system. 'She has no criminal record, then,' Kelly says. 'According to our system she's clean, we have nothing on her.' She types Emily Bride's name in, but the result is the same. 'This was a bit of a waste of time. Let's see if Shane comes up.' But Shane Clemente is not on the FBI system either.

'Either they're truly clean, or they're very good at hiding their involvement with the organisation,' Brady muses.

'I have an idea; we can search the Health Professions Counsel site to look for any infringements or cases against them.' Kelly says and searches for Scarlett on the Health Professions Counsel site. 'Okay, well, she's quite a distinguished physical therapist and is recommended as one of the top therapists in the country.' She continues to read. 'She was also a speaker at a medical seminar.'

Brady stops her. 'Wait, scroll back up.'

'What is it?'

Brady moves closer to the screen and reads about the Chicago Annual Medical Association Improvement seminar. 'Can you search that specific seminar for me please?'

'Okay, what did you see?'

'I just want to confirm the date,' he says. Kelly searches the seminar and a page opens with the seminar. It was three days long and all the speakers and topics are listed with short quotes from each. 'Look at the date of the seminar, it was hosted on the same day that Freddy was murdered. Can you find a guest list?'

'You think Emily might have attended?'

'Maybe.'

Kelly searches, but the guest list is not available on the site. 'Hmm no nothing,' she says. 'However if they did go together, then hopefully they both flew there.' She starts to search through the FBI mainframe for Emily Bride and Scarlett White's flight and travel history and they're in luck, both of them flew to Chicago over that time. 'Okay well, we have at least confirmed what we already knew. Neither of them could have done it themselves; not the first one, in any case.' They also notice that on the night of the stakeout, Emily and Scarlett flew to Bora Bora, and their flight was scheduled to leave at eleven o'clock, which means that they were also out of town for the last murder, Nathan's murder. 'I don't think we'll find much more. It seems like their return flight is booked for three days from now, we have a window of opportunity here.'

'What are you suggesting?'

'The tickets were bought on Emily's credit card, and that lists her address; we should search her house discreetly.'

'Okay, but if we get caught she'll sue us for breaking and entering.'

'Not if we have a warrant.'

'And we have one? Right?'

Kelly switches the computer off while she talks. 'Not yet, I have a contact, I'll get one, he'll send it in the morning; we just have to make sure we don't get caught now.'

Brady seems shocked. 'Now?'

'Do you have somewhere else to be?'

'No.'

'Then if you're up for an adventure, would you like to join me?'

'We'll have to get something to eat on the way, I'm ravenous.' Kelly and Brady leave the FBI safe house, and on the way, stop at a small Asian restaurant where they order takeaways. They talk and laugh, with the windows open, and the air flowing through the car, it feels like a holiday. Emily's house is free standing, and elegant. The low, white picket fence provides little security, but adds a nice artistic touch to the garden. Contained inside the fence is a beautiful garden with roses and flowers of all colours, each bush trimmed to perfection to complement the large evergreen trees and grass. Cobblestone lays the path to the front door, with little motion sensor driver fairy lights, that slowly glow as you walk by them. Low light globes inside the trees, together with the fairy lights create a beautiful scene, such as what you might find in gardening books. The house is a single storey, with a high, red tile roof. Off-white walls make the mahogany wood window frames and door the stars of the show. Security measures to keep those who are outside from coming inside, are virtually non-existent, only a simple lock keeps the door closed. Brady makes short work of the lock; he picks it with very little effort, and wears gloves so as not to leave any prints. 'There we go Miss Young, after you.'

'Oh, how polite of you Detective, to let me enter illegally first.' Kelly winks as she walks through. 'What a pretty house.'

'Expensive taste.' Brady looks up at the ceiling, high as the roof, creating a large open space above their heads.

'If we're going to find anything here, it will be easy, this lady seems to be somewhat compulsive about everything being in place.'

'I agree, let's do this structured; I'll take the rooms, and you tackle the kitchen, dining area, and lounge,' Kelly holds up a finger, 'and remember, we need to leave everything exactly the way we found it.'

'I agree. I hope we find something.' Brady whispers as Kelly disappears towards the master bedroom. For a long while they search, they quietly go through every cupboard and every drawer, but find nothing, nothing that would indicate her involvement anyways. There's no safe, no hidden compartments, nothing under the mattresses, nothing out of the ordinary.

But then Kelly discovers a tape hidden between some clothes. 'Brady! I think I have something.'

'What is it?'

'A tape.'

'What's on it?'

'No idea, is there a video player in the lounge?'

'I think I saw one.' The two walk to the front of the house and switch on the large television. 'Here let me put this in for you.' Brady takes the tape from Kelly. With a click, he inserts the tape into the cassette player, and pushes play. 'We can't really consider this incriminating evidence, can we?'

Kelly slowly replies, 'No. This won't help.'

On the tape is a secret, but neither dark, nor useful. The tape isn't wound back entirely. Soft music plays in the background as the corner shot of the camera catches Scarlett kissing Emily on her neck. Emily is wearing only a white thong, and Scarlett is clad in a shirt and no pants. Kelly and Brady did not expect this, but they continue to watch. Scarlett's long plum hair is tucked neatly over her right shoulder and softly slithers down Emily's tiny body as Scarlett moves from her neck, to her nipples, to her navel. Scarlett's hand reaches up to Emily's breast as she moves down, kissing Emily's thigh. The camera angle perfectly catches Scarlett's tight and appealing bum, with her underwear neatly sitting between her butt cheeks, showing every line. Brady feels uncomfortably aroused, and so does Kelly. With one finger, Scarlett pulls Emily's thong to one side, licking ever so gently, Emily pulls her lower back up and throws her head back, the stimulations seems orgasmic. Kelly's nipples now show visible through her shirt and Brady's pants become tight. Emily puts her hand on the back of Scarlett's head, encouraging her to go faster as two of Scarlett's fingers disappear inside Emily, Scarlett still licking as her hand moves back and forth. 'Okay I think we get the picture,' Kelly mutters in a low and unfamiliar tone.

'Yes,' Brady shoves his hands in his pockets to try and hide his erection. 'Listen, I know this is probably the most inappropriate time to ask, but would you like to have dinner with me tomorrow night?'

'Finally.'

'Finally what?'

'I've been waiting for you to ask me.' Kelly wraps her arms around Brady, attempting to give him a hug, but his erection pushes into her stomach and she quickly releases him. 'Right. Tomorrow.'

'Sorry about that.'

'No need to apologise, it's a normal reaction for a man to present with... that, when he watches a lesbian sex tape.'

'Any sex tape,' Brady jokes, trying to lighten the mood a little.

Kelly starts to blush. 'I think we can go now, don't think we'll come across anything else here.'

'Probably not.' Brady says walking to the door. 'In the car I'll call Peter and tell him that Emily and Scarlett didn't do it, hopefully they have good news about Shane.'

'I'll be with you now, I just want to put this tape back where I found it.'

'I'll wait for you in the car.' Brady walks out. *Fuck man why did she have to hug me straight after we watched Scarlett finger Emily? Nice ass though, both of them.* He sits in the car and dials Peter's number.

'Hello.'

'Pete.'

'What's up?'

'We dug into Emily and Scarlett a little, they were out of town, they couldn't have done it themselves.'

Peter's voice is muffled over the telephone. 'Then I don't think they were behind it either.'

'Why do you think that?'

'Shane was at some or other conference for medical practitioners during the time of Freddy's murder. And he was in surgery during the time of the second one.'

'Emily and Scarlett were at the same conference I would guess.'

'In Chicago?'

'Yes.'

'Okay I think for now we can exclude these three. What do you think?' Peter waits.

'I'll speak to Kelly about it now, but I agree.'

'Have you asked her on a date yet?'

Brady stutters. 'What... how... why would you ask that?'

'The chemistry is obvious Harris.'

Brady looks around and sees Kelly come from the door. 'I need to go, here she comes, but yes, we're going for dinner tomorrow.'

'Enjoy,' Peter replies and puts the phone down.

Kelly slams the car door closed. 'Ready to go?' She asks.

'Yes let's go. I spoke to Pete over the phone now.'

'And?'

'They excluded Shane from the suspect list; he was with Scarlett and Emily in Chicago and in surgery for the second murder.'

Kelly gives a tight smile and frowns at the same time. 'Not what we were hoping to find, but I guess it's still a result.'

Chapter 32

Brady waits at the door of the car in front of Kelly's hotel. She looks amazing. Her hair is loose, she's wearing a spring cocktail dress, yellow and white, with low-heeled shoes; her lips are a sort of light rose red. With her dark eyeliner and beautiful deep purple eyeshadow, she looks absolutely stunning. 'Wow, you look stunning.'

Kelly lightly blushes and smiles, 'Hey handsome, you don't look too bad yourself.' Brady holds the door for her to get into the car.

He hops into the driver's seat and says. 'I hope you're hungry.'

'I am indeed, where are you taking me?'

'There's an old restaurant in the French Quarter, Antoine's, it was opened in 1840 and it was suggested to me by a friend. He said that it is his most favourite restaurant in the world.'

'Okay, at least we know they're experienced.'

On the way Brady pulls out his pipe. 'Would you mind if I had a puff while we drive?'

'Not at all. I like the smell of pipe tobacco, it reminds me of my grandfather, which tobacco do you have in there?'

Brady hands her the tightly packed unlit pipe. 'It's a sixty percent black Cavendish and forty percent Virginia blend with a hint of vanilla.'

Kelly smells the tobacco from the top of the pipe. 'That smells very, very nice.'

'It's a blend I can find only at one tobacconist, I went in one day to buy some tobacco, and being a regular, my tobacconist suggested this, he said it was the highest quality tobacco he had. So I had to try, and since then I haven't smoked anything else.'

'Highest quality, must be expensive?' Kelly asks.

'It's not cheap, but it's not the most expensive tobacco I've smoked; it's affordable enough to smoke on a regular basis,' he says. Kelly hands the pipe back and he pulls out a box of matches, lighting the pipe while steering with his left knee.

'Hmm, yes it smells as good lit as it does unlit.' She looks intrigued. 'How do you know how much to pack in the pipe?'

'There are different methods that people use to pack their pipes, I fill the bowl to the brim.' He puffs a couple of times in quick succession and lets the coal die, then press it with his pipe tool. 'Then I press it in, and they describe the technique as pressing with the strength of a child.' He lights the pipe again and puffs balls of smoke. 'Then you fill the bowl again to the brim and press it with the strength of a woman.' He closes the bowl with his index and middle fingers and puffs twice, then opens the bowl, the tobacco is now perfectly lit. 'Then you fill it for a last time and press it with the strength of a man.'

'Why don't you pack it tight from the start?'

'By packing light, then tighter, then even tighter the third time ensures that the bottom tobacco isn't packed too tight.'

'Oh, now I get it, that makes sense,' nods Kelly. Shortly after this, they stop across the road from the restaurant. 'This place is beautiful.'

'It is!' Brady says, excited. They walk to the front door and they are met by a friendly employee. 'Good evening Sir, table for two?

'We have a reservation. Harris.'

The man opens the reservation book and scrolls down quickly. 'Reservation for eight, just in time, follow me Sir; Madame.' He leads them to their table and pulls out the seat for Kelly. 'Can I get you something to drink?'

Brady takes Kelly's arm, 'What would you like?'

'Do you serve cocktails?' she asks the waiter, leaving Brady's hand on her arm.

'Yes Ma'am we do, is there a specific one you'd like?'

'Long Island iced tea?'

'We do indeed, one Long Island iced tea.' He scribbles in his book. 'And for you, Sir?'

'I'll have a double Jack number seven on the rocks please.'

'And starters? Sorry I am asking so early but we are quite busy tonight so you might wait about thirty minutes for the starters to come.'

'Okay we'll quickly scan through the menu, if you can get us the drinks in the meantime, thank you.' Brady replies in a friendly way.

'Coming right up Sir.'

'This is a long menu.' Kelly says as she starts paging.

'Hmm, what are you in the mood for?'

'Difficult to say, they have quite a nice variety here, and the descriptions look delicious.'

Almost five minutes fly by and both Brady and Kelly are still staring at the menu. The waiter returns with the drinks. 'And do we have a verdict?' he asks as he places the drinks on the table.

'All of it?' Kelly jokes.

'First time here?'

'First time, for both of us.' Brady replies.

'Can I make a suggestion?' the waiter asks.

'Suggest away.'

'Would you like lamb, shrimp or oysters?'

Both Kelly and Brady answer at the same time. 'Shrimp.'

'Aha! Then it's easy, I would suggest the Crevettes Remoulade.'

'Okay?'

'Chilled Louisiana gulf shrimp in our Antoine's unique remoulade dressing.' The waiter licks his lips. 'I would recommend that, it's truly enchantingly delicious.'

Brady and Kelly look at each other, practically drooling. 'Two please, one for me and one for the lady.'

'Coming right up, I'll try and hurry the chef, make some fire underneath his bottom.' He winks and giggles and walks off to the kitchen with the order.

'If he's that excited about the meal, then I can't wait.'

'Neither can I,' Kelly says.

'Can I ask you a question?'

'Sure. What would you like to know?' Kelly replies. Brady then starts asking questions about her past, her parents, and her childhood. Many good stories came out, but also some negatives. The more Kelly tells Brady about herself and her interests, the fonder of her he becomes. In his eyes, she is perfect in every way. He has never met anyone more compatible with him than Kelly. Her small build and pretty smile makes her desirable, but the part that fascinates him the most is her personality. Kelly Young is a pure soul, she is perceptive in every way, not just in her job, she's sensitive to change and can easily pick up how people feel. She's also meticulous. In her personal life, she is protective over those she loves and romantic towards her lover. She's also selfless, independent and secure. A wonderful and attractive person altogether.

'Miss Young?' A man asks.

Kelly turns and quickly jumps up. 'Judge Vance, good evening, how are you, Sir?'

'I'm well thanks and you?' Judge Lucius Vance replies.

'I'm good thank you. Judge, this is my friend.' She points at Brady, indicating for him to get up. 'Detective Brady Harris from the New Orleans CID.'

Judge Vance sticks his hand out to Brady. 'It's a pleasure to meet you Detective, Lucius Vance.'

'The pleasure is mine, Sir.' replies Brady shaking firmly.

Judge Vance turns to Kelly. 'You look wonderful tonight Miss Young.' He looks around as if he wants to tell her a secret. 'Chateaubriand.'

'Sir?'

'Chateaubriand.' He repeats. 'The main course for you and your… friend.' He smiles and winks at her. 'It's a meal to share, and a meal to die for, Chateaubriand.'

'We'll definitely try that then.'

'Have a good evening Agent.' Judge Vance turns to Brady. 'And a good evening to you too Detective.'

'Thank you sir.' Brady says.

'See you soon Judge.'

Judge Vance walks off. 'Oh and Agent, let me know if you need anything else,' says the Judge as he walks off.

'Who was that?' Asks Brady.

'That is my contact, he's the one that gets me all the warrants. His name, as you heard, is Lucius Vance, and he's a high court judge from New York. He works very closely with the FBI.'

'Why on earth is he in New Orleans?'

'I have absolutely no idea.'

A figure appears from the side. 'One Crevettes Remoulade for the lady, and one for the gentleman.' The waiter places the food in front of them. 'Can I refill your drinks?'

Brady looks at Kelly, and she nods. 'Yes please,' Brady says.

'And can I take your main course order?'

Kelly answers. 'The Chateaubriand please.'

'Very good choice, Ma'am.'

'Can I just ask, a friend recommended it, but what exactly is it?'

'Grilled centre-cut tenderloin of beef, served with potatoes, sautéed mushrooms, and Antoine's Marchand de Vin and Béarnaise sauces. Our most popular meal to share, very nice choice.'

Kelly smiles, 'Thank you.'

'Oh my word, you should taste this shrimp!' Brady says to Kelly.

'While they are eating, Lucius returns to their table. 'Miss Young I'm sorry to interrupt your meal; I have a friend that could help you with your investigation.'

'All right…' She replies hesitantly.

'Now I must explain, I met him a couple of years ago, he was part of some or other investigation unit, nice guy, but strange, very strange.' Lucius pulls his eyebrows up and pauses. 'However, even though he might be a bit cracked, he's clever, and I mean, *really* clever. If you get stuck, let me know and I'll authorise the use of an external party for the purpose of the investigation and I will put you in touch with him.'

'Thank you Judge; I will let you know if we struggle; what's his name sir?'

'Nicholas Hollingsworth.'

After dinner they each have one more drink, Brady has a Brandy Alexander, which is a mix of brandy, dark crème de cacao and ice cream, and Kelly has a Golden Cadillac which is Galliano with white crème de cacao and ice cream. 'This is delicious,' she says.

'We should definitely come back here.'

'Does that mean there's a second date?'

'Only if you want.'

Kelly reaches over and kisses Brady softly on his lips, she pulls back, looks him straight into the eyes and kisses him again, this time allowing her tongue to wander into his mouth for a brief moment. Her tongue is cold from the ice cream and he can taste the sweetness of her drink over his own. 'I hope that answers yours question.'

Shocked and surprised he says, 'Unexpected.' He pauses. 'But definitely not unwanted. Second date it is.'

'I'm very intrigued by Judge Vance's suggestion.'

'Me too,' Brady replies. 'What's your take on it, do you think we should consider it?'

'He wouldn't give bad advice, but I think if we don't manage to figure it out by ourselves then it wouldn't hurt to try?' She says, half questioning.

'Okay, let's do it that way then. I like how the Judge says the guy is very, very strange, I wonder what he's like.' He laughs.

'Probably walks around in his underpants all day.'

Brady coughs. 'Does that make a man strange?' He pulls a funny face. 'That makes me strange then.'

'Hmm it does, doesn't it? But I'm sure I can accept you walking around half naked.'

'I could say the same for you.'

'We'll have to make a plan then,' Kelly says naughtily. 'Thank you for the evening, it was great.'

'It's a pleasure, are you ready for me to take you home?'

'I think so, yes.' She smiles at Brady. 'I can make you coffee in my hotel room if you'd like?' Kelly asks.

'Perfect.' He catches the waiter's eye; he comes over. 'Thank you for the food and drinks, can I have the bill please?' Brady says.

'Coming right up, Sir.'

Chapter 33

'The usual.'

'Two?'

'Yes.'

'Happy smoking, man. Remember the rule, if you get caught, you didn't get it from me.'

'It's just marijuana, and no one will lock me up for two joints.'

'I'm just saying.'

'Cheers.' Anthony hands the dealer some money and walks to his car. *Lock me up for two joints, it's not worth any cop's time.* Anthony lights up one of the joints and stands behind his car, puffing away. *This is some good stuff, smooth.* A black, expensive-looking car stops next to him, the engine so quiet it's almost entirely silent. A man who appears drunk staggers out of the driver's seat. The man stands next to the car looking around, it's dark and the parking lot is empty. 'He just left,' says Anthony.

'What?'

'The dealer. He just left, do you want a drag of mine?' Anthony takes another drag of the joint.

'Oh.' The man replies. 'Sure.' He walks over to Anthony. Anthony hands him the lit and hot-dragged joint and the man takes one puff and hands it back. 'Nice.'

'New flavour that he stocks. He calls it blue purple or something like that.' Anthony takes another drag. His heart beats faster and his head feels light; in a brief moment, everything's become very interesting to him.

'Listen man I'm going to head out, do you want to finish this?'

'Sure.'

'Man of few words.' Anthony starts to joke. Before he can pass on the half-smoked joint, the man hits him over the head with the bottle in his hand. Anthony stumbles and the man grabs him from behind choking him with an expertly executed martial arts choke. As soon as Anthony loses consciousness, the man ties his hands and feet with industrial cable ties, gags him with a cloth and throws him into the black car's trunk.

Sometime later, Anthony regains consciousness, he realises he is in a warehouse, it's empty. 'Welcome to my playground,' the man says, but Anthony can only mumble. 'You're a repulsive human being,' the man says and removes Anthony's gag.

'What do you want man?' Anthony asks nervously, sober.

'I just don't like you,' the man replies. He takes a knife from his pocket, the blade is curved and sharp.

'Please man don't do this. What have I done to you?'

'Nothing. You're my entertainment for the night.' The man walks closer and sticks the curved blade into Anthony's stomach.

'Ahh!' he screams. 'What the fuck man?' He yells even louder. The man circles him silently, Anthony tries to twist away, but the man sticks the blade into his back, again, again, and again. 'Fuuuck!' Anthony screams. The man steps on his hand with a hard thump, fracturing Anthony's wrist; he takes the blade and stabs him in his groin and blood immediately gushes out. With every second Anthony gets weaker and weaker. The smell of blood fills the space around Anthony, coppery, metallic and sharp. The floor is cold and the blood from Anthony's wounds quickly coagulates, leaving a sticky pool around him. The man walks closer and sticks two of his fingers in the blood, cool but not cold. He licks his fingers. 'What the fuck man?' Anthony lethargically comments.

'It tastes sweet.'

'Please let me go.'

'It's the first time that I've tasted someone's blood.'

'Please, man…' Anthony's feeling very weak. The man looks at him, staring with pure evil in his eyes. 'Please.' But the man walks over and stabs him unstoppably and repeatedly in his abdomen and chest, viciously ripping into his body; blood from the rapid, successive movements showers blood on both Anthony and the man. Blood now running from Anthony's mouth, but the man doesn't stop. Anthony in all of his terrible weakness tries to move away, but there's no escaping the unforgiving blade. Anthony stops resisting, and the man slows down; with his hands bloody, he pulls Anthony's head back and slices his throat. Anthony for a couple of seconds still attempts to breathe before taking his last breath, the air gushing from his open trachea froths as it exits through the blood. The man cuts the cable tie from his hands, and neatly cuts a triangle with the apex facing towards the hand on Anthony's left wrist.

'Nine one one, what's your emergency?'

'I just killed someone.'

'Excuse me Sir, just repeat that?'

'I just killed someone, you can find his body at the location you're tracking this phone to now.' The man puts the phone down and burns it together with the cloth he cleaned his hands with, and his clothes. He leaves the warehouse naked, gets in his car and disappears.

'Agent Kelly,' the captain says over the phone.

'Captain, when you call this late, then I'll assume there's another homicide.'

'I've already spoken to the other detectives; Brady offered to pick you up, be ready in ten minutes, I think our man just killed again.'

Brady and Kelly stop at the scene of the crime thirty minutes later; he gets out with his pipe clenched tight between his teeth, adjusting his hat so he can see better. Kelly walks closer to the barrier tape, soft, but brisk with a pair of surgical gloves in her hand. 'Thank you, Officer,' she says as the officer lifts the barrier tape over her head. 'I don't see Peter's car?'

'I think he went to pick up Lily.'

'The poor girl, she's being dragged into something she was never prepared for.'

'She agreed to it. Look I'm not saying it's the best idea Pete's ever had, but if he's right, if she is connected, then we'll make progress faster.'

'I know,' Kelly replies. The smell inside the empty warehouse is atrocious and the scene horrific. 'Hmm.' Kelly comments, recoiling in disgust, her hand covering her mouth and nose.

'You okay?' Brady asks solicitously.

But the conversation is interrupted by the captain. 'This is a fuck storm. We can't keep this from the press much longer. The forensic team calls him the Weekend Killer. Agent Young, have we made any progress with this case?'

'We've excluded some suspects, but the killer leaves no evidence; that makes it difficult Sir, as you can understand.'

'I know, I'm trying my best with the press, but we need some results now. Imagine a story where New Orleans' finest with the aid of the FBI can't catch a killer, we don't want that.'

'We understand Sir,' says Brady.

'What have they found so far?' Kelly puts her surgical gloves on, ready for inspection.

'Same shit, different scene, nothing. No evidence, no prints, no weapon, nothing so far, just a poor soul bled to death.' Captain Deloitte, is leaning over her shoulder and looking at the corpse, almost with guilt. 'We need to find this guy—innocent people are dying here.' He sees Kelly walk over to the body, with a look of disgust on her face. 'ME says that there are thirty-nine stab wounds in total.'

Kelly looks up at Brady. 'He's evolving.' She gently turns one of the victim's wrists, then the other, then looks at his feet that are still bound. 'This is strange don't you think?'

'What?' asks Brady.

'This victim was bound throughout the whole thing, you can see the marks on his wrist as he tried to pull out of them, probably the same ties used on his feet.'

'Not probably,' the captain butts in. 'They were the same, we have the cable ties in the van, evidence, but they're clean.' The captain rubs his chin, shaven smooth. 'When you said that he's evolving…?'

'It's just a confirmation of what we already suspected, with every murder he becomes more brutal. It seems like it went from an act of necessity to an act of pleasure, that's what I mean by "evolving",' says Kelly, never looking up, but carefully examining the body; she's used to the smell now.

'Hey guys, can I bring her in?'

'Pete! I don't know hey, this one seems bad. Thirty-nine stab wounds.'

Peter disappears and returns quickly. 'She says she can handle it.'

'It's your call, Detective,' says the captain.

'Lily, you can come in, but if you want to leave, just say the word and I'll take you out.'

'I'll be okay I promise.' Lily walks in and she's faced with an intimidating picture: a bloodied body, stabbed almost forty times without defence. Next to the body is FBI agent Kelly Young. Kelly puts her hand out in a welcoming and comforting manner, indicating for Lily to come closer. 'Hi,' Lily says, timid but friendly.

'Hello Lily,' Kelly replies. 'Remember all you have to do here is see if you recognise anything, anything at all.'

'I'll see if there is something, but I really don't see why I would be connected.' Lily feels uneasy with the dead man, with the scene, with the blood; she walks around the body looking at his hands and feet and the triangle. She looks at his face, frozen in an expression of panic and terror. 'I don't know him.'

'Are you sure?'

'I'm sure.'

'Detective Jones,' Kelly calls out professionally. 'We need to reconsider Lily's involvement.'

'I know. It was a long shot.' Peter walks over putting his arm around Lily. 'Let me take you home, I'm sorry for putting you through this.'

'No need to apologise, Pete, I get why brought me here, but I promise I don't know anyone besides your cousin.' She pauses and looks for his reaction when she mentioned Freddy; no change in his mood. 'I mean I didn't know Fred, I knew *of* him.'

'Well it was worth a shot, thank you for your time.' They leave the warehouse.

'Captain, I have a suggestion.'

'What is it Miss Young?'

'The other night a contact of mine suggested that we use an old acquaintance of his, the man's name is Nicholas... Nicholas something. I can't remember his surname now, but in any case, Nicholas was apparently part of some or other special investigation unit and my contact recommends his use. My contact's a judge and he'll write us a letter of authorisation to use him if we want?' She bites her lip. 'From what I understand he's quite brilliant.'

The captain thinks for a short while. 'I see no reason why not, I mean we tried the whole thing with Peter and Lily, let's give this a shot; find him, make him part of it. This guy becomes more and more brutal with each kill, we need to catch him by any means necessary.'

On the way home, Lily sends Michael a message. 'Who are you texting?' Peter asks.

'Michael.'

'Michael? The artist Michael?'

'Yes we've kept in touch, he's a nice guy.'

'Oh okay, what is he saying?'

'No, no, I asked him to go for coffee tomorrow, but he suggested we do dinner tomorrow night.'

'Do you trust him?'

'Of course, don't you?'

'I don't know him,' Peter says, not looking at Lily.

'You can relax, Pete, he's really a nice guy, you don't need to worry about me.'

Chapter 34

Lily's phone rings, it's just after seven in the morning. 'Hello.'

'Hey Lily it's Michael here.'

'How are you?'

'I'm good and you?'

'Good thank you, what's up?'

'I was thinking, I know it's early, and also late notice, but I was able to borrow a boat for the day, would you like to spend the day with me on this boat?'

'Where on earth did you borrow a boat?'

'It doesn't matter, are you keen?'

With excitement in her voice. 'Yes of course! Where are we going to go?'

'Lake Pontchartrain.'

'What about sharks?'

Michael laughs. 'It's not a rowboat, and it's not the ocean either.'

'Okay what time will you pick me up?'

Michael pauses for a moment. 'Well… I was pretty confident that you would say yes.'

'Uh-huh.'

'I'm already waiting outside.'

'Oh my word! I just woke up, I need to shower, get dressed, do makeup.'

'Shower. Forget the makeup, we're going on a boat, and you're beautiful enough. Dress comfortably, it's only going to be me and you.'

'Do you have a skipper license?'

'I wouldn't be able to borrow the boat without it.'

'Give me fifteen minutes.' Lily says and puts down the phone.

Lily takes longer than fifteen minutes, but regardless they arrive at the Southern Yacht Club just before eight. 'Here we are.'

'A yacht club?' Lily says confused. 'You said you got a boat.'

'It's a small yacht, you'll see.' They walk in and Lily waits outside while Michael does the administration at the front desk. She feels a bit out of place, everyone seems to wear expensive clothes and here she is in her comfortable long beach pants and loose shirt; her hair is still wet from the shower and she has no makeup on. 'Are you ready?'

'I'm ready.' Lily replies. They briskly walk along pier, passing the yachts, big ones, small ones, long ones, broad ones, but the one thing they all have in common is that they all seem pretty expensive. 'There are some really nice boats here.'

'Very nice, the people here have quite a bit of money.' Michael stops next to one of the yachts. 'This one is ours.'

Lily looks up at the yacht with amazement. In front of her is a 1996 Burger Raised Pilothouse called *Breeze*. 'It's massive!'

One of the crewmen welcomes her and Michael. 'Hello Ma'am.' He helps Lily onto the yacht. 'Mister Lafayette, it's good to see you again.'

'Thank you, are you guys ready?'

'Yes Sir.'

'Do you do this often?' Lily asks.

'I told some white lies to you. The yacht is mine and we're only coming back tomorrow morning, but before you panic, I've already spoken to your parents.'

Lily runs over to Michael and playfully punches his arm. 'You're sneaky you know that.'

Michael smiles and leads her in. 'Let me show you around while the crew take us out on the water.' On the inside, *Breeze* has a timeless and classic look. It has hand-finished butternut interior and raised panels. The interior is soft and rich, open and uncluttered. The yacht is gorgeous. On the outside and decks, it is mostly painted pearl white, with details in Kingston grey. 'What do you think?' Michael asks, standing next to Lily on the deck with wind blowing through their hair.

'I'm still shocked by the fact that you own a yacht.' She looks him straight in the eyes. 'But it's very, very nice, thank you for bringing me here.'

'You're the first one.'

'What do you mean?'

'I've only ever come alone before.'

'That explains why everyone was so excited to see me!' She hugs Michael. 'This is nice, I need the time away.'

Michael is now curious. 'Why do you say that?'

'You remember my friend Peter?'

'I do.'

'He thought that I might somehow be connected to some crimes in New Orleans, so he's been taking me to crime scenes to see if I recognise anything or anyone, but it's horrible.'

'Lily, are you a criminal?' Michael jokes.

She laughs. 'Maybe.' She looks behind her to see that no one is listening. 'I want to tell you something.'

'Your tone makes it sound very serious…'

'Yes it is.'

'All right I'm all ears.'

'But you have to promise me that you won't tell anyone.'

'I promise.'

'And I mean *no one* can know; I'll be in trouble.'

'Okay, I promise.' Michael can pick up the distress in Lily's behaviour. He's concerned.

'Peter and his friends are investigating murders in New Orleans.'

'Murders?' he asks, loud and shocked.

'Yes, and they've been taking me to the crime scenes because Pete felt that there was perhaps some connection to me. Something to do with a piece of old jewellery I have, now the bodies are marked with a triangle on the wrist.'

'Bodies? You mean you've been to more than one of these scenes?'

'Yes, but Pete and his team said that they doubt there is a connection after all, so I probably won't be going back.'

'Lily that's terrible. I'm sorry you had to see those things.' Michael rubs her back. 'Do you want to tell me about what you saw?' She nods. 'Okay let me get us a bottle of wine and you can tell me all about it.' Michael walks off and comes back not long after that with two glasses and a bottle of Chenin Blanc in a bucket of ice. 'I'm all yours,' he says and sits her down on one of the tanning chairs; he sits on the one next to her, facing her. He pours them some wine.

'I don't get why this guy kills these people, he's brutal, and evil.'

'Why do you say that?' he asks, sounding interested.

'Apparently he went from killing them quickly to pretty much torturing them. The last person had something like forty stab wounds.'

'What?'

'Yes. The first one had no blood they say; the body was entirely clean, and only the throat was sliced, but since then he's been killing them more viciously every time.'

'Why is this not on the news?'

Lily shrugs. 'I have no idea, they just don't want to share it with the press at this time. I don't think they have many leads to be quite honest.'

'Probably not, otherwise they wouldn't have used you,' Michael comments.

'That's exactly what I was thinking.'

'I can't believe there's a serial killer in New Orleans and none of us even knew about it. It's interesting how his MO's changed.' Michael sips his wine.

'That's what the FBI agent also said.'

'FBI?' He raises his eyebrows. 'The FBI is involved?'

'Shows you how little they have on this guy.'

'That's a bit of a concern, I hope they catch him quick.'

'I don't understand the killer though.' She frowns and downs the glass of wine, then fills it up as she talks. 'Who would do something like this; who gets a kick out of killing people like that? And like that! I mean I wasn't exaggerating when I called him pure evil earlier.'

'In our library we had many books, and among those books was a book on why killers behave the way they do and how they think, now I read some of it when I was younger, you know when you watch scary movies or read scary books, it intrigues a man. Anyway, I can't remember all of what I read, and as I say I didn't even read all of it, but one of the things I remember them comparing was nature versus nurture. One serial killer even said that killing became the same thing as having sex, so I think that even though they come across all bad, they do enjoy themselves in some weird way.'

'What is your opinion?' asks Lily.

'My opinion?'

'Yes your opinion.'

'My opinion is irrelevant.'

'Okay... so what did they say about nature versus nurture?'

'I think if I remember correctly they said that this is one of the oldest debates, whether a person is born bad, or if they become bad. There's a great debate about that in psychology and one man made a comment to say that a psychopath is born and a sociopath is created, but for you to have a serial killer, you need an element of both nature and nurture. It's just easier for those who are a little bit unstable to be influenced to commit those crimes.' Michael's tone is impartial. 'I mean Albert Fish said that none of us are saints. I think he was trying to say that all of us at one point or another do something bad, or something that is socially frowned upon.'

'Are you defending them?'

'No. I'm just telling you what the book said,' Michael smiles at her and looks at the water. 'Beautiful don't you think.'

'Amazing. Maybe he was poorly educated.'

'No, it has nothing to do with education, some of these killers were – and probably still are – intelligent.'

'Pete said that he's becoming more and more violent and brutal. Do you think he's trying to get caught?'

'I don't think any killer wants to be caught; I mean if that were the case, they would want to be punished for their crimes, and that implies they feel bad about their actions. I think perhaps they would prefer to be recognised by someone, if not everyone. I must say this killer you speak of really fascinates me.'

'You don't think they feel bad?'

'Why would they?' Michael responds. 'Each one of them is driven by something in some way. I would say if you can figure out what drives this specific killer, it would be easier to catch him.'

'They have no leads though.'

'He seems to be planning these things well.'

'He should just leave me out of his plan.'

'I could protect you if you wanted me to?'

Lily laughs, the alcohol has now taken effect; she's not used to drinking, her head feels a bit fuzzy. 'How can you protect me from a serial killer?'

'We can stay on this boat until he is caught?'

'Can we?' She leans forward. 'And what will we do on this boat until that day?'

Michael comes closer, almost kissing her, he takes off her shirt, then unbuttons her pants, he pushes her back onto the tanning chair and pulls her pants off. Then looks her straight in the eye and says, 'We'll tan.' He smiles. 'You are attractive, but I refuse to take advantage of a girl who had had a bit too much,' he winks at her.

'Such a gentleman,' she replies as he walks behind her and puts on some Caribbean music.

'Here you go,' he hands her a glass.

'What's this?'

'Vodka with passion fruit cordial and lemonade.' They listen to music and tan and drink and talk for ages; somewhere during the day, lunch was served, honey roasted chicken salad with nuts and rocket and strawberries. They do something that she's never done before, watch the moon rise. 'This is one of my favourite things to do, we give the moon so little credit.'

'I've never thought of it that way.'

They stand on the side of the boat, the water-cooled breeze is sharp; Lily is still in her bikini and Michael can see her shivering every now and then. He fetches a throw to cover her. While walking back he notices how tiny her bikini bottom is, just a thong, and her bum is now lightly reddened by the sun. 'I see you're cold,' he says and places the throw softly over her shoulders.

'Will you rub some aloe vera after-tan gel on me before dinner?' She says, now sober.

'Of course, I'll fetch it quickly, it's in the master bedroom.'

'No need, we can do it there, then I can also get dressed for dinner.' But then she realises she has no bag. 'I didn't pack!'

'I came prepared; I bought you a cocktail dress for tonight and the crew can wash your clothes for tomorrow.'

'I'll have no underwear.' She comments, soft and suggestive.

'I didn't think that one through.'

She touches Michael's arm. 'I'll just not wear any tonight then.' She bites her lip. 'I changed my mind, I'll quickly shower and get dressed, we'll have dinner and then before we go to bed you can rub the gel into my skin.' She frowns. 'Where am I sleeping tonight?'

'Wherever you want.'

'Where would you want me to sleep?'

Michael smiles. 'I don't think I need to answer that one.'

'It's okay, I think we're on the same page.' Lily walks off and disappears. After her shower, Lily joins Michael in the dining room of the yacht. Her hair is still damp and she's barefoot. Having no underwear she keeps her arms at her sides, to ensure the short black dress doesn't lift, but her nipples are visible through the unpadded top. 'It's comfortable.'

'It's beautiful.' Michael pulls out her chair. He calls the waiter over with a wave and dinner is served. 'I hope you enjoy seafood; we're having lobster.'

'It's a first for me.'

'You've never had lobster?'

'Never.'

'Oh wow, well there's a first time for everything.' The lobster is soft and melts in the mouth; the chef prepared it to perfection with lemon butter and a small side of fried rice and a green salad. During dinner, the two are very quiet, both in anticipation of what will happen after dinner.

'That was delicious, thank you.'

'It's a pleasure.' Michael gets up. 'A nightcap?'

'No thank you, I think I'm ready to turn in for the night. Are you coming?' Lily asks looking over her shoulder with her legs crossed, and holding onto the doorframe.

Michael feels warm. 'I'm coming.' He follows Lily to the room.

Lily crawls onto the bed; standing behind her, Michael can see the bottom part of her vaginal lips as the dress pulls up onto her tight bum.

She looks over her shoulder. 'Are you just going to stand there and watch?'

Michael is quiet as he takes off his shirt, and undoes his pants; now only in his underpants. Lily puts her head on the pillow, and with her bum still in the air, the dress slides up and over her back, everything is now visible, even her breasts can be seen.

'I think you can take everything off,' Lily says and starts to rub herself with her fingers. Michael still quiet, not saying a word, takes his underwear off, his penis is erect. He gets onto the bed, but he doesn't enter Lily, first he lies down on his back, with his head between her legs, he pushes her knees apart and her clean shaved vagina is just above his face, he can feel the warmth and the moisture on his lips.

Chapter 35

Peter walks to his car; it's late, around nine at night. *This was a long day, I'm exhausted,* he thinks to himself. The car smells funny inside, a faint but noticeable scent; fruity even. His doors lock and the smell increases, he tries to escape but the doors won't open. From what seems a distance he can see three people standing there as his vision starts to blur and he becomes euphoric. His mind has adjusted to the smell now, he can't smell anything out of the ordinary.

'Wake up,' a deep voice says, but it feels more like a dream than reality. Water gushes over his head. 'I said wake up!'

Confused, Peter mumbles, 'where am I?' The lights are haloed and dim, the voices muffled. 'Where am I?' He finds he is tied to a chair, he can't free himself, he's weak and the ropes around his arms and legs are tight.

'A warehouse.'

'Why am I here?' Peter feels nauseous.

'Why do you think you're here, Detective?'

Peter leans forward and vomits. It tastes like bile, bitter and strong. 'I don't know.' He vomits again. 'Why am I here?'

'Think, Detective!' the man responds aggressively.

Peter's vision improves, the haziness has been overcome by the adrenaline. 'I don't know.'

'I'm sure you'll figure it out soon enough.'

'Is it this investigation?'

'Bingo.'

'They're going to catch you.'

'You think so?' the man asks, never coming close enough for Peter to see his face. A knock at the door. 'I'll be right back.'

'I'm a police officer, man, just let me go!' Peter screams at the man as he walks away. With the man gone, Peter can focus on freeing himself. *Fuck, fuckfuckfuck. I need to get away from here.* He looks around, but in the dim light it's difficult to spot anything; he looks at the space in his immediate vicinity. There is nothing useful lying around. He tries to lift his right leg, then his left, both are tied at the ankles, tight; when he puts pressure on the ties, he can feel the circulation being cut off. But the chair is warm; wood. He does the same with his wrists, but no luck, his right arm is not as tightly bound as he left, but even with the little bit of play, he can't manage to get his hand through. He pulls harder but he can feel the rope split his skin. *I need to think of something else. This isn't working.* He leans forward again, seeing his vomit between his feet, and squats up hard, the chair is loose, but he can't get upright. Peter leans back into the chair, trying to shift his weight onto the back legs of the chair, then with his toes pushing hard into the concrete floor, he tries to swivel himself to see if there is anything behind him. His efforts are working, but not efficient, with every motion, he turns less than half an inch. Voices can be heard in the distance, faintly. Peter can't really make out what is being said; the deep voice he recognises, that of the man, another voice whispers, and the last voice—difficult to hear but it is definitely a woman's voice. Focussing hard on those voices, he almost forgets that he's bound to a chair. *The woman, that voice, it sounds so familiar but I just can't put my finger on it.* They must be walking way now because with every passing second, the deep voice grows softer, the whispers are already gone, and the woman's voice may now only exist in his mind, he's not even sure if he can still hear her talk, or if he's imagining her responses. This is good, with them gone, Peter can try again. The muscles in his neck strain and his spine clicks as he throws his head over his right shoulder, trying desperately to see what's behind him, he closes his left eye hoping that his right one can focus better alone. He does the same over the left shoulder. It seems like there's nothing. Peter leans forward again and with great force throws his weight back in the chair leaning backward as far as he possibly can, his feet lift and his balance moves over slowly; he starts to fall. The moment the chair hits the ground, the right arm rest cracks at the joint. Peter is winded, but determined, he rips hard up and down until the arm rest gives way. 'Thank you, thank you, thank you,' Peter whispers at the ceiling. He needs to move quickly now, before the man returns. The splintered wood cuts his arm as he pulls his wrist over the broken bit, but his right arm is free. Still on his back he slowly unties his left arm. Then with both hands free he pulls himself onto his left side and yanks the ties from his ankles. He looks around, still nothing useful. Dust, the smell of dust is distinct, this place is old, and abandoned. *The chair, it's my only option now.* Peter walks back to the chair and steps hard on one of the legs. *It's short, and light, I'll have to make it count.* Peter tiptoes over to the door, the light in the passage can be seen through the gap between the door and the floor.

'Hey!' he screams, standing against the wall. If the door opens, he'll be hidden behind it.

'Heeeeeeey!' he shouts again, hoping to lure any one of them to him. Footsteps now audible, and just before the door opens, he can see a shadow break the sliver of light underneath the door. As the man appears in front of Peter he bashes him behind the head with the leg of the chair, the man goes down, immediately unconscious. Peter hits him two more times behind the head, enough to injure him severely and keep him unconscious, but not enough to kill him.

'Piece of shit,' Peter says to the unconscious body and pats him down for any weapons, but the man is unarmed. Peter takes the piece of wood and walks out the door.

'Detective.'

'You're fucking with me right!' Peter yells, in rage and incredulity. 'Right?'

'You stopped coming to therapy, and I understand that you were angry at us, but your therapy must continue for you to catch this killer,' Dr Alexander Rayne says smoothly, with Diana standing behind him.

'This was another one of your twisted games.' He puts the leg of the chair on his shoulder like a bat. 'Who did I just beat to a pulp?'

'A hired hand.'

'Diana?'

'Yes?' She responds, and for the first time he can sense fear in her.

'What the fuck did you guys do?' Peter's face is filled with anger; it's difficult to read him in this moment. He slowly walks closer and points the piece of wood at them. 'I should be beating *you*, not the hired hand.'

Dr Rayne puts his hands up. 'Come now, Detective, this was for your own good.'

'For my own good?' Peter laughs angrily and manically. 'For my own good!' he screams again. 'Explain to me Doctor, please, just how was any of this for my own good?'

'We just wanted you to experience fear, Detective, that's all.'

'*We?* You and Diana?' He leans to one side to see all of Diana.

'Please, Peter, calm down—'

'You shut up,' he barks. 'I'm going to fucking kill you!' He turns to Dr Rayne. Diana starts to cry. 'Oh! Now you can cry?'

'I didn't sign up for this, I warned you!' Diana screams at Dr Rayne.

He slaps her hard. 'Quiet.'

'Did you really just hit her?' Peter asks.

'Peter, please I don't want to be part of this anymore,' Diana wails.

'Before I decide how to handle this situation Doctor, I would like for you to explain to me just how Diana got involved with you.'

Dr Rayne cocks his head, 'Detective.'

'You better tell me before I beat it out of you,' says Peter, more composed now. But Dr Rayne doesn't respond. 'Diana?' He turns to Dr Rayne. 'And if you interrupt her, so help me. I'm tired of your shit Doctor, and all I have to say is that all of this was self-defence.' Dr Rayne shrugs.

Diana cries while talking, 'I was depressed, and my mother took me to him. Over time he made me do things. In the beginning it was just talking, but eventually he made me give him oral sex, then sleep with him... after that, it spiralled out of control; he raped me twice. I want out, but I stay with him!' Diana is nearly screaming now.

Peter looks out Dr Rayne, then charges him and hits him in the face with his fist, knocking three of his teeth loose. 'You have a week to disappear; if I ever see you again in New Orleans, I will kill you, do you understand me?'

'Yes.' Hands to his face as blood gushes from his mouth.

'One week. You're an animal.' He puts his arm around Diana. 'Come, you can stay with me until you're back on your feet.'

'It's too much.'

'No it's not, come stay with me.' He looks at Dr Rayne. 'Your buddy in there will live, but he's your problem.' Peter and Diana walk out of the warehouse and leave in Peter's car.

Chapter 36

The next morning Peter comes to work, tired, stressed, and for the first time he's late. ' Morning Pete. First time you're late, you okay bud?' Brady asks.

'Sorry guys, I just had a rough day yesterday, but I'm okay now, thanks for asking,' says Peter a little despondently, but his face shows a degree of relief and satisfaction.

'Now that we're all here,' Kelly bumps Peter with her shoulder in a playful manner, 'there was a suggestion the other day to use a previous and retired investigator. The man's name is Nicholas, he used to be part of some or other investigative unit, and I've been given the details of where to find him. Now I know that we'd rather do this ourselves, but right now I think the more help we can get, the better.'

Brady steps forward, standing large and with authority in front of his colleagues. 'I agree with Kelly, I think we should give it a bash, we try this guy out, and if it works we keep him; if not then we send him off.' Peter and Andy look at each other then get up. 'Where are you guys going?'

'Well, Kelly said she knows where to find him,' Andy says, walking to the door.

The other three, Peter, Brady and Kelly follow Andy to his car. Inside the smell of smoke lingers faintly, but apart from that the car is spotless. 'Here's the address Andy.' Kelly hands him a piece of paper with an address written on it.

'He lives in quite a secluded area,' he says, studying the piece of paper. 'I know where it is.' Andy throws the piece of paper into the ashtray. After about twenty minutes of driving they turn off onto a gravel road. Peter's been staring out the window in silence for most of the trip, even though he says that he is okay, it's obvious that something is still bothering him, something is eating away at his mind—maybe it's Diana, maybe it's Dr Rayne; it could even be the case. The road is rough and they have to go slowly, it's evident that not a lot of people drive in and out on this road, the grass growing in the middle path can be heard hissing as it scrapes at the bottom of the car. A couple of bends now, left, right, long right, over a hump, now a gate can be seen, a large metal gate and on the inside of the security fence, trees, lots of trees, old ones and new. 'This is it,' confirms Andy.

Brady jumps out to check the gate; Peter's still staring into the middle distance and Kelly looks at him with worry. Brady tugs at the gate and it rolls effortless on its rail. 'It's open,' he says, sliding the gate open. It is a heavy gate, but the rail and wheels are well maintained, it rolls without difficulty. Brady climbs back into the car. 'I'll leave it open for now, if we need to leave quickly, we can.'

'We're coming to see a retired investigator, not a retired terrorist.'

'It's good to trust, but it's better not to trust.' He turns around looking at Kelly. 'We don't know him. So I don't trust him.'

'Fair enough, he is apparently a little bit strange in any case.'

'What do you mean by strange?' Peter asks, speaking for the first time since they left the office.

'My contact just said he's a bit weird, but he's apparently also very, very crafty.'

Andy proceeds slowly, focussing on the long and twisty driveway, trees on both sides. The other three are looking around. They take a sharp right, then a sharp left and the trees come to an end. A large open space with evergreen grass and plants confronts them, it's paradise. But the small house seems lost and forgotten on the enormous plot. 'Kelly.'

'Yes.'

'Is that him?' Andy asks pointing to an old wooden shed with a raised flag, unrecognisable to them. Next to the shed a man trots along with a broom between his legs like he's riding a horse. He's wearing socks and underpants and an old rag of a t-shirt. A pot is on his head and a wooden spoon in his hand, he waves it around like a sword, hacking endlessly at the air around him, then he sticks the spoon in the air and rears his broom of a horse. Kelly is silent; all of them are. 'He's not weird,' Andy says, 'he's fucking crazy.'

'It does seem a little like he may have lost his mind since your contact spoke to him,' Brady says, trying to keep from laughing as the man in socks and underwear races his broom horse across the lawn with the pot hopping on his head. 'But we're here now and we might as well at least speak to the guy, if he manages to understand us.' He can't keep it in; Brady starts laughing, and one by one everyone in the car starts to laugh. 'Andy,' Brady eventually gasps, 'take us forward.' Andy parks the car, the four get out with their eyes red and faces wet from all the laughing. 'Okay we need to control this now,' Brady wipes and straightens his face. 'Kelly will you take charge for us on this one?'

'I guess it was my idea.' She walks over to the strange man, the three detectives following. The man stops his horse, brushes its neck and places the broom gently on the floor. He walks over to the four.

'Hello Sir, my name is Kelly. Are you Nicholas Hollingsworth?'

The man takes the wooden spoon and pushes the pot towards the back of his head, the pot starts to fall and clangs as it hits the floor. The man's beard is grey and unshaven, his hair is also grey and long; he looks like a wizard. His green eyes are strikingly perceptible through the ash-grey hair and his skin is oddly pale for someone who's running around in the sun. He looks about fifty. He only takes two seconds to scan the four, and then, in perfect Japanese, he greets Kelly. 'Good morning, Agent.'

Kelly frowns and replies in Japanese, 'good morning.'

He continues in fluent Japanese. 'Agent why do you surround yourself with these baboons?'

Kelly finds him funny and giggles, but replies in Japanese. 'They're my colleagues. If I may ask, how did you know I was an agent?'

'I wonder what they're saying,' Peter whispers to the other two.

'Your badge and gun,' still with the fluent Japanese. 'The other three have their badges displayed like paintings on their belts, yours is tucked neatly in your left inner jacket pocket, I can see the faint outline. Same with the gun, their guns are out there on display for everyone to see and they are full-size versions; yours is on your right hip hidden under your jacket, and is compact, for concealment. You don't need the extra barrel length do you, Agent? You guys from the FBI get enough shooting practice. Now a question for you Agent Kelly... Agent Kelly who?'

'Young.'

'Beautiful. Tell me Agent Young, why is the FBI assisting New Orleans's finest?'

Kelly switches the conversation to English. 'There is a murderer – serial – we are having trouble catching him. Judge Lucius Vance gave me your details.'

'Lucius! My old friend.' Nicholas says. His voice displays his excitement in an impeccable British accent. 'Let me get some clothes Agent, and we can be off.' He starts to walk away

Brady steps in, with Peter following. 'Wait hold on a minute Sir; we just want to talk to you.'

'Oh nonsense, Detective, you need my help and that's why you're here, clearly the beautiful agent Kelly Young is in charge here. Agent? Do you want me to come with you?' He strides on ahead.

'You spoke Japanese, why?'

Nicholas realises that this is a test to prove to the others why he needs to be on the case. He turns around, facing them again. 'You all judged me because I was running around here, but let me tell you, I'm writing a play, and the best way to write a play, is to act it. Now to answer your question Agent—although most westerners like to generalise and just call you Asians.' He pauses and looks at the three detectives, staring at them to make his point. 'There are differences. Your facial structure is longer and more of an oval shape, where Chinese descendants have a square facial structure and the Koreans a rounder face, giving them that perpetually youthful look. You also have beautiful big eyes with a more pronounced nose, where the Chinese have small eyes and small noses, and the Koreans also have small eyes, but with small and *long* noses. Your cheekbones are low and Koreans have high cheekbones. You speak perfect English which means you were schooled in English. Asian nationalities are proud people and prefer the children study in their first language; that means that you were born in America, your parents moved here before your birth, and that is also why you were able to join the FBI, you're an American-born citizen. Your English is perfect as I just said, but despite that, I can hear a faint nasal pronunciation of certain words that is obviously as a result of habit, which means that even though you were schooled in English, you spoke Japanese at home.' He looks at the three detectives who seem very uncomfortable. 'Don't even get me started on the three of you. Luckily all of you know about Agent Young's and your relationship.' He points at Brady.

'How did you figure that out?' Brady asks.

Nicholas smiles. 'Agent? Shall I put some more appropriate pants on?' But Kelly only smiles. 'Good, I'll be ten minutes or so, I also need to pack for a couple of days, you never know how long this might take.' He points to Andy and Brady. 'The two of you can smoke while you wait for me; I know you smoke a pipe.' He says to Brady. Then he looks at Andy. 'You also smoke pipe, but prefer cigarettes when you're out and about; don't throw the remainder of your habit on my lawn.' He picks up his pot and broom, and rides his horse into the house.

'How the fuck did he know that?' Andy asks.

Kelly smiles. 'I saw him look, I'm pretty sure that it's because you both have tobacco-stained teeth, but only you have stained fingers,' she says to Andy. Andy looks impressed. He lights a cigarette.

Ten minutes go by and Nicholas returns, he's wearing Converse All Stars sneakers, an old and faded black pair with tuxedo pants and a stretched tie-dyed shirt. 'I'm ready.' He walks right by them to the car, throws his bag in the back window and sits in the middle of the back seat. He leans out the door a moment later, 'well are we going now or what? And Agent Young you can tell me all about these murders in the car.' The other four join him, Andy in the driver's seat, Brady next to him in the front, to Nicholas's left sits Kelly, and to his right is Peter. 'All right, let's hear it.'

Kelly starts. 'We don't have much, to be honest. Four people have been killed so far, four that we know of. The first one was probably the most memorable one, I wasn't here during the investigation of the first, but I read the file. The first one was unusual because there was no blood; literally, no blood at the scene, no blood on or in the body, no evidence. He had defensive wounds and the COD was a slit across the throat. The second was much the same, except with the absence of defensive wounds and this time the man was killed in his own home and there was lots of blood. We assumed because of the arrest of Nathan Brown – who presumably sold crime scene cleaning kits to the killer under the table – that it was the reason the second scene had blood. The third was Nathan Brown himself, we brought him back out of protective custody... well that was the plan, but he was already back in town by then. We suspected he was the killer, but, long story short, he's also part of an organisation of influential people who he crossed, and then he was beaten, cut and then same story, a slit throat in his own shop. The last man was killed in an abandoned warehouse—brutally, he was stabbed almost forty times. He was also bound and his throat was cut at the end.' She hands Nicholas some pictures, one of each victim's throat, and one of each victim's wrist. 'He marks his victims with a triangle. He always cuts it into the left wrist with the apex of the triangle pointing to the hand.'

'Your suspects?' Nicholas inspects the pictures, close to his face.

'Peter suspected that it may be someone in the Savage group; we later found that they are connected to a much larger and more dangerous organisation. The three detectives used profiling to compile a list of people who they thought could be the killer. The murder of Nathan Brown confirmed the suspicion that the killer is part of the group, because the group blamed Nathan for drawing attention to them, and the next day he was killed.'

'Okay.'

'Our problem is that we can't figure out how he chooses his victims; Peter thought of a connection, but it went cold. And he leaves no evidence… we have nothing. At this time, he kills who and when he wants, and we have no chance of catching him.'

'Hmm… yes he does seem to be quite the attentive killer.' He takes Freddy's picture, then looks at the other three, then again at Freddy's. 'What about the other one?'

'I don't follow,' Kelly says, now confused.

'The other one, the other *killer*, Agent; anything on him?'

Andy turns his mirror to better see Nicholas; Brady turns around, now even Peter is staring. Nicholas keeps his focus on the pictures, but he knows he has four pairs of eyes on him. 'Sorry? There's only one as far as we know. He changes his MO with every kill, becoming more and more brutal. It was thought that he's starting to enjoy himself.'

'No Agent, you're wrong, there are two killers. The first one with no blood, it was meticulous, there were also defensive wounds, not because the victim tried to escape, but because the killer gave him the opportunity. I see here in the picture is a note, the first victim was struck on the back of the head and then in the face to knock him unconscious; he never saw it coming, so how is it that he had defensive wounds? Because the killer cut him loose; he gave him the opportunity to escape. The other three never stood a chance. Also, you can see there was a change in the blade, with the last one, at least, a curved blade was used. Serial killers with that level of perfection in their execution never change the tool, it's risky and sloppy, they have a ritual, and the ritual makes them successful. Everything you just told me indicates that the first victim was not the killer's first murder, he has killed many before to be able to do it with such excellence. The first victim was on display, it was a message. The next one was a sloppy attempt at a copy, but there are things missing, firstly the body was at the man's house and nothing was staged. Second is the blood. Do you really think a serial killer who makes the blood disappear will suddenly leave it all over the place? No he won't. Then there's the slit across the throat, the second one's blade was different to the first, the depth and width is different, and so it is with each victim. Same with the triangle, the last three are roughly the same depth, but they differ from the first one.' Nicholas hands the pictures back to Kelly. 'This is a good one. You have one masterful killer, and one copycat killer. The copycat is changing his MO because he's not getting recognition I would imagine. Have you kept this from the papers?'

'Yes.'

'So you're the reason he's escalating, he wants the actual killer to see his work, and you don't allow it.' He sees the doubt in their faces. 'Trust me, there are two, and the copycat is the least of your problems. If the killer didn't stage the first one, no one would ever have known that he even exists, we need to find out who that message was for.'

Chapter 37

A man reads this on the last page of the New Orleans paper; not buying it, and not touching it either. 'Sir would you like a copy?'

'No thank you. I need to go.' The man disappears from the newsstand, after reading only Lily's blog; he seems uninterested in the rest of the news.

Later that day, Howard Cox goes outside to have lunch, he buys a pie and a soda which he devours outside the shop, he has an hour and the shop is a fifteen-minute walk from the office. Howard looks around, the street is quiet, and then pulls out of his pocket, a number for a prostitute who stays close to the office.

'Hello, sexy,' he says when she answers the phone.

'Mister Cox, when you call me it means we have business to discuss.'

'We do,' Howard says, now standing in an alley with his back to the street, hiding his conversation from society, which is what he must do, since he is a respected businessman.

'What would you like to do?'

'Well my wife gets home early today, so I was thinking that since I am already in the neighbourhood, what about a quick blowjob?'

'Can you be here in ten minutes?' Silence. 'Mister Cox I don't have all day, be here in ten and I'll swallow for you.' Silence again. She hears a strange noise and the sound of the phone dropping onto the street. 'Hello. Hello!' She hears him pick up the phone. 'Hello, are you okay?' She hears breathing on the other end, and then the call is disconnected.

'Let's go, Howard, we have much to discuss.' A man pulls Howard's body behind a dumpster. The heels of Howard's expensive black shoes drag on the ground. Behind the dumpster the man effortlessly picks him up and places him in the trunk of a car, binding his hands and feet. The chloroform will keep him asleep for the trip.

Howard wakes up, bound to a trolley, the same as Freddy. 'Where am I?' he says in fear.

'It's the first time in a while that I've opened the skylight. Look how big the moon looks tonight. I usually keep everything closed during the proceedings, but I had to answer a question for a friend. Do you like the smell of the fresh cut grass coming through the top windows?' says a man from behind him

'Help!' Howard screams when he sees the open windows.

'That won't help.'

'Help!'

'Scream all you like, but trust me, we're far from everyone; no one can hear you,' the man replies calmly.

'How much do you want?'

'How *much*?' a sigh, 'Howard, money won't buy you out of this.'

'I'll pay you double.'

The man keeps quiet, gathering his thoughts. 'You're assuming someone paid me. I took you because I wanted to; this is for no one else,' the man says, and Howard doesn't respond. 'I will never forget my first time, I really thought that I was going to get caught. But this is not that time, oh, I apologise for being rude, I would stand in front of you, but I usually only show you my face at the end, and tonight is a full moon.'

'Please man, let me go. Why me?'

'You should know why you. I must be honest, anyone would've worked but Lily asked me a specific question, and therefore I have to answer it.'

'Lily? Tomlinson?'

'Aha! Yes, Lily Tomlinson; you see, whenever I do something for her, I leave a little… mark. And it seems from her blog that someone has attempted to copy my work.'

'But why me?'

'The fact that you know Lily's name means that you crossed paths: tell me how, again.'

Howard starts to explain, hoping it would buy his freedom. 'It was just a joke. I kept on scaring her.'

'To what end? What happened to her?'

'She had to see a psychologist.'

'Psychiatrist,' he corrects Howard.

'It was a joke, I'm sorry.'

'Tell me Howard, what happened at the psychiatrist?'

'The guy molested her.'

The man keeps quiet for a moment. 'Yes he touched her breasts while she was under hypnosis. Luckily for her, she thought it was a dream.' The man closes the skylight and walks around to face Howard. 'She's lucky that he didn't do anything else. It was between you and him, but I seem to have lost track of Alexander. Doctor Alexander Rayne, the child molester. When I find him, I will bring him here.'

'Please just let me go. I'm begging you.'

'She was only a child.'

'Please.'

'Here's how this is going to work, I am going to let you go, and the keys to the door are in my back pocket. If you can take them, you're free.' The man is calm and contained. Then he unties Howard.

Howard just falls on the floor and starts to cry, 'I can't do this.'

'You're not even going to try?'

'Please!' Howard cries loudly. But he doesn't move, he stays curled up in the foetal position, sobbing.

'Howard there have been twenty-eight people in this room before you, and this is the first time that the person didn't even try.' The man walks behind him, grabs him in a choke hold and picks him up by his neck, he holds him for a while from behind, but Howard doesn't resist. 'I will end this quickly out of mercy.' The man pulls the blade out from behind his back and in one quick and seamless motion he slits Howard's throat. Howard falls to the floor holding his neck. The blood streams through his fingers, warm and unstoppable, and moments later he loses consciousness. The man ties his feet and hoists him up with his head hanging over a funnel, the blood swirls into the bottle below, marked "Howard Cox". He clicks the button of a recorder. A breeze enters through the window, flowing gently. 'I'm standing here in the cold, dark night with my eyes closed, absorbing all of the sweet senses. I feel the wind on my skin, touching me softly and dragging its fingers across my body, better than the most perfect, unimaginable lover ever could. A touch so perfect it sends impulses down my spine, calming and nurturing. I smell soft and clean, almost soapy, cologne, mixed with the smells of iron and grass. When I take a deep breath, it fills every space from the tip of my nose down to the bottom of my lungs. The taste in my mouth so natural, raw and metallic, the sort of taste you get only with vigorous exercise. Unpleasant yet so perfectly suited and wanted. I hear the wind slowly moving through the leaves outside, gently pushing each one ever so slightly out of position. I also hear dripping in perfect harmonious synchrony with the wind combined with the crickets. An orchestra conducted by nature. I open my eyes and look down at my creation: art. In my hand, the knife dripping with fresh blood; the body still seems to be warm. The blood, blackened by the glimmer of moonlight, seeps slowly from his neck, I don't think there's much left. It's almost time to cut the triangle. Oh! How it all comes together now. Do you see it? Smell it? Taste it? Do you feel it little Lily? Don't worry, I won't leave you with such a mess, I'll clean him up first. I leave you this voice recording so you can understand what went through my mind. This one was for you.'

Then he picks up the left arm and cuts a perfect triangle with the apex pointing to the hand.

The phone rings. 'Hello.'

'Peter it's Kelly here; there was another murder.'

Peter jumps up. 'Where?'

'I'll send you the address now, but Peter you need to bring Lily. You were right. The call came through and Nicholas and I were close to the scene. He was also right, there are two killers.'

'I'm on my way.' Almost an hour later, Peter and Lily get to the scene. The body was placed neatly under a tree.

Nicholas runs to the car, dressed like a homeless man. 'Is this the girl, Detective?'

'Yes this is her.'

'Come child, walk with me,' Nicholas says to Lily. She walks with him and he escorts her to the body. 'Do you know this man?'

Peter catches up with the two. 'Yes Sir,' she grabs her mouth. 'He used to scare me when I was a child, he kept doing ghost pranks and ran after me with a knife, but he never touched me.' She starts to cry.

'It's okay my dear, I know this is difficult, can I ask you to do me one more favour?'

'Yes, Sir.'

'Listen to this recording and tell me if there is anything you recognise, anything at all.'

'Okay Sir.' With a gloved hand, she plays the recording, everyone now quiet, also listening. *Another one, another signature-marked body, dumped. This one is different though, this one was left for me to find, for me to admire and indulge in. How does one choose between the living and the dead? How does one choose who lives and who dies? He knows. He knows this question exists within me and that's why he left me this body to find. This one seems more like the first one. Over time the modus operandi, the MO, has changed. But the evidence is just so unclear. No one knows any more. I just wish that I could see how I fit into this, why am I one of the puzzle pieces? I'm just a regular girl; I'm just Lily. Pete does me these favours though, letting me onto the crime scenes even though I'm not even related to law enforcement. He believes I'm somehow connected to the killer. Not sure how yet, but I guess he's the detective. I truly don't know what to do. They already checked the recorder for prints and unsurprisingly there were none found. The voice is muffled; it can't be recognised. He's so careful, so meticulous, never makes a mistake. He believes the killing was done elsewhere, the body's bled dry and not a single drop can be found where the body's staged, almost like he didn't want to spoil his thoughts on the recording with an actual picture. In a very strange way, it's artistic. He always cuts a triangle into the wrist, the left one, it's the sign. This one is a little different though, it's almost like he waited for the body to be nearly bled dry before he drew it. The triangles are usually messy, this one, however, is perfect. Only a little bit of blood has seeped into the cuts, leaving the triangle red and distinguishable from the rest of the skin, but not ruined by a bloody mess. This one is perfect.* 'No Sir, I don't recognise anything.'

Nicholas sighs. 'That's okay.' He looks at Peter. 'You were right, Detective. Congratulations. There are definitely two killers though.' He says to the group, 'This one and the first are the only two that are linked to the girl, and they were done exactly the same. The other three were, without a doubt, done by someone else.'

Chapter 38

"Dear Lily.
I hope this letter finds you well. I understand that you might be confused at this moment and that for a brief period you will probably compare me to the monster that you encountered, however I must tell you that I am nothing like him and when I take a life, I do it with good reason. I stand by my word and you should not fear me; I mean you no harm. One day you will understand my decisions and one day you will see the world through my eyes. You are worth more than all the gold in the world.
Please will you convey a message for me? Tell Peter, Brady, Andy, Kelly and Nicholas that I don't appreciate cheap imitations of my work. I took offense at this other man and he abused my meticulous system for attention. I will find him, and I know that the team won't stop looking for him either, so let us see who gets to him first.
P.S. Thank you for your blog and for your kindness."

Chapter 39

'Sugar?'

'No thank you, I drink my coffee black,' says Nicholas.

Andy puts his feet on his desk and leans back in his chair. 'The captain will be in soon, then we'll introduce you and you can tell him about the second killer.'

'Thanks, old chap.' Kelly hands him a cup of coffee, he puts his nose over the edge and inhales deeply. The vapour becomes two strings as it enters his nose. 'Gosh Kelly this coffee smells incredible.'

'Thank you.'

Nicholas gets up and walks around the office, inspecting each desk. The team just stares at him. He looks at the blinds, then through them at the window, and then through the window. 'Peter…' Nicholas keeps staring through the window, calling Peter over with a wave of his hand.

'I'm coming.'

'Isn't that your friend?' He points to a girl outside.

'Lily? Yes it is, why is she here?' He runs out to get her. The team keep staring at Nicholas, and he, oblivious to them, continues to stare out the window.

'Nicholas.' Peter calls with Lily at his side.

Nicholas turns around and there next to desk, behind Peter is Lily, as white as a sheet. 'Oh dear young lady, what's wrong?' Nicholas asks while walking closer to her.

She sticks her hand out with all the letters she received. 'I never thought much of it—' she starts to cry. 'But the last one, it's him.'

'It's who my dear?'

'It's the killer, he's been writing to me all this time, and I've been responding with my blog.' Lily continues to cry and hands the letters to Nicholas.

Nicholas opens them and scans through them quickly. 'Interesting. Lily, my dear, can I keep these? Just for the night.' Lily nods. 'Thank you, I will return them to you tomorrow, I just want to analyse his handwriting.'

'You can do that?' Brady asks.

'Oh yes. I have studied graphology for many years. Lily do you have any other information on this man that could help us?'

She thinks for a while. 'No, Sir.' And just before Peter speaks, she interrupts, 'actually, maybe Michael could help.'

Peter asks. 'Michael? *Your* Michael?' Lily nods.

'Why do you think he might be able to help us?' Kelly asks.

Lily looks at Nicholas and points to the letters. 'Because in a similar way to how he writes to me, he also communicates with Michael; he gives Michael paint and he's also given him some paintings.'

'Interesting…' Nicholas rubs his head, making an even bigger mess of his hair. 'Can someone take me to see this Michael? I would very much like to meet him and look at these paintings.'

Brady pulls Kelly closer, 'we'll take you.'

'Splendid. Peter I suggest you speak with your captain when he comes in to arrange some sort of protection for Lily.'

'He said he won't hurt me.'

'Are you willing to bet your life on that?' Nicholas says, walking off and not even looking at her. 'Come now you two, it's time to meet Michael.' The three drive off and shortly, Brady parks the car in front of the art gallery. 'Is this it?' Nicholas asks.

'This is it.'

They get out and walk into the gallery. Michael is busy painting, as usual, but he takes notice of the three investigators. 'Good morning,' he says.

'Good morning: I presume that you're Michael?' Nicholas takes charge of the conversation.

'That is correct. How can I help?' He puts his paintbrush down and wipes his hand on a white cloth stained with different colours.

Nicholas doesn't answer immediately; he wanders over to look at some of the paintings.

'Lily came to us with some information that you have connections with the same man that writes letters to her.'

'I do.' Michael's face speaks of betrayal.

'You see, the reason that she shared it with us – the fact that you have contact with him – is that we are investigating a murder and she is somehow connected to the killer—he writes to her. I then asked if she had any other information and she said that he sends you paintings. Is that correct?'

'Paintings and paint yes.' Michael picks up a bottle and hands it to Nicholas. 'That's the paint, every now and then he gives me a bottle. However, unfortunately, I don't have letters for you.' He seems more comfortable now with the secret that Lily shared.

Nicholas takes the paint and swirls it in the light, then opens the bottle and smells it. 'A very particular colour don't you think?'

'I've never seen anything like it, and I've been looking to buy more, but I can't find it anywhere, I think it's a special mix.' Michael points to the two paintings at the back. 'The man also sent me those.'

Nicholas walks closer, he touches the paintings, then smells them; slowly he sticks out his tongue and tastes the paint. 'Agent Young and Detective Harris.'

'Yes?'

'Don't you want to take this two pictures to the precinct as well as this bottle?'

'All right, but why?' Brady asks.

'Detective don't you find it strange that the bodies are always drained of their blood? And we keep wondering why... *this* is why. This is evidence, evidence of a murder, of the original killer. This paint.' He swirls it again in the light. 'I'm pretty sure it contains the blood of the victims, and those paintings, go smell and taste them, those were painted with only blood.' Michael looks at the paintings, then at Nicholas. 'The lab will confirm my theory.' He walks out and as he passes Kelly, he throws the closed bottle into her hands. 'See you later.' Nicholas sticks his hand in the air, calling a cab and then disappears with the letters in his pocket.

'Sorry Sir, we have to take them.'

'I understand.' Michael replies. 'As long as it keeps Lily safe, you can burn them for all I care.'

Back home, Nicholas opens each of the letters and spreads them on the floor. With a pen in one hand and a magnifying glass in the other, he analyses the handwriting, and it takes him most of the night. The next morning he walks into the office. 'And what did the lab say?' he asks abruptly.

'They confirmed it's human, we're waiting for DNA confirmation of whose blood it might be.'

'Great. Do you want to hear my report on the handwriting?' He asks hyperactively, seeming almost drunk. It's evident that he didn't sleep. 'Right, so this handwriting was very complex; notwithstanding that, I put a profile together. Our man is somewhere in his late twenties or early thirties. He has dark triangular slashes below the base line with lighter pressure above that fades into long upstrokes. He also has large pressurised I's with cradles at the bottom and the first humps of his M's are larger and angled with the second hump being smaller and rounder. The first letters of his sentences are also not connected to the others and the writing is upright and flows with a fast pace. The writing is neither too big nor too small.' He takes a moment. 'All of that tells us that our man would be artistic and charismatic. He definitely has a superiority complex and probably thinks that he will never be caught. He's assertive and dominant, yet at the same time, calm, but intelligent and pays great attention to detail. He most probably had some or other childhood trauma; lost a parent, or maybe both. It is evident that there is a lack of attachment to the parental figure in his home and he was probably a lonely child.'

'You got all of that from his writing?'

'The question still exists whether the handwriting is influenced by the personality, or if the handwriting dictates it. I agree with the former. But yes, graphology is a study of psychology that is ninety-seven percent accurate.' Nicholas's face is filled with satisfaction. 'It's not much on its own, but the moment we have suspects for the original killer, we can apply this profile and match that to our man.'

Chapter 40

The whiteboard is not very heavy and Peter is able to carry it himself upstairs to one of the empty precinct offices. The room is empty, apart from the five silver metal chairs. It has white walls and a bright white light; it used to be dim and yellow, but Detective Anderson changed the bulb.

'Sorry again that we had to meet here guys, but I have someone staying with me now for her own safety.'

'Lily?'

'No. Diana. You don't know her,' Peter says to Brady. Nicholas is wearing a cap today and a faded and stained blue shirt, at least two sizes too big. The cap is a red and white trucker cap with the classic naked lady silhouette on the front. 'Nice cap.'

'I'm a mother trucker,' Nicholas jokes. He waits for Peter to set up the board against the wall and then walks closer. He inspects the board with the utmost concentration, and puts his face so close that it seems like he may need glasses to see. 'Hmm...' He rubs his chin. 'Very interesting.' He moves to the next bit, then scratches his head. 'Very interesting indeed. Can I assume that none of these people meet the profile I gave you on the graphology report?'

'No one matches that report.'

'But all of them meet the other killer, right?'

'Yes.'

'The whole Savage family and a group of names I assume to be the closest to them in this... club. Rob,

William, Jacob, Kathy, the mayor... the *mayor*?' Nicholas turns and frowns while looking at the team. Then shrugs. 'And I assume the others, Gilbert and Victor; Ryan, Benjamin, Oscar and Edward are those that you expect to actually perform the murders under the orders of the others?'

'That is correct.'

'I like it.' Nicholas quickly moves back and sits down. 'Obviously this works on the basis of exclusion, so who do we investigate next?'

'Anyone really, I don't think it matters.'

Some silence as everyone stares at the board, trying to decide, then Nicholas looks around, and answers. 'Edward. Hmm, yes, I like that name, Edward Valentine.' He puts an exclamation mark after the surname Valentine. 'Let's investigate him next; who is this Edward Valentine?'

Kelly hands Nicholas a picture and Brady gets up; he stands next to the board waiting for Nicholas's attention. Nicholas scans the picture, blonde buzz cut, blue eyes, a piercing in the left eyebrow, medium height it seems, fit and lean in build. He looks up and Brady starts to explain. 'He's a very captivating person; he's alert and confident, definitely intuitive and smooth. He seems quite hungry for power too.' Brady licks his lips and starts to explain why he chose him and his connection to all of this. 'Quite some time ago we were at Peter's party and he had this theory that the person who committed the murder had to be part of the group. The three of us then went around— of course, sorry, I have to add that the Savage family hosted the party, and I can't remember why, but regardless of their reason, they said the most important and influential people would be there. We then went around speaking to people, without anyone knowing our plan and tried to profile them to see who would possibly fit the profile.' Brady took a sip of water. 'Benjamin Black is quite the criminal and Oscar Reid does business with him; I then overheard Oscar and Edward speaking and from that conversation gathered that he is in Benjamin's pocket. Knowing all of that, and taking his personality into account, I thought that he is significant enough to be on the list of suspects.'

'Have you considered the fact that none of these people may be the killer?' Nicholas asks.

'It's gone through our minds, but since we had nothing to go on, we reasoned that this is at least something.'

'Hmm yes, that makes sense.'

'In the interim, I have gathered some information on him. He doesn't really have a fixed job, he's a chef and he does private contracts, and that obviously brings to mind the question of where he gets all of his money.'

'Look if he is part of this group then I agree that he would make for a good suspect, but you must consider the fact that he is not a hitman for hire; he might have some other function in the system, something entirely unrelated, we need more information on this man. Miss Young, can you help out with that?'

Kelly gets up. 'Let me quickly log into one of the bottom computers and see what I can find on the FBI system.' She walks out.

Brady continues, 'That's where Kelly came in, we searched the names on our system and when we searched for Benjamin, it flagged the search on the FBI's system because they are investigating him for unrelated crimes.' Nicholas nods. 'Since then we've been stuck, really.'

'Let's think about it for a second, he does seem like the type of person that could probably be involved in some or other criminal activity, but at the moment I'm not entirely convinced that he is a killer. If we're lucky, Miss Young will find something to prove him innocent or guilty. Detective Jones, where can I get a cup of coffee?'

'I'll quickly make you one, how do you take it?'

'I think today I will do cream, yes, cream with no sugar, and strong, please.'

'Coming right up, do you guys want some?' Peter asks.

'I'll come help you, I'll make a cup for Kelly also,' Brady says.

Anderson talks as he walks out, 'I'm going for a smoke while Kelly's busy.' They all leave and Nicholas is left alone in the room. He looks at the board and the biggest question in his mind is how the mayor is connected to all of this. He is also not convinced by the idea of Edward Valentine, it just doesn't make sense; the picture, the profile, it makes no sense at all. Nicholas looks at the picture again, analysing every aspect of the photo. He looks at Edward's expression, and he can see the dominating look, but even with that he also looks a little bit too friendly, he seems proud, more than anything else. And pride doesn't make him a killer.

After a couple of minutes, the team returns, including Kelly; they're laughing. 'What an idiot,' Peter says.

Thinking they're talking about him, Nicholas asks defensively, 'Who's the idiot?'

'One of our friends was downstairs. We told him there's a bug in the bottle of milk, and as he looked inside it, Brady squeezed the bottle, squirting his face full of milk.' He laughs out loud. 'But he's a good guy, love him to bits.'

Relieved, Nicholas turns to the agent. 'Miss Young, what have we found?'

'He was caught shoplifting when he was fifteen, but that's it, he was never prosecuted because he stole an X-rated magazine. The state prosecutor just laughed and let him off with a warning, and made him pay for the magazine.'

'And at the time of the murders?'

'Nothing found, nothing to prove him innocent or guilty.'

'So what do you guys think?' Nicholas asks. 'Personally, I think that he doesn't seem like the type, if he committed the murders it would only be under orders; he doesn't seem like the type to act on his own.'

Peter frowns. 'I think we can put him on ice.'

'Agreed,' nods Anderson. 'He seems like a little fucker, but not like a killer. I think we can focus on the rest.' They all agree and remove Edward's name from the list, leaving Gilbert Wilburn, Victor Quinn, Ryan Hunt, Oscar Reid, Benjamin Black, and Thomas Savage as the remaining six suspects. 'We are still a little fucked you know.'

Nicholas smiles. 'Because we're only working on the copycat?' he asks.

'Yup.' Anderson responds.

Chapter 41

After excluding Edward, everyone goes home with a feeling of success and accomplishment. The cab drops Kelly at her hotel, she chose not to drive with Brady tonight. It's late and she's exhausted. Walking briskly, she enters the hotel lobby, but there's no one at the desk. Strange. She enters the elevator and inside is a woman with a straight face, she doesn't move. The numbers show as they reach each floor and Kelly starts to feel awkward with the woman behind her. Then as the doors open, two men are standing in front of the door and before Kelly realises what's happening, the woman grabs her from behind, holding a cloth over her face. Kelly's not knocked out immediately and tries to fight the woman, but the two men seize her arms and hold her down; she loses consciousness. She smells a strong smell, one she's smelled before, in training, it's ethyl chloride spray, that's it, she wakes up next to the docks with her hands cable tied behind her back and her feet chained to a weight; a cloth as a gag so she can't speak. 'It's time you leave us the fuck alone,' a masked man says aggressively. Kelly is trained well and even in this dire moment she tries to memorise certain landmarks, she knows trying to get away is futile, all she can do now is hope they don't throw her in the water, she'll drown; never be found. 'Did you hear me little Asian?' the man asks. 'I'll say it again.' He grabs her face and puts his face almost against hers, she can smell he recently had coffee. 'Leave us the fuck alone. No more playing games;

tell your people to stop searching for us.' She knows that someone told them that she searched for Edward on the FBI system, the organisation's connections run deeper than what she thought, but she knows they won't kill her, not today, this is only a message. The man takes her phone and dials nine-one-one, then drops the phone next to her. 'Next time you're dead,' he says and walks to the car. It's too far away, she can't make out the registration. The car disappears into the darkness and moments later she hears the siren of a police cruiser, they're driving fast. Luckily she was left unharmed.

'Ma'am are you okay?' A police officer shouts, jumping out the car, gun in hand. His partner walking with sights aligned around the premises. She doesn't respond, he removes the gag. 'Ma'am.'

'Call your captain, and take me to the precinct. My name is Kelly Young. I'm an FBI agent.' The man does as she asks and races back to the precinct, it takes no longer than ten minutes, but by the time she gets there, the whole group is there, all but Peter, he's still on his way. 'I'm okay,' she says as she walks in. 'They did nothing except threaten me.'

'I'm going to fucking kill them!' Brady screams.

But Nicholas advises, 'Calm yourself detective. She's safe now.'

Captain Deloitte seems angry. 'This just got out of hand, they're targeting our own, we need to catch this guy as in yesterday.'

'Captain I will not rest until he's caught,' says Brady.

Kelly takes his arm. 'We need to be careful now, don't let this steer us off course, I'm safe now—'

'I agree with Miss Young,' Nicholas interrupts. 'However, we shouldn't be scared, that's what they're hoping for. Having said that though, I do think that she must stay with someone, it's not a good idea for her to be alone.'

'She can stay with me, and we can go to the hotel to fetch her things,' Brady says promptly. 'Have we checked the hotel's security footage?'

'Pointless. I chose it specifically because it didn't have cameras,' says Kelly. 'Let it go, we know who's behind it and we also know that they won't be stupid enough to get caught.' She looks disappointed. 'It's quite evident that not only is this organisation still around and very active, but also that the whole thing where the FBI said that we've got them on the run is false; they have someone inside.'

'Inside the FBI?'

'Yes.'

Chapter 42

'Good evening, Benjamin.'

Benjamin Black looks around, but has no idea where he is. The room is dark and he can't see the man standing in front of him. Benjamin's bound. 'Where am I?' He remembers getting in the limo with a driver from the Royal Aces casino, his casino. He's vision's blurry and he feels nauseous. 'Where am I, man?'

'That's not important.'

'How did I get here?'

'I drugged your bottle of champagne, the one you drank in the limousine.'

Benjamin's body is weak and he tries to pull himself loose, but the attempt is futile, he's tightly bound. 'Fucking untie me!'

'I would love to; you're not entirely my type, but you'll have to do for now.'

'Your type?'

'No I'm not gay. You see Benjamin I need information—information that I suspect you might have.'

'Why me?'

'You're reckless. Come to think of it, I reckon the drugs I gave you wouldn't even have been necessary, but better to be safe than sorry.' The man walks around and stands behind him. 'Now as you know the police and the FBI, jointly, are investigating your little club. I would like to know who he is.'

Benjamin unaffectedly seems confused. 'Who are you talking about?'

'The person who kills.' The man yanks Benjamin's head back by his hair. 'The one who kills then takes credit for being me.' And lets him go.

'Fuck man, ask John!' Benjamin screams.

'I don't generally torture people, but you must understand that these are rather special circumstances,' says the man and hits Benjamin hard in the ribs.

'Fuck!' Benjamin screams still struggling to wriggle free. It's impossible to free himself. 'Look man I'm not all that loyal to them, I'll tell you what you want know, for crying out loud.'

'Tell me about the group and tell me who possibly could be killing in my name.'

'John.' Benjamin grimaces; the blow must have fractured at least one of his ribs, maybe more. 'John likes to pretend he's in charge, but he's just a puppet. The real puppet master is out there somewhere, he's somewhere in this town.'

'Who is he?'

'I couldn't tell you, only certain people are privileged to that information, and that includes the Savage family.'

'Who could be the killer?'

'I don't know.' The man steps beside him and pulls his hand back, but before he can land the punch, Benjamin starts to scream. '*No, no, no, no!* Look I fucking swear on my life that I don't know.' The man just stares at Benjamin, but he can't make out his face; the man moves only in the shadows. 'If I knew I would tell you, I don't like them killing people when it draws attention to us, I'm already under enough pressure from the FBI.'

'Is there anyone who you think it could be, anyone who looks like he or she would kill people?'

'Fucking Thomas, John, Ryan? I don't know. They all could.'

'Who's Ryan?'

'The butler. He does whatever John tells him to.' Benjamin tries to pull free again, struggling vigorously. 'Please man, I've told you what you wanted to know, now let me go.'

'And the operation?' asks the man, calmly.

'What do you mean by operation?'

'I mean what is the purpose of the group? What do they do? Why do they do it? Tell me about the group.'

Benjamin hesitates, and when he does, the man hits him twice, hard. 'Okay, okay, okay! Fuck! Fuck you man!' Benjamin grunts in pain. 'I only...' He continues to groan. 'I only know some of it. They're international and they have a finger in almost all pies... illegal business. I run a casino, strip club, and brothel, that's my part.'

'Brothel?'

'Yes, the girls who dance, they're all whores. All I know is every now and again, someone drops off another girl, don't know where she comes from or how she got there, but I'm sure you could use your imagination. There's no leverage over a man like taking his kid and turning her into a sex slave.' Benjamin starts to laugh. 'And that's just *my* job, who knows what else they do?'

'You actually do fit my criteria.' The man muses, changing tack suddenly.

'What do you mean by that?' Benjamin asks nervously.

'It means I'm going to let you go now.' Benjamin smiles in relief. 'Oh no, I'm not letting you go *entirely*; you see that door?' The man points right across the room,

Benjamin nods. 'That's the only way out of here, but it's locked and the keys to that door are in my back pocket. If you can take them and unlock the door, you're free to go. Simple.'

As the man walks around him to untie him, Benjamin says. 'Probably won't be a fair fight.'

'Would you like a knife?'

'No, you misunderstand: it won't be fair for you.'

'Good! Finally, a challenge.' The man unties Benjamin and walks back. Benjamin shakes his shoulders, loosening them up a bit, then the man switches the light on.

'You?'

'Yes, me.'

Benjamin laughs. 'I hope that you can fight, boy, because I'm going to fucking tear you apart.' Benjamin crouches into a kickboxing stance. He runs closer trying to kick the man with a powerful sidekick, but misses him, only just. The man retaliates but Benjamin blocks every punch and every kick, for the first time he has a worthy opponent. For about a minute, arms and legs fly, the man, then Benjamin; the man again. But neither of them is successful in knocking the other down. The man comes at Benjamin again, but Benjamin waits for him, grabs his arm and throws him to the ground; Benjamin now on top of him, he punches, but the man blocks him. Finally, he tries to choke him, but the man levers his left foot into Benjamin's pelvis. He grabs Benjamin's arm and throws his leg over him, placing Benjamin in a triangle choke. Now the struggle. Benjamin tries to free himself, but the harder he tries, the tighter the man squeezes with his legs, and after a couple of seconds, Benjamin starts to feel dizzy, and weak. His head feels thick, and finally, he passes out. But the man doesn't let go, he holds on for a bit longer, and tighten the crushing grip of his legs. Then, he lets him go, takes his knife, and with Benjamin lying prone, gently tucks the blade under his neck, and swiftly slices as he pulls out. The burning sensation, wakes Benjamin, he tries to cover his throat, but it's too late, he can't breathe, and the carotids bleed extensively, but briefly, before Benjamin starts to feel weak again. It's only been a matter of seconds. The man walks over and ties Benjamin's feet together, and his arms to his waist. Benjamin now drifting in and out of consciousness, he feels a dragging motion, and a nauseating pull upwards, he's now upside down and all he can see is the top of a funnel, he coughs, spraying blood on the floor; he coughs again, but soon after, his eyes close. The man cuts a triangle in Benjamin's wrist, with the apex pointing to the hand, and as the blood continues to run into the funnel, and the container below, the man quickly, but effectively cleans the floor around him. He takes the bottle and puts a label on it with Benjamin Black's name, then walks over to the fridge to place the blood next to that of the others.

Chapter 43

'What do we have guys?' Captain Deloitte asks. He crosses the yellow police barrier tape, and looks at the scene, he already knows; the question is just formality. The lights from the police cruisers flash unsynchronised: blue, white, blue, blue, white, blue, blue. A high hum is heard from the barrier tape as wind passes over and under it, vibrating the tape.

'Another murder, Sir,' says the ME.

'COD?'

'Same as the first, and the last.'

'So, we're dealing with the real deal here; are my detectives here?'

'Yes sir, they took a walk around the premises, the mad man wanted to have a look around.'

Captain smirks, smothering his laugh through his nose. 'Mad man,' he whispers to himself. Before he reaches the body, the group returns. 'Evening gentlemen, and Agent Young.'

All are pleased to see him and greet in synchrony, but Nicholas's voice is heard above the rest. 'Captain! Good to see you,' he says. They reach the body simultaneously. 'Tell me, what do you see here that's significant?'

Captain looks, and looks. 'No! Isn't that… what's his name again? Umm the man from the group, the… umm, the casino owner?'

'Correct, Benjamin Black. Our killer is holding up his end; he's hunting.'

'Anything… evidence?'

'What do you think?' Nicholas asks. The captain merely gives a wry turn of his mouth. 'Don't worry, we'll get him, eventually. We should focus more on the copycat, he's the one killing random people.' Nicholas bends down next to the body. Benjamin is supine in an anatomical position, bruising can be found over his right ribs, and some petechial haemorrhage is evident; apart from that, nothing, no other defensive wounds either. And then as expected, an expertly executed slice across the carotids and trachea, direction left to right, and a triangle in the left wrist, no blood. 'Benjamin could fight.'

'Why would you say that?'

'Look at the bruising over his ribs, high, and broad, there was more than one unguarded blow, which was done while he was tied up I would guess. He has no other defensive wounds, yet there is petechial haemorrhage, from strangulation. The question is why would the killer strangle him, and then cut his throat? And the answer to that is, he let Benjamin go, there was an altercation, but Benjamin was a worthy adversary.' Nicholas rubs his beard. 'Come to think of it, the killer unties all of them, think about the wounds of the previous victims. He gives them the opportunity to leave first, then subdues and kills them. Remarkable. You do know that is our first clue, right?' he says excitedly, looking around. But he is met with blank faces. 'He's a fighter, we're looking for someone in this city who can really fight, and I mean *really* fight. He must be magnificent and confident in that to have let the first one go, do you know what I mean? What was his name?'

'Freddy.' Peter answers.

'Yes, yes, Freddy. Think about it, Freddy was a large and strong man, and to let him go, then subdue him, that takes confidence, and skill.'

Kelly interjects, 'If you think that Benjamin was as good a fighter, then we should send a cruiser to all the hospitals and clinics in the area, maybe we're lucky and Benjamin left a mark.'

'Look if he's that good, it might be a waste, but send one,' Captain Deloitte says.

'Captain, there's not much more here, we can get the ME report in the morning, but we know what we'll find, this guy is clean, so I want to ask you a favour.' Nicholas says. He steps closer and softly says, 'Take me to the Savage home.'

'I'm not sure if that's a good idea.'

'Take me, please.' He looks like a relapsed drug addict, begging for a next fix. Nicholas always wears strange clothes that don't match, today is shorts with his coat and a white shirt, Converse sneakers and long socks.

'Why do you want to go there?'

'I'm going to convince them to give us alibies for some of the names on that list.'

'Why would they help us?'

'Just take me; I'll show you.'

Captain Deloitte is in two minds, on the one hand it seems like a good idea, Nicholas has a good argument, but he's not sure, he thinks for a while, *well what the hell, they have nothing, they cannot lose.*

'All right. When?'

'Now.'

'Now? It's ten at night.'

'I'll wait for you in the car,' Nicholas says, heading there. Captain Deloitte follows and takes him to the

Savage family's mansion, it's a twenty-five-minute drive from their location. At the gate, they're let in, much to his surprise. But Nicholas seems unsurprised and simply sits there, scanning the property.

'Good evening, Gentlemen,' Ryan Hunt says, calm, monotonic, but inviting.

'Hi… Nicholas.' Nicholas shakes Ryan's hand.

'Ryan Hunt, pleasure to meet you.' He looks at both of them. 'How can I help?'

'We'd like to speak with John,' Captain Deloitte says.

Ryan nods. 'Follow me.' They walk through the doors, once through, they notice a closed door on the left. Ryan opens it, and in the office, sit John and Sandra Savage. 'They're here to see you.'

'Thank you Ryan, just close the door behind you.' Ryan closes the door and sits in on the meeting.

Nicholas looks around slowly; he looks at Ryan, then Sandra, then John. The office is decorated in dark cherry wood, with a large glass desk and a brown leather couch set. The walls have been entirely converted to bookshelves filled with books and the light is bright. 'As you well know, we're investigating murders in the area.'

'*We?* Does that include you?' John asks.

'Where are my manners?' says Nicholas. 'My name is Nicholas and I'm a private investigator, of a sort. I'm just consulting at the request of a friend.'

John says hesitantly, 'Yes… we are aware of the investigation, is this another interview?'

'Not entirely. I have some names, and I would like to discuss some of them with you. I would like – if possible – for you to give me some alibis for them. It would make our investigation much, much easier.'

'Nicholas, we are not interested in helping you when the department could not come to us from the start.'

'You might be now…' Nicholas now silent. John tries to intimidate him, but with no luck.

'How so?'

Nicholas gets up. 'Never mind, we're leaving.'

John looks at Ryan, then says, 'Sit, please.'

Nicholas looks at Ryan sitting in an upright chair, with an absolute blank face. Then he sits and says, 'You might want to help us now, before you're all dead.'

'Is that a threat?'

'Not so much a threat as a warning, John. There was another murder; another one of your own.'

'Who?' he asks, looking shocked.

'Well let me tell you the story first. It seems that there are two killers. We suspect one is in your organisation, but he's not the concern, he's merely a copycat that will be caught. The other one, however, has made it clear to us that he does not appreciate the fact that this copycat killer exists, and has challenged us to a race, to see who gets to him first.'

'Who was killed?' John looks nervous.

'Benjamin Black.'

John sits back with his eyes closed for a moment, then looks at Ryan as Ryan exits the room. 'Damn, he was a good friend.'

'But not such a good citizen,' Captain Deloitte comments. Sandra sits in silence throughout the whole conversation, but she is follows closely.

'Will you help us exclude a couple of people?'

'Fine.'

Nicholas gives him a list of the inner circle members, he's smart not to give the names of who they think could be the trigger man. 'There we go.'

John reads through it. A pause. He hands it back. 'Get your pen.' Nicholas takes out his pen ready to scratch the names out. 'Evelyn wouldn't; her cousin was a casualty, not her. Scarlett and Emily were out of the country. I would think Rob wouldn't either; he wouldn't kill Benjamin; Benjamin was his biggest client. My son Thomas is on that list, but you are more than welcome to find his medical records, he was in a… hospital.'

'Psychiatric?' Nicholas asks.

'Yes,' John answers, then continues, 'Kathy and William I can't provide alibis for, but Jacob's been out of the country for months now trying to set up another branch of some import and export company.'

'Which one?'

'I can't remember; three letters.' John cringes.

'PCL?' Captain Deloitte asks.

'Yes that's it.'

'It's owned by Oscar Reid.'

John sits forward, the name rings a bell. 'Yes that's it! Oscar. Jacob and Oscar are out of town, so not them.'

'And Ryan?' Nicholas asks.

'Our butler?' John sounds incredulous.

'Yes.'

'Don't be ridiculous.'

They all sit for a while. 'Thank you for your time, and thank you for your assistance. Good luck and I'm sorry for your loss,' Captain Deloitte eventually says. 'Come Nicholas, we got what we came for.'

'Yes you're right. Thank you, John; Sandra, please give my thanks to Mr. Hunt.' They walk out alone to the car. On the way back to the precinct, Nicholas says, 'John's not the leader, he's just another member. Ryan on the other hand, *he* intrigues me.'

'Ryan?'

'Yes, he seems more like the leader type, but I don't know, he also has no alibi, John's word isn't good enough.' Sometime later they stop at the precinct, Nicholas walks over to the detectives, it's late, but they're still there working the case. 'Here.' He gives Kelly the list. 'Confirm if Thomas was in a psychiatric facility during the time of some of the murders and check if Jacob Taylor and Oscar Reid have been out of town.'

'Will do.'

'Find me upstairs,' he says and walks to the room with the whiteboard, he sits there in silence for nearly twenty minutes, then Kelly returns.

She leans into the door. 'All checks out, I'll call the guys.' Nicholas doesn't respond, he only stares at the board.

The other four enter the room. 'All right we can take Jacob, Oscar and Thomas off, which leaves us with Gilbert Wilburn connected to Kathy Larson. And Victor Quinn connected to William Smith, *and* Ryan Hunt.'

'Go home guys.' Nicholas says. 'I'm going to stay here and go through the files, we'll continue tomorrow.' He gets up and takes the names of Jacob, Thomas, and Oscar off the board.

Chapter 44

The next morning the team returns early in the hope of finding something, *anything*, that would help them. They all look exhausted. Brady and Kelly spent the night together and seem cheerful to some extent, Andy looks tired as always, but Peter has restless nights because of what Alexander Rayne did to him. Everything he did was for nothing, it didn't help the case one bit, and now on top of everything else, he is stuck with Diana, a bird with a broken wing. Diana's nice, but psychologically she's been changed and Peter can see it. They walk into the upstairs office and there he sits, Nicholas, in the exact same place he sat when they left last night. He went through the files as is evident from the pile on the table.

'Morning, Sir,' Peter says.

'Hello team,' Nicholas responds and they all mumble greetings back; he doesn't hear them, he only stares.

Kelly hands him a cup of coffee. 'Were you up all night?'

'I was indeed, and I found something interesting.' They all sit down and listen to him attentively. 'This group that you call the Savage group, it has been around for a good number of years. So last night I sat and I looked at that spider map of yours.' He points at the whiteboard. 'And it got me thinking, how is Mayor Richard Briarheart connected to all of this?' He looks at each of them, then smiles. 'He is a heavily connected man and would be an absolute asset to such a group wouldn't you say?' The team members nod in agreement. 'So how do you get one of the most powerful and influential men in the city to do your bidding?'

'Bribery.' Kelly answers. 'Or blackmail.'

Nicholas jumps up. 'Yes!' he shouts, 'that's the one, blackmail. The problem is you first need something with which to blackmail someone, and guess what I found?'

'You found exactly that.'

'Kathy... Principal Kathy Larson. When you look at her now, she's slightly overweight; she's caring and helpful according to her file, but—Peter my boy please pass me her file, behind you.' He points at the file and Peter reaches back to get it for him. Nicholas opens it and removes a picture, looks at it himself for a moment, then holds it in the air. 'Look at this luscious blonde girl, this is the same Kathy twenty years ago.' In the picture Kathy poses naked for a camera, covering her private bits with her hands she stands with her legs open and her lips pouted for a kiss. 'This was the blackmail. You see, Mayor Briarheart had one of these in his house, and Kathy claimed to have one almost like this, but in a hotel room, with our dear mayor holding those bits that she herself covers in this picture.' He puts it back in the file. 'Kathy joined this group at the age of nineteen, and at the age of twenty-one, her task was to seduce Richard, who at the time was merely a politician, and get it on camera. In doing so, Kathy climbed the ranks, and Richard got... persuaded, to join the group. And this is where Gilbert Wilburn becomes a strong suspect. Gilbert was a troubled child, and he somehow got his hands on a picture like that.' He points at the closed file. 'He then thought it would be a good idea to show Kathy this picture. Thereafter, she took him under her wing—oh and I forgot to mention she was one of his teachers. Nevertheless, she had him join the group and it seems, from what I've read, that he's always been in love with her since that day of the picture. But here's the juicy bit, he stated that he would do anything, *anything in the world* for her; he said that he would even kill himself if that was her wish. Now you're probably wondering why Kathy would have all those people murdered, right?' They're all on the edge of their chairs, amazed by what Nicholas has accomplished in one night. 'I'll take that as a yes. Kathy was placed in charge of the introductory phase of joining the group, and this entails coming up with tasks for the new recruits to do, and sometimes they can be quite... how do I put it? Disturbing to the individual concerned. These tasks can range from having sex with people to committing fraud; it all depends on what they want to accomplish in that time. Now here's a task for you guys: I have a theory, and you're going to prove it. After all this, I then went back to each victim linked to the copycat killer; I still can't find why he would copy someone, but I may have found how he chose his victims. It seems to me that the group does not take it well if you try and to leave, and I suspect that each one of the victims attempted to do exactly that: leave the group. There is obviously little to find on the matter, but I want each of you to take a victim killed by the copycat, and find out whether they joined the group, and then wanted out.'

'I can do one better,' says Kelly.

'Yes?'

'The FBI has an informant in the group.'

'My dear girl, you need to make a very important phone call,' says Nicholas. 'Why haven't you just asked him to find the killer?'

'He has very clear objectives and is only involved to some extent; somehow he got into finances, and his only objective is to report what he finds, nothing else.'

Peter asks. 'Finances?' He frowns.

'Yes.' Kelly's tone prohibits Peter from asking any more questions, and he lets it go.

'All right then,' Nicholas says excitedly, 'it seems, Miss Young, that you have better connections than all of us. Please call your connections, and when you're done, we'll be here.'

'Okay I'll be back in a moment.'

'Let us know if you need help,' Brady says

Nicholas smiles when he recognises young love. 'Go with her; keep her company.'

After some time, Brady and Kelly return and find the other three laughing and joking; furthermore, not only does Nicholas look strange, he also acts a bit strange. 'Guys.' Kelly calls for them to keep quiet. 'You were right,' she says to Nicholas. 'Our connection doesn't have access to that part of the group, as in he doesn't know who is in charge of handling the situation when someone tries to leave, however he did say that they don't take it lightly from his understanding. Also, you were right again: Kathy Larson oversees new recruits and the introductory period which is six months. He said that he doesn't think she takes people leaving lightly though, but he's not sure, he said that she might very well be. He also said that what you found was correct in terms of Gilbert, apparently, they call Gilbert "Kathy's pup". He does whatever she asks, and our connection agrees that he would make for a strong suspect.' She seems excited. 'Then I gave him the names of the victims.'

'And?' Nicholas asks. Kelly keeps him in suspense.

'All of them were new recruits; all of them tried to leave.'

Nicholas claps his hands together once with a great force. 'And there we have it! Now we have something to work with.' He licks his lips. 'Our greatest suspects on this list would then be Gilbert Wilburn and Ryan Hunt; get us everything you can on Victor Quinn and William Smith, let's see if we can exclude them, and if so, we bring the other two in for questioning.'

Kelly gets up suspiciously fast and says. 'I'll get everything I can on William Smith, you guys can investigate Victor Quinn.' She walks to the door.

'Would you like me to join you?' Brady asks.

'No need, I'll manage,' she replies and disappears from the office.

'That was weird,' he says.

Peter looks at the empty door, then at Brady. 'It seems that William Smith might be the FBI informant. Think about it, the informant is in finances, and now that strange behaviour, I will bet you my salary we won't find anything on Quinn.'

Nicholas sits down. 'You boys can relax, I agree with Peter, and I think she'll do one better. She's going to bring proof that William is clean, and she will bring us an alibi for Victor Quinn. Victor is a tool for the FBI, not this organisation, Victor just doesn't know that yet.' The three detectives sit down and continue to drink their coffee in silence, waiting for Kelly's return. The smell of coffee fills the room, and they're all in their own worlds, only now and again the occasional noise of one sipping coffee breaks the silence. Then Nicholas speaks. 'Don't let her know we know of William. It would put her in a tight spot.' None of them responds, but in their minds, they all agree.

The silence persists until Kelly returns. 'Okay I spoke to someone from FBI HQ,' she says. 'It seems that both William and Victor are in the clear. Victor ran a night tour on one of the nights of the murder; William was apparently on that tour as a gift from Victor after they met to discuss the finances of the company, which means that neither of them could've done it.' She looks at the four men sitting there. 'Have you guys done anything?'

Nicholas answers before one of the others can, 'We thought we'd have a coffee break first, but you were so fast that we hadn't even opened a file. But good work Miss Young, good work indeed. Can I ask for you to call my old friend Lucius, get a warrant for us to bring Ryan and Gilbert in, and then Anderson, will you arrange for two cruisers to pick up those two gentlemen please? Peter and Brady, you can help them, I'm now going to lie here on the floor and nap until they're here.' He waves his hands to indicate they must all leave. 'Come, come, you have to excuse me now.'

Later that afternoon Peter wakes him up. 'Nicholas,' he whispers. 'Nicholas,' he says. 'Nicholas!' he shouts.

Nicholas jumps up. 'What is it? What's wrong?'

'They're here.'

'My gosh, Detective, you gave me a fright; what time is it?'

Peter looks down at his watch, his hands a bit shaky. 'It's ten to four.'

'Good heavens! I slept all day.' He vigorously rubs his face and groans; Peter smiles, trying not to laugh. 'I'll meet you in the interrogation room,' he says and slowly gets up. First, he walks to the whiteboard, takes

William's and Victor's names off the board and then walks down to the interrogation room. 'Where are they?'

'We've put Gilbert in room one and Ryan in room two.'

'Who's leading the questioning?'

'Peter,' Brady answers promptly.

'Can I join him?'

'He's waiting for you in room one, you'll start with Gilbert.'

Nicholas walks to room one. The door handle is round, metal and cold. He opens it and enters the room. The inside of the door doesn't have a handle. 'Hello Detective,' Nicholas says.

'Gilbert, this is Nicholas, he's one of our colleagues, he will be joining us for this interview.' Gilbert sits in silence. 'I have your file here…' Peter starts to read in silence and every now and again he says, 'Hmm, interesting.' Finally, he closes the file. 'We already know quite a bit about you, we know you were born on the twenty-fourth of March in 1970, which now makes you thirty. We also know that you are quite assertive and stern and that you lecture Philosophy at the University of New Orleans. We already know that you are part of the Savage group and you are well connected to Principal Kathy Larson. We suspect that you are in love with her to some degree, and we also know that the group calls you her little pup. Now, since you can see we've done our homework, I would like to ask you some questions.' Gilbert says nothing; he only looks at Nicholas. He's not intimidated.

'Detective I think I'll wait outside,' Nicholas finally says. Then as he gets up and whispers in Peter's ear, 'He won't talk with me here, I think they've all been warned about me.' Nicholas walks to the door, knocks twice and the door is opened.

'Okay now that we're alone. Is it true? Everything I just said?'

'Yes.'

'Is it also true that you stated you would not only kill others, but also yourself if she asked?'

'No, I only said I would kill myself if she asked me to.'

'Would you kill someone else if she asked you to?'

'Yes.'

'Has she?'

'No.'

'Have you killed anyone of your own accord, or at someone else's request?'

'No.'

'Can you provide your whereabouts for these dates and times?' Peter puts a piece of paper in front of Gilbert with the dates and times of each of the copycat murders.

Gilbert looks at them all, licks his lips then answers, 'No, I can't remember.'

'Are you willing to answer these questions under polygraph assessment?'

'If you can provide a warrant, then yes, but right now you're fishing.'

'Tell me about this organisation.'

'There's nothing to tell, not everyone knows everything, and I'm a lower order member, I don't have privilege access to any information.'

'So, you don't know anything?' Peter asks.

'No.' Gilbert answers, his face straight; he doesn't even flinch. 'Detective, you're wasting both your and my time. If you have something, then book me, if not, I'm leaving. As I said before, this is a fishing expedition, we could have had this conversation in my office. Now, if there is nothing else…?'

'You can go,' Peter says and the door opens. Peter walks to the team. 'I was hoping he would drop something.'

'He did,' Nicholas says.

'What?'

'Well now we know that the lower order members only follow tasks, and that he's only willing to take a polygraph if there is a warrant for one; innocent men don't mind taking them, unless this lot just despises the police. We also know that he can't provide alibis for all of those dates.' Nicholas looks at the second room. 'Speak to him, I won't be joining you, then when you're done, and if Ryan remains a suspect, we place them under surveillance.'

Peter walks away saying, 'All right.' He enters the room where Ryan sits playing with a box of matches. 'Hello Ryan, I'm Detective Peter Jones.'

'Hello Detective, where's Nicholas?'

'Would you like him to join the interview?'

'Interview? I thought this was an interrogation? But yes,' says Ryan. Moments later, Nicholas appears in the door. 'Hello Nicholas.'

'Ryan, how are you?'

'I'm all right and yourself?'

'Good thank you. Why am I here?'

'Because we both know you're running the show here,' says Ryan.

'And who's running the show on your side?' Nicholas asks.

'Hmm...' Ryan smiles. 'All right, Detective Jones, fire away.' He picks up the box of matches again and looks down. 'And skip what you know, only ask me what you want to know. My time is precious.'

Nicholas interrupts. 'Why is your time so precious if you are a butler?'

'I have... things... that require my attention.'

Peter starts, 'How exactly are you connected to the Savage family?'

'I'm their butler, as Nicholas said.'

'And do they give you tasks to perform outside of their home?'

'Sometimes they do, yes.'

'Have they ever asked you to kill someone?'

Ryan smiles and then chuckles. 'No detective, they have not.'

'Have you ever killed anyone?'

'Many. I was in the military.'

'Have you killed someone recently?' Peter asks and slides the piece of paper with the dates and times forward. Ryan looks at them and smiles, then looks at Peter, but doesn't answer. 'Can you provide your whereabouts for these dates and times?'

'I was home, working, I'm a butler, remember? Ask John or any of his family members, I'm sure all of them will vouch for me.'

'I'm sure they will, is there anything or anyone else that could prove you were home during those times?' Nicholas asks.

'No. Right then, gentlemen, this has been fun, but I'm terribly sorry that I have to leave now.' Ryan says looking at his watch. 'I have a meeting to get to, besides if you had anything to go on, and I mean if you really had something concrete, someone would be in cuffs. Have a nice day.'

Peter gets up with him. 'We're not done yet.'

But Nicholas drags him down by his belt. 'It's okay Peter, let him go. I'll see you soon Ryan.'

'I should hope so,' Ryan says and leaves.

The rest of the team enters the interrogation room. 'Both are confident,' Nicholas says. 'Place them under surveillance, it's definitely one of them.'

'Which one do you think?'

'Difficult to say, but I do think that Ryan is hiding something, he's taunting us; there's more to Ryan Hunt than what we think. Try and get more on him. Miss Young, speak to my friend Lucius, get us a warrant for twenty-four-hour surveillance. We'll keep an eye on them for now, and maybe we can use them to catch a bigger fish.'

'I'll be right back,' says Kelly.

Nicholas stands around for a while, his thoughts racing, and his finger tapping on his chin in a slow but predictable beat. The men wait for Kelly's return to hear whether or not they have approval for the surveillance. 'Peter,' Nicholas says, 'I'm fairly confident that we will get this warrant; don't you want to do me a favour?' He asks very artfully. Peter nods in silence, willing to do anything. 'Won't you take me to your friend, Lily? I'm going to need her help with something.'

'Okay...'

'We can kill two birds with one stone here you know. We already know that the original killer reads her blog, so why not say what we want it to say? Why not call him out?'

Anderson's not convinced, his hoarse voice echoes. 'He'll know that it was us.'

But Nicholas smiles in satisfaction. 'And that's okay.'

'We've got it,' Kelly announces, walking into the room.

'Perfect. Peter, on second thought, all you have to tell her is to add a little something from me in her blog, for the rest of it, she can say whatever she wants.'

'What do you want her to say?'

Chapter 45

"To the mystery man.
It is imperative that we meet one day, my world is changing, and I'm scared that one day, there will no longer be a place for you in it. I have spoken to some of my friends; this monster I told you about, well they're on the hunt, and they have an idea who he is. But I fear that even if they find him, there is another, but one that wears a mask and who believes with that mask, no one will ever know who he is.
It seems to me that I have become the centre of so many worlds, but I'm not certain that it is in my best interest and I fear that someday soon, I will have to escape them all.
I look forward to hearing from you soon. xoxo"

Chapter 46

"**Dear Lily.**
I hope this letter finds you well. It would be sad to me if you were to leave. I enjoy our interaction; however, I also understand your point and I will merely hold thumbs and believe that all will work out as it should.
If ever you need comfort or protection, all you need to do is speak to my friend Michael, he will look after you, always.
P.S. Tell your friend Nicholas, that I got his message."

Chapter 47

After a long day, Peter comes home. It's late and he's exhausted, but Diana's light shines bright from her room, she's still awake. Peter walks in and slams the case file on the table, then leans on it with both hands and closes his eyes, he still must cook and shower. But Diana emerges from her room. 'Hey Pete.'

'Hey there.' His voice is filled with exhaustion and irritation.

'Shame, you look tired.' She touches his shoulder gently. 'Why don't you jump in the shower and I'll make you something to eat, then you can eat and go straight to bed?'

'You are too good to be true Diana.'

'I just know the feeling where it feels like you're taking on the world. And a nice warm meal always does the trick.' She smiles at him. 'I must warn you though, I'm not the world's greatest cook, but I make a killer bacon omelette,' she jokes.

'I love omelettes,' Peter says, trying to smile.

Diana nudges him in the direction of the bathroom. 'Go shower.' Peter walks away in silence and drags his feet all the way to the bathroom, then half-heartedly closes the door, but it swings open a slight bit, and Diana can see his naked body get into the shower. She can't help but think of the night in Alexander's office, with the girl. Free range eggs, extra-large, she cracks three of them in a bowl, then adds a pinch of salt, ground black pepper, a hint of cayenne pepper, Italian herbs, and crushed garlic, then whisks the combination and heats the stove. While the stove heats up she takes the back bacon from the fridge, it's cold but not frozen. She dices it. The smoked bacon goes well with salted butter and chilli. She adds a bit of honey and a dash of balsamic vinegar, but it seems bland, something's missing from the mixture. The stove is now so hot that it's gone red, she turns it down. *Shallots! That's what I'm missing,* she thinks, and looks for some in the kitchen. The diced shallots get added to the bacon and now... now it seems perfect. Peter's shower is still running, and steaming. Diana then adds a block of butter to the pan and waits for it to melt. Then, she adds the bacon concoction on low heat with a lid, to steam the bacon before she fries it. Diana walks to the table, the smells come together beautifully and fill the whole room, for a second she glances at Peter through the small gap, his body is shining and steaming from the hot water; he's taking his time. Diana smiles then leans against the table. She feels the case file beneath her hand. She looks at the shower door, he's still in there, then looks again at the file. She can't, he would be angry. But the thought burns, *one peek can't do anyone any harm.* She opens the file, and then goes through a couple of pages. Diana goes cold, and a chill runs down her spine, she looks like she's seen a ghost. Her body is frozen and she feels lightheaded. She grabs the file, losing some of the pages as she runs to the bathroom. Diana flies into the bathroom. 'Pete!'

He gets such a fright that he nearly slips as he turns around, grabbing his private parts to try and hide them. 'Diana!'

'I went through your file.' She holds it up in front of him, and the fear can be seen in her eyes.

'That's supposed to be confidential!' He turns the water down. It looks like Diana is going to burst into tears. 'Hand me the towel.'

She gives him the blue towel. 'Peter you need to listen to me, you have no idea what you are dealing with, let this go, let's leave town tonight, you and me. *Please.*'

'Leave town? Diana what are you on about? That's an ongoing investigation, I can't just leave, it's my job to investigate this.'

'Peter please, please listen to me. Let this go, and leave town, tonight.'

'What am I missing here?'

Diana opens the file and holds a picture out in front of him. It's Ryan's picture. 'This man.'

'Ryan Hunt?'

'Do you know about the organisation?'

'Yes?'

'He's the leader! Peter please, this man is dangerous, he kills for fun. He made the group that John Savage runs promise never to kill, because killing is his pleasure and reserved only for him. He's as evil as they come.'

'Fucking hell Diana, you just solved this case.' Peter starts to shake. 'Let me put some clothes on, I need to speak to Kelly and Nicholas about this.' He drops the towel; he doesn't care if Diana sees him naked now, and she doesn't even notice.

'You're not listening to me, don't pursue this.' She urges.

'It's my job,' he repeats. Half dressed, he walks to the phone and calls Nicholas.

The phone rings and rings. Then Nicholas answers. 'Hello.'

'Nic. Pete here. We have a break in the case.'

'The copycat or the real one?'

'The copycat, it's Ryan, Ryan fucking Hunt is the killer, he runs the organisation and he made the Savage group promise never to kill, the privilege is reserved only for him.'

'How do you know this?' Some excitement can be heard in Nicholas's voice.

'Diana.'

'How does *she* know this?'

Peter takes the phone away from his ear and whispers to Diana, 'Where did you get this information?'

Diana replies, almost crying, 'Alexander was part of them.'

Peter talks into the phone again. 'Doctor Rayne, she was with him and he was part of the group.'

'Where's Diana now?'

'She stays with me, remember?'

Some silence follows. 'Okay Peter, call Agent Young and ask her to meet at your house, on the way she can pick me up, I'm not far from her, let's hear what this young lady has to say. Then we can pick him up. Remember Peter, we will rely on her testimony.'

'Okay, I understand, I'll call Kelly and see you now.'

'All right, Detective.' Nicholas puts the phone down.

'Diana they're coming here; you need to tell us everything.' But Diana keeps quiet then walks to the kitchen and switches the stove off and leaves the file on the counter. Peter can see she's disappointed in his decision. Her shoulders are drooping; her eyes filled with tears. He dials Kelly's number, and the phone rings, and rings, and rings, then the call is disconnected. 'Fuck,' he whispers to himself and dials again. The phone rings, and rings, then disconnects. 'Fuck!' he shouts. He dials the number again, but the same thing happens. Peter races to the room and grabs the first shirt he sees and hurries to the kitchen. 'Diana I'll be right back, I need to go to Kelly and pick up Nicholas.'

'Can I come with you?'

'I'll be right back,' he says, taking his keys, and disappearing through the door.

'I'm not safe here anymore,' she whispers softly, desolately.

Peter races off to Kelly's hotel to pick her up, and is not surprised to find Brady already there. The three then fetch Nicholas and in the car Peter asks Brady to call Anderson and the captain, and asks him to tell them to meet at Peter's house. 'We'll have to be smart to catch him,' Peter says.

'It won't be difficult,' says Nicholas. 'Remember we now have someone to testify against him, but Agent Young, we'll have to arrange for protective custody through the FBI for Diana,'.

Kelly turns sideways in the front seat, looking back at Nicholas 'I'll make sure everything is in order before it gets out that we have someone, I will speak to Judge Vance now when we stop at Peter's house, I'll call from there and make the necessary arrangements.'

'What the fuck!' Peter screams as he pulls into the driveway. 'The door's been kicked in!' He stops and reaches for his side. *Fuck! Left my gun in the safe.* He thinks. 'Are you guys armed?'

'Yes,' Brady and Kelly reply, but Nicholas just shakes his head.

'I left my gun in the safe. She's here alone.'

'Okay Pete, you and Nicholas stay here in the car, Kelly and I will clear the house.' Brady says quickly.

Kelly and Brady get out the car and one behind the other crouch and move into the house with their pistols held out in front of them. Their shadows can be seen moving through the house, but no gunshots are heard. Moments later Brady appears from the right side of the house and Kelly from the left. Peter gets out, he already knows the result. 'She's gone Pete,' says Brady, 'and your house is trashed.'

'The case file is scattered all over,' Kelly says, putting her pistol back in its holster; Brady still holds his in his hand.

Peter crouches next to the car, then bursts into tears. 'She wanted to come with me. And I told her to stay,' He cries in rage and fear. There is a silence, as no one knows what to say.

'Detective, do you have a forensics kit in your car?' Nicholas eventually asks him.

'In the trunk.'

'Okay. Agent Young, you and I will check the most obvious places in the house while we wait for the forensics team. Detective Harris, call it in and wait here with Peter.'

'Copy that Sir.' Brady pulls out his phone and steps away, gun still in hand.

'Was there blood?'

'Not that I could see during the sweep,' Kelly replies, Peter just nods. Then Kelly and Nicholas enter the house. After some time, they return to Brady and Peter who are sitting on the hood of the car, both smoking; it's Peter's first time. 'Peter,' Kelly says gently, 'we'll have to see what the other team finds, we only found small traces of powder from gloves, nothing else that could lead us to a suspect, but I'm sure we all know who's behind this. I'm sorry.' Peter just bites his lip, shakes his head but doesn't respond.

Nicholas hands him an evidence bag. 'Your phone was tapped,' Nicholas says. 'That's the bug, military grade, and that's probably why they came for her.'

'They heard when I called you,' Peter says numbly.

'Yes. You were lucky that you weren't here, but we'll find them. And let's just hold thumbs that we find her too.'

'I wouldn't bet on that…' Peter says despairingly. The sirens can now be heard and soon the blue and red lights start flash against the front wall.

Chapter 48

The house is quiet, and so is the neighbourhood. In the early hours of the morning in New Orleans all the musicians have gone to rest. The forensic investigators found nothing more than Kelly and Nicholas found in the house. It seems that whoever did this came in and took Diana with little difficulty, and little resistance. Peter's in two minds, he wishes he had taken her advice, but now that she's taken, he's glad that there's no blood. But not even that is a good thought. Who knows what they'll do to her? Her room's light still shines bright and Peter sits on the couch in the lounge with a glass of whiskey, staring down the passage at the glow. His mind is blank, and all thoughts are being blocked out. His team was adamant that he should not stay at home, but he wouldn't listen. Eventually, the Captain arranged for a cruiser to stay outside his house with regular patrols around the house. The two officers are lean, young, and trigger happy, perfect for the situation. Every now and again Peter closes his eyes and imagines Diana walking to the kitchen, he imagines her cooking her omelettes with bacon, he imagines the divine smell wafting through the house. Diana. Beautiful Diana. He should've listened to her. *Why did I leave her here alone, it was stupid, fucking idiotic. Who leaves someone alone in a house with a killer out there? I should've just listened to her. Her blood is on my hands now.* Peter looks over at the window, and there goes the first officer around the house, the other one stays at the front door. Peter looks over to his other side, it takes the officer about thirty seconds to appear at that window. The officer passes on the other side and Peter hears a clapping sound, sort of like someone hit a broomstick against a tree. Peter ignores it, and looks back at the other officer, but the one patrolling doesn't appear. Peter checks his watch, twenty seconds late now, the officer still doesn't appear. His heart starts to pound, then he whistles and pulls his gun from his pants.

'Psst.' He gets the officer's attention. 'Keep your eyes open,' he whispers. The officer nods and starts to shine the torch mounted on his pistol's picatinny rail around. The two are now vigilant, but the other officer seems to have vanished. Peter sneaks through his house in a crouched position. His sights are aligned as he switches lights off as he goes. For a second he hesitates when he puts his hand on Diana's light switch, and then turns the light off. His military training kicking in now, with his back against the wall, he forcefully closes both eyes for about a minute to adapt to the dark. Then, that noise again, but this time closer, whatever it was, it's just outside Diana's room, but Peter can't see anything, it's too dark on that side. Peter now getting worried, he's stuck in the house with no way of communicating with the officers. He remembers that he left his phone on the couch, he should notify someone. Before he moves he feels beneath his gun on the torch for a switch, he then slides it to the front switch. This will create a tactical strobe and not a torch, but it's still off. His right index finger is on the trigger, already halfway pulled, and his left thumb is on the on switch for the strobe, he now slowly makes his way back to the lounge to fetch his phone, and from there the plan is to exit the house through the front door. It's so quiet that he can hear his own footsteps, and his breathing. He hears a creak in the lounge, it's close, and in a reflexive movement he pulls the gun in line and turns on the strobe. He sees a face, but before he can pull the trigger, Peter's on the floor and the gun with the strobe is near him, but out of reach. He can now feel a cloth being pushed over his mouth, the man is strong and Peter can't resist.

Ethyl Chloride burns the nose when sprayed up the nostrils.

'Wake up!' a masked man screams, and Peter starts to cough, his nose burning. 'Hello Detective.'

Peter looks around, it's his own bathroom, and he's in the bath. 'Don't do this.'

'Do you know who I am?'

'I could guess if I had to.'

'And who would you think I am?'

'Ryan. Ryan Hunt.'

The man pulls the mask off; it is Ryan. 'Well done Detective.' Peter's hands and feet are tied together with tactical cable ties, there's no way out of them. 'You've been a pain in my arse lately.' Ryan sits down on the toilet, relaxed and calm, Peter is on his side in the bath, but it's impossible to change position or get out, he can only see the top half of Ryan's upper body over the edge of the bath. 'Quiet now hey?'

'What have you done with Diana?'

'Oh, sweet Diana.' Ryan lifts his head and sniffs the air with his nose pointed at the roof and his eyes closed. 'Her perfume is still prominent in your home.' He turns and twitches with excitement. 'You know I've heard that the other one – the other killer – talks with his victims first, this is really my first time talking to my victim like this. It's an exhilarating experience I must tell you.'

'Where the fuck is Diana?' Peter asks aggressively.

But Ryan smiles. 'Where do you think?' Then leans his chin in his hand, resting his elbow on his leg. 'If you are here, where do you think she is?'

'Did you kill her?'

'Of course I fucking killed her!' Ryan gets up and opens the tap, the hot one, and only the hot one. 'The little bitch told you about me, and I warned Alexander about her, but he insisted she could be trusted. For a while I did trust her, but since you came along and started messing with her mind, she became more of a liability.' All the cold water is now expelled from the pipes and the hot water starts to fill the tub; it burns Peter's skin. 'Everyone always opens the cold water first, but this works better, don't you think?'

'Please, it's burning me.' Peter tries to move, but every time he does, it burns him somewhere else. 'Please!'

'I'll tell you this much though, she was a sweet girl, and I knew her, so I just shot her in the head and dumped her body, but you... you are going to feel every bit of pain I've imagined for you.' Ryan sits closer and listens to Peter moan from pain, the water level is now close to his face, but Peter pulls his head up, keeping it out of the water. Ryan looks at him for a moment then stands up and starts to kick down on Peter's head; one of the blows fractures his jaw and knocks his head down in the steaming bath. Ryan stops for a second and looks at Peter's dazed face, then starts to kick him again. Suddenly, the power goes off, the water is still running, Peter is now coughing from the blood and water in his airway. Moments go by and the light stays off, but the tap is now closed, and the plug pulled out, the water is draining and Peter can see the light of his cell phone on the toilet, and it's dialling. Then a woman can be heard over the speaker.

'Hello. Hello?' It's Kelly's voice. With his fractured jaw, he can't talk; instead, Peter screams loudly.

'Peter? Peter!' She calls out and he replies with a loud scream again. 'Are you home?' She asks, then with great difficulty he is able to scream back something that sounds like yes.

'I'm coming, just hang on!' she screams and puts the phone down. To Peter it feels like a day goes by before he sees the flashing of all sorts of lights against the wall. The ambulance crew arrives first.

Ryan wakes, tied upright to a trolley in a dark but large room, the same room as the others. From behind him, he hears a calm, composed voice. 'Welcome, Ryan.'

Ryan laughs. 'You just couldn't let me have him, could you?'

'You have a misguided perception that you can just kill whomever you like.' The man replies tranquilly.

'Oh, *I* have a misguided perception? Who do you think you are?'

'I'm just a man, hunting people like you, Ryan.'

Ryan looks around, but sees nothing useful. 'People like me?'

'Yes, you step on people for your own gain, you kill whomever you like; you torture people, you are the best example of the worst kind of person on this planet.'

'And how are you any different?' Ryan asks.

'In every possible way.' The man walks around him.

'Oh, you're kidding me, right?' Ryan frowns and looks surprised. 'You were the last person I would expect to be standing there.' He licks his lips. 'I must congratulate you though.'

'Oh yes?'

'You truly have fooled the world. They all think you're so innocent, the shoulder to cry on.'

The man keeps quiet for a while and so does Ryan, they just look at each other and then the man asks, 'Why did you initially copy me?' Ryan looks around, he's thinking. 'I mean you've been killing people for longer than what I've been around.'

'Tell me about it, I even killed people at your father's request.'

'I think he asked only because he was a gentleman, but they weren't requests.'

'Oh, so you knew about your daddy's sins?' Ryan pulls up his arms, then looks at his hands, indicating that the man should untie him. 'I know how you do things, you'll give me the opportunity to fight my way out of here, but I also know I won't win, so I'm not going to try. I know I'm dying here tonight, so untie me, like the gentleman you purport to be.'

'I don't purport to be anything; this is who I am.' The man walks closer and cuts Ryan loose. Ryan shakes his hands to get the blood flowing a bit. 'Would you like a chair?'

'Please.'

The man drags a chair from behind the standing trolley. 'There you go.'

The chair is metal, it's cold on the back of Ryan's legs. Metal is easy to clean. 'So, tell me, apart from everything else your father gave you, did he also give you the reins of the organisation?'

'You are running the organisation.'

'Oh come on!' Ryan's tone becomes offensive. 'Don't fucking play games with me, we both know I'm just the face; I'm not the boss, not the real boss.'

'I like how you made everyone think that John was in charge.'

Ryan smiles. 'Smart hey? I have someone like that in every city.' He taps his fingers. 'So? Did your father put you in charge?'

The man drags another chair closer. 'He tried, but I declined.'

'Of course, you don't care about your family's legacy.'

'I do, but since he left—'

'Died,' Ryan interrupts bluntly.

'Yes, since my father passed, you people have changed his vision. You've turned the organisation into an evil entity, and that is exactly what he did *not* want it to be. He wanted to change the world, and you people started using the connections and contacts for your own, personal gain. Then one of you, and I will still find out which one—' The man becomes angry, 'had him killed because he resisted your evil nature.' The man rolls his sleeves back to just below the elbows. 'I will hunt and kill every single one of you until this organisation is but a distant and vague memory.'

'Of that I have no doubt.'

'Now answer my question: why did you copy me?' The man now sits forward, aggressive for the first time, it is clear that he has taken offense at the act.

'If I knew it was you, I wouldn't have, but, I guess the way you did it intrigued me. I wanted to explore that avenue.'

'I only kill people like you.'

'No, you kill any predators who even as much as fantasise about your precious little Lily.' Ryan now copies the way the man sits. 'What do you think she would do if she found out that it's been you all along?'

'You don't dare to speak her name!'

'Or what?' He points at the man's hand where he holds the knife. 'You're going to stab me? If I could go back and change one thing, I would start with your sexy little girlfriend, and fuck her first.'

The man looks at Ryan, and then in one swift movement slices Ryan's throat. Ryan grabs his throat, but there's no stopping the bleeding. He gargles and gasps for air. 'I told you not to speak of her.' The man gets up and serenely walks over to fetch the chain. He ties it to Ryan's feet; Ryan's not resisting. Then he pulls Ryan off the chair, but before he hoists him upside down, he gets the funnel and bottle ready. 'This is for your blood.' He shows Ryan, and the fear can be seen in Ryan's face. 'I'm nothing like my father. I'm a god among men.' Then he ties Ryan's hands to his waist and hoists him up over the funnel. Just before Ryan loses consciousness, he cuts a perfect triangle in his left wrist, with the apex pointing to his hand.

Chapter 49

That morning Lily gets up. She puts on her tights, running shoes, and a bright pink shirt for visibility. The tights show every line of her muscular legs and bum, her panty line can be seen running up halfway over her butt cheeks. She opens the door and with a fright, screams and slams it shut again. Lily starts to cry, she rushes for the phone to call Peter, but there's no answer, she doesn't yet know that Peter is in hospital. Her father comes running down the stairs with his gown flapping open. 'What is it?' But Lily cries and shakes and points at the door. 'What's wrong Lily?' he asks again as he slowly opens the door. On the front porch is the pale body of Ryan Hunt, with a letter on his lap. 'Oh my! I'll call the police,' he says, horrified, and slams the door shut. He dials. 'Hello, please you need to come… the Tomlinson house. There's a dead man on my porch.' The lady on the phone replies and then puts the phone down.

Sometime later three police vehicles stop in the driveway, in one of them is Kelly Young. She runs to Lily. 'Are you okay?' she asks.

Lily cries, 'he has a letter on his lap.' Kelly puts on gloves and takes the letter, opens it and hands it to Lily.

"Dear Lily.
I have come to realise that I may not be the best thing for you. You see, this man, this body, he is one of the monsters you keep talking about. And I suspect that you already know I am the other one. I

know this is a very unconventional gift, but this man is my gift to you.

I need to tell you, however, where I found him. He was busy torturing your friend Peter and I've seen the way you look at him; he is important to you. He was going to kill Peter and I decided to intervene. Your friends will give you all the details, but Peter is safe now, he was injured, but he is safe. I did not care for him much, but I saved his life for you, everything I do, I do for you, Lily.

P.S. Tell Agent Kelly Young that she is an absolutely brilliant FBI agent and that she deserves only the best. She will find all the information she seeks on the organisation in the public library. There is a book there, hand written in a glass case on display. The title of the book is not important; it's fake. My father wrote that book, and inside it she will find the names of every person connected to the organisation up until twenty years ago. But in my experience with the group, they will all still be there, and that would be a great starting point to dismantle them."

Chapter 50

A couple of days later after the dust settles, the team meets back at the office. The captain had given them some time off to process everything that happened with Peter and Ryan Hunt. Their mood is off and gloomy. Anderson walks in, he's late again, but this time the office is empty. He leans into the captain's office. 'Morning Cap. Where's Brady and Kelly?'

He doesn't even look up at Andy. 'Check the conference room.'

'Thanks,' says Anderson and makes his way through the office. The smell of coffee fills the air, like every morning. Then up the stairs and a quick left down the passage. There's Brady outside looking into the conference room through the big glass window. 'Morning.'

'Hey.' Brady replies. He stares at Kelly through the glass, the unpolished and hazy glass window. The conference room doesn't get used much. 'She might be leaving.'

Andy squeezes Brady's shoulder. 'Sorry bud.' He pauses for a while, looking at the book on the table. Kelly reads from it to someone over the phone. 'Is that it?'

'Yep.'

'Does it contain what the letter said it would?'

'To the fucking tee.' Brady folds his arms in front of his chest. 'Who would've known that everything we were looking for would be in the library?'

Anderson looks around and puts his hands back in his pockets. 'Where's the mad man?'

Brady gives a snorting laugh. 'I don't know, he called Kelly and said that he's got some things to take care of; he'll join us later.'

'How long has she been in there?'

'I don't know; she was in already when I got here.'

In her peripheral vision, she can see Brady and Andy talking, but she tries to ignore it. 'Was that enough proof?' She listens to the man on the other end of the phone. 'Okay I'll see if I can make a copy of this book to put in the safe house and then I'll post it straight away.' The man interrupts her. 'Yes?' She nods, and looks surprised. 'Of course, Sir!' She gets excited 'Thank you Sir.' She looks up at Brady for the first time and winks at him. 'Yes, Sir. Yes, I understand, Sir.' The man asks a series of questions. 'Brady Harris… we are involved, but I understand the policy.' The man interrupts her again. 'Thank you Sir, I'll explain everything to him and then let you know.' She puts the phone down after saying goodbye, then gestures for Andy and Brady to enter. Kelly jumps up and hugs Brady for a couple of seconds. 'Morning guys.'

'Hey.'

Kelly takes Brady's hand. 'I got a promotion!' she shouts, beaming. Brady smiles, but she can see that something bothers him; the smile is fake. 'I'm moving to another division.'

'I'm happy for you.'

'And I'm happy for you, too.'

'What do you mean?'

'Since I'm moving in division, there's an opening, if you want it?'

Brady's eyes fill with tears; he can hardly speak. 'You're... joking, right?'

'What do you say, Agent? Are you coming back with me?'

He smiles, it's what he's always wanted, to join the FBI. 'Of course!'

Kelly sits down. 'Okay so before we go, I have spoken with my superiors and I've requested to see this case through, so the moment we finish the case, we can go.'

Andy slaps Brady on the back. 'Congratulations!' He laughs and cries at the same time. 'Now you're moving up in the world my friend, you fucking deserve it!' Then shakes his hand. 'Well done, my boy.'

'Thanks!' The room is filled with joy. 'It's a dream come true.'

'I have an idea,' Kelly interrupts.

'Yes?'

'Do you guys still have the guest list from Peter's birthday party?'

'We do yes, why?'

'We need to work through some files. I think we should take the profile Nic wrote and see if we can link that to any of the guests who were there that night.'

'It should be with everything in the other room.' The three make their way to the room where they've been working since Diana moved in with Peter. When they walk in, Nicholas is there, engrossed in something. He's wearing a beanie in the shape of a panda bear's head. 'Nicholas!'

'Good morning team. I was on my way to explore the city, it's changed so much since I was last here, and of course this time has been focussed on work. But then it got me thinking. These letters that Lily keeps getting, why risk it? Why risk getting caught just to hand deliver a letter? Then I also started to wonder why risk painting those paintings using the blood of his victims and risk getting caught when delivering them? Remember in my profile of him, that I constructed from his handwriting, he has had a broken childhood, which explains the link with Michael, the artist… Lily's boyfriend. But how is *he* connected to Lily?'

Kelly sits next to him on the floor and Brady and Andy sit on chairs. 'Are those all the letters?' She asks.

'Yes, and this one in particular intrigues me. The first one.' He hands it to Kelly. 'He says there that it is not a letter of love, nor is it a letter of hate. Then he says that he admires her. And then he goes on about how she's received more declarations of love than most cities, and then, the interesting bit. He tells her that her mind is worth more than gold; including the way that it works.'

'Okay?'

'I think his plan all along was to corrupt her, to take the most loved person he knows, and turn her into something else. Look at the next letter.' He hands Kelly another letter. 'He shows her how heavily connected he is, and arranges for her to be exposed to the world through Francis. We need to speak with Francis Linwood when we are done here, I can't believe we missed this small detail. But anyway, then he mentions that he knows she met Michael; how does he know that? Then again he tells her not to fear him.' He hands Kelly another letter and she passes the other two along. 'Here's the third letter. And this is after she's spoken about him twice in her blog about how she admires his gentlemanly nature, and of course that's not who he really is, and what he really is——he's a killer, right?'

'Right.'

'Now look at what he says there. He promises again that he means her no harm, *after* he broke into her room and placed the letter there while she sleeps, then while there, he adds another section. First, he thanks her for her letters to him, then he adds that her father must revisit their security measures. Do you notice the change in tone? He went from wanting to corrupt her, to caring for her. Then he asks her where he can leave the next letter; he gives her the opportunity to catch him, he exposes himself to her, or risks exposing himself at least.'

'You're right,' Brady says, nodding as he is piecing it together.

Nicholas gets excited. 'Now look at the next letter.' He hands Kelly the next one. 'Now, this one is after he left the recording of his experience as he killed that man—I think it was Howard Cox he murdered. He was Lily's therapist at some stage. He tries to convince her that he is not a monster and that his actions are validated. He then says that one day she will see the world through his eyes, but that she still should not fear him. Why did he now suddenly worry about her corruption again?'

'Because he was angry about the whole copycat?'

'Exactly!' Nicholas nods at Brady. 'And then he thanks Lily for her kindness.' He hands Kelly the fifth letter. 'Then, in the second last letter, he shows emotion. It is a short letter, but he tells her that he understands her decision to leave and retracts from her. He then pushes her towards Michael; why? Because he trusts Michael, more than he trusts himself with her.' Nicholas hands Kelly the last letter. 'In the last letter he tells her that he is not good for her, and that he now realises that he is one of the monsters she fears. He then gives her an odd gift, the body of Ryan Hunt; he kills one of the monsters, leaving only himself. And then he tells her that he saved Peter's life. Do you guys see what's happened here?' He holds his hands up in the air. 'He fell in love with her. His whole mission was to destroy the perception of love, probably because he never felt it, and then because she was kind to him, he starts to feel loved.'

'In a strange way, it's quite sweet,' muses Kelly.

'I suspect that instead of him changing her, she changed him,' Nicholas adds. 'I don't think that he'll ever kill again.'

'We need to keep a close eye on Lily,' Anderson says. 'If you guys are right, he might even attempt to see her one last time.'

Nicholas nods. 'Detective, you're absolutely right. In fact, I think you may be one-hundred and ten percent correct with that thought.'

Anderson gets up. 'I'll arrange for surveillance.'

'Before you go.' Nicholas stops him. 'He also gave Kelly information on the organisation; he's somehow connected to them. Be careful.'

'Will do.'

'Okay so while he does that, the three of us can quickly go over to the New Orleans Weekly and speak with Francis. If we're lucky, he might have some details on the guy.'

The New Orleans Weekly is housed in a surprisingly large building and the paper has many employees. The building on the outside has lush gardens filled with trees, plants and flowers of all sorts. On the inside the walls are colourful and freshly painted with large resting and working areas for the employees, but the office of Francis

Linwood is old fashioned and bleak. 'Detectives! Good morning, how can I assist you?'

'Good morning, Francis.' Nicholas says. Kelly and Brady echo the greetings. 'Nice building you have.'

'Oh, I'm fortunate that the mayor gives us lots of funding.' Francis is a friendly person.

Nicholas looks around. 'Your office looks very different to the rest of the building.'

'My father, rest his soul, told me to always hold onto that which made you who you are.' He looks around and smiles with pleasure. 'I haven't changed a single thing in here, I've only cleaned. And of course added a new chair.' He laughs. 'Back then the chairs were chairs, these days they feel like thrones.'

Nicholas sits down, he feels comfortable talking with Francis. 'One day you and I should have coffee. But unfortunately today we're here on business.'

'Oh?' Francis sits down, concerned. 'Everything all right?'

'You know about the ongoing murder investigation; I take it?'

Francis sits forward, looks around and talks quietly. 'I do, and I've kept it quiet around here; I don't let anyone publish anything on it, as the department requested.'

Nicholas senses that Francis feels he is in trouble. 'No need to worry old chap, I actually come here with some questions regarding Lily.'

Francis sits back in his chair. 'Lily?' He looks a bit confused. 'She's a brilliant girl; she in trouble?'

'No, no, she's not in trouble. It's come to our attention that someone arranged the job here for her?'

Francis goes pale. 'Yes, indeed. Are they involved?'

'Who?'

'The Savage group?'

'Did they arrange for the job?'

'Not in so many words.' Francis takes a pack of cigarettes from his jacket pocket and offers one to Nicholas, he declines, then he offers to Kelly and Brady, Brady takes one. He lights the cigarette and drags it until the coal is red. 'When I told you that the mayor gives us lots of funding… he made a deal with me some time ago, he's a good man, he's just in the wrong circles. They have something on him, but I fear that he now rather likes being part of that group. You see, he merely carries out tasks, and the deal was that he and the group will fund us, in quite a large amount, if, occasionally, we do them favours, jobs, articles, nothing major. Then one morning I get a phone call, the man was friendly, but stressed that it is in the best interest of the group if I employ Lily. I've spoken with this man before, and he's hassled me. But to be honest Nicholas, I couldn't give you a name even if I wanted to. I've never met the man, and he's never introduced himself.' He sucks on the cigarette again, then kills it in a large wooden ashtray, expensive looking. 'The best I can do is tell you that he didn't seem old. His voice was soft, not too deep; he spoke in a friendly tone, calm. In all honesty, based on his phone calls with me, I would never have guessed that he is part of them.'

'If you heard his voice again, would you recognise it?'

'Certainly.'

'Have you ever spoken with anyone in person, and thought that it might be him?'

Francis looks into the middle distance and thinks for a short while. Shakes his head. 'No, no I truly don't think so, and I never really paid attention. I'm sorry.'

'Not a problem.' Nicholas gets up. 'Well thank you for your time. When the investigation is over, I'll come by and we can have a social chat.'

'You're always welcome here, all of you.'

As they walk out Kelly says, 'Oh one more thing, if you think of anything, please call.'

'Of course my dear.' Francis smiles at Kelly and the three leave the office. For a while Francis stares out the window and when he sees their car leave, he picks up the phone and dials a number. It rings for a while. 'Hello my friend.' The man greets him back. 'This is a courtesy call, tread carefully.' Francis listens to the man's reply. 'They were here, and I suspect that they probably have seen all of the letters you wrote her; just be careful, Nicholas is not someone to be taken lightly.' The man says something again. 'Thank you my friend.'

Chapter 51

"Dear Lily.

I regret to write this letter, but I've been thinking and I can't let my actions influence you, I have decided to leave. I should never have come, and I should never have involved you. I plan on seeing you and all those I adore most, one more time. Would you do me a last favour and go to the coffee shop around the corner from the Pure Imagination Art gallery at nine o'clock tomorrow morning? It's a small coffee shop, but it's my favourite. Don't worry, you won't be there alone, you're not the only one I've invited. I truly hope that I will see you there tomorrow.

P.S. I do apologise for the trauma I've caused you and that you will forever remember me as you described me in your first blog."

Lily runs to the phone, it's early in the morning, but she has to call. She dials the number for Nicholas's hotel. For some reason, apart from Peter, she trusts him most. The phone doesn't ring long. 'Sir Nicholas, it's Lily.'

'Morning sweetheart, how are you?'

'He wrote to me again. He wants to meet tomorrow at nine at a coffee shop near Michael's gallery.'

But before she speaks again, Nicolas says. 'I know.'

'What do you mean you know?' She goes cold, maybe it's him.

'I also got a letter, with the same time and place. I'll pick you up and we can go there together; I don't want you going alone. I'll see you at half past eight tomorrow morning. And Lily, don't be scared.'

'Okay.' She puts the phone down. *Why would Nicholas tell me not to be scared? And why would he be invited?*

The Final Chapter

The weather forecast foretold a sixty percent chance for rain and heavy thunderstorms. For the moment, there's light rain, it is slightly misty, and not very windy. However, it is a cold day and Lily can feel her toes burn inside her shoes while she waits outside for Nicholas to pick her up. Her nose is so cold that she constantly wipes it, in case it runs. But her skinny jeans and thick, layered coat keep her nice and warm. The beanie she wears is the one that Peter gave her a couple of years ago, it was on a night out to the movies and Lily had felt okay when she left home, but then the weather turned and he bought it for her. This weather today is perfectly suited, it reminds her of that night, and of Peter. He's such a good friend, and they could have had more if only Freddy didn't die. In a way she blames J for it, because that was the first person he killed. Peter changed after Freddy's death, he became hungry for revenge and distracted and distant from the rest of the world. That can't be changed though, it's all said and done. She checks her watch, Nicholas is three minutes late now. She considers going back inside where it's warm and dry, but she decides to wait for him right there. She looks around; it's so quiet today, odd, usually by now the musicians can faintly be heard from the front porch, but not today, few play outside when it rains. It's difficult to find cover on days like this. A yellow cab stops in the street, five minutes late. Nicholas opens the door and gets out, he's a strange man, wearing shorts with a bomber jacket and one of those old pilot beanies. What an odd character. 'Are you coming?' he shouts, holding the door for her. Without answer she walks briskly and gets in the cab, it smells like coffee and fish, and the heater is on. Nicholas joins her and slams the door closed. 'Sorry I'm late, I didn't come to New Orleans with my own car, so I had to wait for a cab myself.'

'That's all right.' Lily's friendly as always. 'Are you nervous?'

Nicholas moves around trying to get comfortable, the jacket is more a liability than anything else. 'Nervous? No my dear. And you shouldn't be either. Think about it, if he was going to do anything to either one of us, he would've done it by now, I mean he broke into your house without waking so much as a ghost.'

Lily giggles. 'A ghost you say, that's the first time anyone has ever said it like that.'

He smiles and winks at her. 'Someone has to swim upstream.' Then gets serious. 'So tell me, how is it going with your degree?'

'Well thank you, I'm home more these days with everything that's happening, but I'm still top of the class, and if you perform well enough through a semester than you don't have to write exams.'

'My word, now that is interesting. Pretty and smart, you're a lucky girl. You know way back when, when the dinosaurs still roamed the earth and I was a young boy…' Lily laughs at him, he smiles, and continues, 'we didn't really care much for university. That was only for the rich kids, well that's what me and my friends thought anyways. To us all we cared about were war and guns, and gangsters, and hippies and so forth.'

'I can see you as a hippie,' she says.

'My dear you have no idea. We would sneak out at night, not to go clubbing, no, no, no, we would sneak out and smoke hash, and then... well the rest is not important.'

'Oh, please tell me.' Lily is very intrigued.

'Back then in our circles, we didn't commit to relationships, so, we would puff a bit, then whoever felt in the mood that night, we would do some stuff.'

'You had sex after getting high?'

Nicholas seems very uncomfortable. 'Well, I didn't really want to put it like that, but yes, that's pretty much it.'

'Have you ever kissed a man?'

'What? A man? No thank you. I'm not gay, I mean I don't mind them—and I had one or two gay friends back then, but it was never for me. My mind never wandered there. It's... it's just not for me.' He looks at her. 'Have you kissed a girl?'

Lily starts to blush. 'I have. But it was a night at university after we, well let's just say you're not the only one to have smoked some stuff.'

Nicholas laughs. 'Do you smoke often?'

'No, it was only that one time and it made me feel sick later anyway.'

'It's better that way. Kids these days.'

Lily turns in her seat, then hits him on his arm. 'What do you mean "these days"?' She looks at him with an intimidating stare. 'You were worse than me, Mister.'

Nicholas laughs, she's a sweet girl. He holds up his hands in surrender, 'Okay, all right, you're right. Do your parents know?'

She sits upright. 'No ways, I can never tell them. Well not never, maybe one day when I'm on my own and married I would.' She turns to Nicholas again. 'Are you married?'

But Nicholas seems unhappy with the question. 'No, my dear.' Something like regret is in his tone.

'Sorry.'

'It's not your fault.'

'I shouldn't have asked.'

'No, you should have. I never talk about it.' He takes a necklace out of his shirt, and a ring hangs between his fingers. 'She's the reason I moved from England to America to become an investigator. We were engaged, but while we were planning the wedding she flew to America for business. She was a smart girl. She was my everything. She went to New York and there she got mugged in an alley while taking a shortcut, they say, and the boy who mugged her also stabbed her. She only got found the next morning. So I came here hoping to track him down.'

'And did you? Did you find him?'

'I always find my man.'

'And what did you do?'

Nicholas bites his lip. 'I beat him, and beat him, and beat him. Eventually a man stopped me, he was a lawyer at the time. My friend Lucius. The man survived, but he's disfigured now. I was lucky that they found evidence and he was locked up, and because of the circumstances, I was sent for mental evaluation and stayed in a psychiatric facility for about five months, then Lucius got me out and motivated for my release saying that they needed me on a case. Of course it was a lie, he just felt bad for me at that stage, but that was the start of a great friendship. And the start of a memorable career.'

'Did you ever meet anyone else?'

'No. She was supposed to be my wife and even though she's not with me anymore, I will always keep that promise to her; I will always be faithful to her.'

Lily can see now that he is very unhappy. She puts her hand on his. 'I'm sure that when she looks down at you from heaven, she loves you still, and visits you in spirit.' The rest of the trip is quiet and gloomy, and Lily never lets go of Nicholas's hand. Last night she thought that it could be him, that Nicholas might be the killer, but today she is convinced otherwise. He's just a broken man, and a broken soul. 'Here we are.'

'Is this it?' Nicholas asks.

'This is it.'

'And there's our seat.' He points through the car window, letting go of Lily's hand.

'How do you know?'

'Because every table has a rose on it, and that one has a lily,' he replies, then gets out and walks around to open the door for her. Here the clouds are grey and heavy, but still no rain, only a distant lightning strike now and then.

As Lily and Nicholas approach the door, the waitress asks politely. 'Your names?'

'Lily and Nicholas,' says Lily.

'Right this way.' She leads them to the table, where the lily is not the only difference. The table cloth is white whereas the rest of the table cloths are cherry red. The plates are red and the other tables have white plates. Lastly, this table is also right in the middle of the room.

'Forgive me, Miss, but why is this table different to all the others?'

'It was requested at booking, Sir.'

'Thank you.'

'Can I get you anything?'

'Can I please have one Americano, double shot, black, no sugar.' Nicholas says and the girl nods.

Lily scans through the menu, then asks the waitress. 'Do you have any freshly squeezed juices?'

'Only orange.'

'That's fine, I'll have one freshly squeezed orange juice,' Lily replies.

'Oh Miss, and a tall glass of water, with ice and lemon please.'

'All right, coming right up,' the waitress says and walks to the kitchen. It's not very busy, not with the weather forecast. But it's not empty. Lily and Nicholas sit in silence until the girl returns with their drinks. 'Anything to eat?'

'No thank you Miss, not at this moment, we're waiting for someone.'

'Just call me if you need anything.'

'Will do, thank you.' Nicholas replies politely. Then he sips his coffee, and Lily drinks her juice. It's evident that both are a bit nervous. They're quiet, and shaky, and fidgety. After a while, and after the coffee, the juice, and the water is finished, they order a second round of the same drinks; still no food. They wait again. 'Thank you, Miss.' Nicholas says when the waiter brings the drinks. 'What time is it? My watch is a little behind,' he lies. His watch is correct.

The waitress pulls out an old pocket watch. Nicholas can see that it's a family heirloom. 'It's now, twenty-two minutes past nine Sir.'

'Thank you.' He looks at Lily and sips his coffee. 'He's late.'

Lily looks around. 'Do you think he's still going to come?'

'I don't know.' He thinks for a while. 'He could've left already.'

'What do you mean?'

'Neither of our letters said that he wanted to meet with us, just that he wanted to see us, and from the outside one could walk past and see this table perfectly. Or he could've sat anywhere here and left, because we don't know what he looks like.' Lily looks disappointed. 'Lily, I want to ask you a question. But I don't want you to take offense.'

'Okay?' Lily looks apprehensive.

'Don't you find it odd that Michael isn't here?'

'Do you think something happened to him?' She asks quickly and with concern.

'Not entirely, no.'

A pause, then, 'No.' Lily shakes her head. 'It's impossible.'

'It's not.'

'Why would you even suggest that?' She asks.

'Let me explain.' He takes Lily's hand. 'My dear, the letters said that everyone he adores most will be here; Michael is one of those people. Why isn't he here? Also have you heard from him since Ryan's death?'

'No.'

'You see? But let me explain; I wrote a profile analysis on the killer based on his handwriting, I'm going to tell you what I found, and if at any point you don't think that's what Michael is like, you stop me immediately? All right?'

Lily's eyes fill with tears. 'Okay.'

'I found a man that would be artistic and charismatic. He suffers from a superiority complex. He's assertive and dominant and yet, at the same time, calm, but intelligent and pays great attention to detail. He has suffered a great childhood trauma, lost a parent, or maybe both. It is evident that there is a lack of attachment to the parental figure in his home and he was probably a lonely child.' He keeps quiet. 'Is he at all like that?'

Lily bursts into tears, and when she stops she says, 'His parents died when he was young, he was then adopted by the Lafayette family, but they also later passed away. They left him all their riches and power, and he has since become one of the most influential people in the city. He's an artist, and he's smart.' She stops for a second, trying her best not to cry again. 'And this coffee shop is his favourite.'

'I refuse to believe it.' She is angry now.

Nicholas calls the waitress over. 'Miss, do you by any chance know who booked this table?'

'Of course, Sir.'

'Who?'

'Mister Lafayette, from the art gallery...'